Killing the Captain

**by
James Hume**

Killing the Captain

Copyright © 2018, Jim McCallum Publishing Ltd. (JMPL)

Editing by Katherine Trail

Cover Design by Victoria Bushby

Book Design by JMPL

First JMPL electronic publication: 01 July, 2020

EBooks are not transferable. All rights are reserved. No part of this book may be used or reproduced in any manner without written permission, except in the case of brief quotations embodied in critical articles and reviews. The unauthorised reproduction or distribution of this copyrighted work is illegal. No part of this book may be scanned, uploaded or distributed via the Internet or any other means, electronic or print, without the publisher's permission.

This book is a work of fiction. The names, characters, places and incidents are products of the writer's imagination or have been used fictiously, and are not to be construed as real. Any resemblance to persons, living or dead, actual events, locale or organisations is entirely coincidental.

English Edition
ISBN No: 9798662893757
Published in the UK by Jim McCallum Publishing Ltd, 2020.

Killing the Captain

For

BABS and DOT

My wonderful, special,

so-talented girls!

Chapter 1. Triumph Group

Richard glanced at his watch. Quarter to nine. Better head for the meeting room. The polished board beside the door carried a paper insert marked 'Triumph Group'. He took a big breath, and entered the room.

Another man stood over by the window holding a cup of tea. Richard hung up his coat and dumped his case, then flashed his widest smile as he approached the man. 'Morning, I'm Richard Preston, from Ayr, in Scotland. Good to meet you.'

The man shook hands. 'Same here. I'm Colin Firth, from Leeds.' He had a broad Yorkshire accent. 'This is my first visit. Have you been a member long?'

'No, it's my first meeting too. Sir Anthony invited me to join after I spoke at an Economic League area managers' meeting a few weeks ago.'

'Wow. What did you speak about?'

'Well, we wanted to show how the League could help businesses recover after the war. I had been to the US just before the war to learn their retail practices. We own the biggest department store in Ayr.'

'Really?'

'Yeah. I liked the way schools over there teach students how businesses create value, and how money flows around the economy. I firmly believe that's one reason why the US is so successful. My speech covered how we could do the same in the UK.'

'Did it go well?'

'Yes and no. The meeting agreed to include my proposals. So to that extent it went well. But Sir Anthony, the Chairman, had assumed Churchill would win the General Election in July.'

'Yeah, so did we all.'

'He even coined the scornful phrase, 'Captain Attlee', to contrast the powerful presence of Churchill during the war, with Attlee, whom he thought was more like a bumbling Home Guard captain.'

Colin laughed. 'I like that.'

'To him, it was obvious that Churchill would win by a landslide. But, as we now know, the country voted Attlee in. Our strategy was blown apart before we even got started.'

'Yeah. That was a shocking result. So, have you come down from Scotland just for this meeting?'

'No, no. We're pretty good at what we do, and I think there are good businesses around that have lost their way during the war. I'm eyeing other department stores in Glasgow, Edinburgh, and here in Manchester.'

'Wow. Good for you.'

'I came yesterday to meet my accountants on how we could fund the target here. What about yourself? What business are you in?'

'I've got four engineering companies – all in Yorkshire – that are major suppliers to Sir Anthony's two giants. At a meeting a couple of weeks ago, he told me about this group. So, when he invited me along, I came. He's so influential. I'd rather have him as a friend than an enemy.'

Richard laughed. 'That's for sure. We're riding on his coat tails here. If he succeeds, we all succeed.'

The door opened. Another five men entered, and introduced themselves. Three were from the Midlands and two were from the Manchester area. One of them said, 'I've just seen our esteemed leader heading for the phone booths, so he might be another few minutes. Let's grab a cup of tea.'

***

The distant voice said, 'Hello?'

'Larry? It's me. Just got your message.'

'Hi, Tony. Sorry I can't make the meeting. I've a problem at the office. Hope it goes well, though.'

'Thanks. We've got a couple of new boys this morning. Colin Firth, from Leeds. We met him a couple of weeks ago, remember? And a guy called Richard Preston from Scotland. He's a retailer. Bit of a softy, I think. Not a manufacturing man. But he has some good ideas on business education that might give us a more respectable veneer.'

'Okay, good. Talk later.'

***

They settled around three sides of the large table, leaving the front seat for Sir Anthony. Richard sat next to Colin at one side. Everyone pulled out notebooks, and joined in the banter about the next day's football matches. Then Sir Anthony arrived.

He strode into the room, tall, a bit overweight, with a florid face, and silver hair shining in the room lights. Well dressed as usual. 'Morning, lads. Sorry, I'm late. Had to make a phone call. Welcome to Colin and Richard. Good to have you with us.'

There were murmurs of support from the others.

'Right. This morning, we want to work out how we can protect ourselves from this bunch of bloody pillocks we now have as a government.

'I mean, I now regard these guys as dangerous for this country. Did you see their latest? They want to extend public ownership, for God's sake. To take over gas, electricity, steel, coal mining, the railways. And that's just for starters. It's a bloody socialist agenda. A total bloody joke.

'There isn't anywhere in the country where the government, local or national, does a good job. Their people can't manage a damned thing. They just form sub-committees and bloody delegate everything.

'They have loads of bloody useless meetings, and only want to expand their own groups to raise their status. They've got jobs for life. Never fired for incompetence or waste. What makes anybody think these guys can run our vital services better than us?'

Sir Anthony had worked himself into a fury. 'This clown Attlee's set to borrow billions to build his 'New Jerusalem'. He should be doing what every other country's doing. Rebuild our infrastructure, and make our export businesses more competitive for the future.'

He thumped the table. 'Instead of that, these new nationalised industries will swallow more and more money, and deliver less and less value. It's just a huge bloody vanity project.'

His face went red with pent-up rage. 'Did you see *The Sunday Times* last week? They showed what's happening in Germany, the losers, compared to Britain, the winners. Two weeks after they surrendered, with Berlin flattened, they had the city's bus system fully back up and running. And it's been like that ever since. Typical German efficiency.'

He thumped the table again. 'What were our people doing that same day on London buses? They were on strike. That's the unions for you. And Captain Attlee's pandering to them with all this socialist claptrap.

'Our children and grandchildren will be paying off these debts forever. It's a total bloody nonsense, lads. We need to do something about it. Let's see, who are the targets?'

He pulled a pad towards him. 'Right.' He opened a newspaper. 'We've got Clement Attlee. He's got to be the prime target. And then we've got the main members of his cabinet.' He read out their names. 'Right, that's the targets. Now, what can we do about them?'

Colin Firth cleared his throat. 'I can tell you for a fact that not all the cabinet agree with Attlee's actions. There's a group that think he's going way too far too fast. We should put some money and support behind *them* to limit these actions to something more sensible.'

Sir Anthony snorted. 'Ah! That'll take too long. We need something more direct, with quicker results.'

A voice from the other side of the table quipped, 'Why don't we just shoot them?'

Everyone laughed.

Then Richard piped up, 'Funny you should say that. My lawyer told me last weekend that one of his team was part of a group taken out to the countryside north of Glasgow to see a super sniper. A guy, just back from the Army, with a snaffled rifle, who could hit a can of beans at a hundred yards. He offered a discreet service to get rid of vermin – including human – for a price.'

Sir Anthony sat back in his chair. 'Wow. What kind of price?'

'Up to a couple of thousand.'

'Is that all? Jesus, that's got to be worth it. Let's find out when Attlee's next in Scotland. Be back in a minute.' He left the room.

Richard savoured the murmurs of approval from the others. 'Great idea, Richard.' 'Good man, Richard.'

A few minutes later, Sir Anthony came back into the room. 'My contact tells me Attlee's in Scotland on the twentieth of next month. Don't know the details yet, but he thinks it's near Glasgow. What do you think, lads? Is it worth looking at?'

'Only if we can guarantee no comeback,' said one

'What about it, Richard? Could you organise that? To take Captain Atlee out?'

Richard swallowed. Shit, he hadn't expected this.

'We'll send the details once we get them. Agreed, gentlemen?'

Everybody nodded.

'We'll each give you £250 cash today, and you go organise it. How would that be?'

The others congratulated Richard.

He lapped up their praise. 'Okay, guys. Leave it with me. I'll see what I can do.'

'Well done, Richard,' Sir Anthony said. 'We'll give you the cash after lunch.'

Richard's joy lasted until he got on the train to Glasgow. Then he realised it might not be so easy to deliver with no comeback. Shit. He'd talk to Daniel. *He'd* know what to do.

***

'Larry, it's me. How's the problem?'

'All sorted, Tony. How did your meeting go?'

'It went fine. Turned out the new guy Preston might be a better cover than I thought.'

'How do you mean?'

'I'll tell you on Monday. Have a good weekend.'

'You too.'

Chapter 2. Adam

Adam Bryson lip-read the woman opposite. She talked quietly to her neighbour about someone called William, who had returned from the war and got his sister-in-law pregnant. Another sad story of post-war family life.

Six years earlier, his own life had changed. He had wakened with a heavy cold. Then realised he'd lost half his hearing. He couldn't hear the radio at normal volume, and his parents only if they shouted close to his ear. His hearing loss wasn't like a cold. It wouldn't get better. So, in his usual upbeat style, he set out to live with it by learning lip-reading.

He attended courses and became very adept. Within a year he scored over ninety percent on his lip-reading tests. But now, in a hearing world, he had to wear a hearing aid. It had an obvious earpiece, a thick black wire to the microphone box in his top pocket, and a heavy battery pack hidden from view in another pocket.

At seventeen, and almost six feet tall, he thought himself quite good-looking, with a great smile. But no one could see past the hearing aid. It seemed to define him as a person in the eyes of others.

And he couldn't get a decent job. The manager at a hardware store hired him to help in the back shop, but because he had problems using a phone, that job ended. He then got a job in a paint factory, but hated that.

Now, six years after that fateful day, he was on a train to Ayr, on the Clyde coast, to join his Aunt Janet. She'd hired him as her aide in a local department store. He had a new chance, and he was going to grab it. And enjoy a salary of five pounds a week.

***

Aunt Janet met him at the station; dark-haired, round-faced, her slim athletic figure in a grey coat. She walked towards him with a big smile and gave him a hug. Then, with her head tilted, spoke straight at him. 'Oh my, I think you've got taller. Welcome to Ayr.'

He smiled back. 'Thank you. Good to be here.'

'Come on then. Let's go.' She took his free arm as they pushed through the crowd and left the station.

She wasn't his real aunt. She'd been his mother's best friend and bridesmaid, and was godmother to him. But after his parents left Ayr to live in Glasgow, they'd seldom seen Aunt Janet and Uncle Harry. Even less during the war years.

He'd last seen her at Uncle Harry's funeral a year ago. It had been a huge affair because Harry had been a business expert and a senior officer in the Masonic Lodge for years, so lots of his colleagues and contacts had attended. Janet looked grim that day, but she now seemed back to her cheerful self.

They walked down to the seafront and along the wide esplanade. Her apartment, in a new glass and steel block, overlooked the lawns, esplanade and beach.

He dumped his case in his bedroom and went into the lounge, a stunning long room with floor-to-ceiling windows the full length, and a balcony with chairs and a table that looked out to the sea and hills of Arran beyond. It was just like one of those adverts in fancy magazines. He'd be very happy here.

'Let's get some sea air,' she said. 'Give me your ration book and we'll get your food. After dinner, we'll go to the tennis club dance. I've arranged for you to meet a group of people your own age, relatives of Amanda, my ex- neighbour. They're a good bunch.'

***

They walked up Myrtle Avenue towards the tennis club. Very nice area, he thought. They stopped for a moment at number 21. 'This was our home for twenty years,' Janet said, with a wry smile. 'Lots of happy memories.'

Amanda met them at the top of the stairs in the tennis club pavilion, and guided them into the bar on the right. At a crowded table, she waved her hand in the air. 'Hi, everybody. You all know Janet, and this is her nephew, Adam. Make room for her while I take Adam across to join the young ones.'

Janet moved to the table, and Amanda took Adam by the arm, and led him back out of the bar towards the lounge. As they crossed the main foyer, Adam glanced up at the list of club champions. Amanda stopped. 'There's your aunt – 1926, 27 and 28. Our only triple singles champion. She inspired me as a young girl. And I also made the list here in 1936.'

Adam peered at the entry: Amanda Ross. He turned to her. 'Well done.'

'Thanks. Worked hard for that.' She smiled at him. 'How long are you here for?'

He shrugged. 'Don't know. I'll see how it goes after a few weeks.'

'Okay. Come on, let's meet the others.' She led the way into the lounge.

Over to the left a band played swing music, which sounded great. They walked towards a small group at a table in the far corner.

As they approached, one of the girls stood and held out her hand to Adam. 'Hello,' she said. 'I'm Philippa. Pip for short. And these are Charlie, Kev, Tim and Katy. Come and join us. This is Adam, everyone.' They all gave a wave of welcome, and he took a seat opposite Katy at the end of the table. No one took any notice of his hearing aid, which was unusual. Maybe they'd known about it in advance.

'Can I get you a drink?' Tim asked, and laughed. 'We need you to come more often, Adam. Aunt Mandy's opened a bar tab for us in your honour.'

'Just an orange juice with some lemonade, thanks.'

Katy studied him through dark hooded eyes. Her long black hair brushed the sides of her cheeks. She was the only one smoking, and seemed more mature than the others. She smiled across at him. 'They're all talking about football. Are you into football too?'

'Yeah, I coach a team in Glasgow. Under sixteens. They've done well this season. Won every game.'

She turned to the others. 'Did you hear that, guys? He coaches a football team that has won every game. You should pick up a few tips.' She turned back to Adam. 'They play in a five-a-side league, and have lost every game so far.'

They all laughed. They seemed a pleasant bunch. He began to relax and looked around. The lounge was busy. Behind Katy, a tall man leaned back against the windowsill. He wore a blazer and flannels, with a white shirt and striped tie.

The band leader announced, 'And now, ladies and gentlemen, please take your partners for a quickstep to our version of Woody Herman's "Golden Wedding".'

The drummer started an insistent beat, and within seconds the dance floor was packed. The band leader kicked in with his clarinet and a haunting melody. Then the rhythm section started, followed by the rest of the band. The drummer went into a long drum solo, his arms and drumsticks flailing. Everyone stood to watch him. The band kicked in again, with the clarinet gradually climbing the scale until it reached the long, high note at the end. Adam felt a shiver down his spine. Even with his hearing aid, the sound was sensational. Everyone cheered and clapped. The band had to repeat the number.

Katy excused herself and left the table. Adam sat down again, and noticed another man with long hair and a thin nose come over, and join the tall man. He also leaned back against the sill, took a cigarette, and then said, 'How did it go in Manchester yesterday?'

Although he was six yards away, Adam could lip-read him easily.

The tall man took a drag on his cigarette. 'We agreed to try and stop this nonsense. We're going to kill the captain. We'll use that sniper guy.'

Long hair looked astonished. 'What? When?'

'Next time he's in the Glasgow area.'

'When will that be?'

The tall man took another drag on his cigarette. 'Let's talk about it after the golf tomorrow.'

Long hair nodded. 'Okay.' He stood and began to move away.

Adam pulled out a notepad, which he used sometimes to communicate, and noted what they'd said.

Katy returned to her seat, and Adam asked, 'Who are the two men behind you?'

She'd glanced at them as she returned. 'The tall man is Richard Preston. He owns the Preston department store, the newspaper I work for, and various other businesses. Probably the richest man in the area. The other man is Daniel Bloomfield, his hot shot lawyer.'

'They're two of the four most powerful men in this town. The other two are probably here too. Why do you ask?'

'Oh, just interested. They seemed a bit . . .different. And the tall man will be my boss come Monday.'

Tim brought the drinks, and they shouted, 'Cheers!'

Katy turned to the others, 'So, do you want to find out how to win every football game?'

They all gathered close, with expectant faces. Adam smiled. 'Well, they're not *my* ideas. The coach for the whole club is a guy called Dougie, who studies football like other people study maths or science. He watches loads of films of clubs from around the world, and he's worked out a system that he calls "two-touch", which he learned from a Spanish club. The first touch is to control the ball, the second to pass or shoot.

'All our teams play that way. I coach the under-sixteens, and we just dominate our league. Football's great when you win all the time. I can show you how it's done, if you like.'

Katy said, 'So it's a kind of Spanish two-step you play. Is that right?'

Adam thought for a moment. 'Yeah, I suppose you could call it that.'

She pulled a notebook from her bag, and wrote on it.

'Is this another story for you, Katy?' Kev asked.

She smiled. 'Only if you win.'

They all laughed again. Kev shouted over. 'Be careful what you say, Adam. It may be taken down and used in next week's paper.'

Pip cut in. 'Why don't you come along on Tuesday night, Adam. See if you can help with their training?'

'Okay. Happy to help.'

'That's great. Maybe win the trophy this year, lads?'

The boys all cheered, and Adam felt pleased to have become part of the group. Katy asked Adam up to dance. He'd never danced before, and watched the others, who seemed to know the steps. He and Katy just shuffled their way round the hall, more or less to the beat of the music. He enjoyed his first experience of holding a woman, and felt honoured that she'd asked him.

'What were you writing when I came back to the table?' she asked.

'Oh, just something I wanted to remember.'

'You mean like our names?'

'Well, something like that. What did Kev mean about the paper?'

'Oh, I'm a reporter with the local weekly *Gazette*. Always looking for stories, wherever they are.'

'What kind of stories?'

'Any type really. But with some human interest where I can use a quirky angle.'

'How do you mean?'

'Well, I don't just report the facts, but the story behind them if I can. I had a story last week, for instance. A woman up in court who had beaten her husband. Very unusual. But she wouldn't give a reason why she'd done it. They found her guilty, fined her and put her on probation. But when we dug behind the facts, it turned out her husband had had an affair. With another man. And that's why she beat him up. So, who was in the wrong?'

'Crikey. How did you find that out?'

'Oh, I've got a colleague, Archie Sinclair. Used to be a crime reporter in Glasgow. He's got lots of contacts, and can find out anything about anybody. And everyone's got a secret.'

He leaned back and frowned. 'Really? I don't think I've got a secret.'

She laughed. 'Maybe you're the exception that proves the rule. Or maybe you just don't admit it to yourself.' She danced closer to him.

Katy intrigued him. She just seemed a lot older than seventeen. After his initial nerves, it had turned out a very enjoyable evening.

At closing time, the group broke up, and agreed to meet on the Tuesday evening at the sports hall. Pip and Katy went off together.

Adam found Janet outside the cloakroom, and helped put her coat on. As they left, they met Richard

Preston at the top of the stairs. 'Richard, this is my nephew, Adam,' Janet said. 'He'll join us on Monday.'

Richard smiled at Adam, and shook hands. 'Look forward to that. Welcome aboard.'

Adam thought he seemed a friendly guy, which didn't match his chat with the other man.

They strolled to the sea front, and along the esplanade to her apartment. 'Cup of tea?' she asked, as they entered.

'Yes, thanks. I want to talk to you anyway.'

'Okay.' She went into the kitchen.

They carried tea trays through to the lounge area. 'You want to talk?' she asked, and sat back in her chair.

'Well, it's kind of unusual.'

'Okay, I can take that.'

He took his notebook from his pocket. 'Because I'm deaf, I lip-read very well. Tonight, I watched two men talk in the lounge. I couldn't hear them, of course, but I know what they said. The two men were Richard Preston and Daniel Bloomfield.'

Janet's eyebrows rose, but she stayed silent. He opened his notebook, and read her the conversation. Her eyes widened. She leaned forward, and put her cup and saucer on the table. 'Are you sure Richard said that?'

He nodded. 'Yeah.'

She pursed her lips. 'This could be serious, Adam. Richard's a close friend, and my boss. And your boss too, come Monday. Are you certain?'

'Yes, I'm certain.'

She studied him. 'It's not that I don't believe you, Adam, but let's do a test with your hearing aid out. How far was Richard from you?'

He thought for a moment. 'About six yards or so.'

She put the radiogram on, turned up the volume, and stood Adam beside it. He took out his hearing aid. She faced him from halfway in the room, and spoke quietly.

'I went to Glasgow yesterday, and bought a new blue coat and a red skirt at Pettigrew's.'

He watched her speak, and repeated her words.

She turned off the radio, and beckoned him to sit. He put his hearing aid back in. 'I'll have to think about this, Adam. He did have a meeting in Manchester yesterday, but I thought it was about buying another store. This sounds much more serious. Let's sleep on it, and talk again in the morning.'

Chapter 3. Janet

Janet Barbour lay staring at the ceiling, facing a sleepless night. *Oh, my God, Richard. What have you got yourself into? Why are you doing this?* She thought she knew the man so well, but the remark reported by Adam was so alien to his nature. At least as she saw it.

She'd known Richard since their teenage years at the tennis club, when they'd formed a mixed doubles partnership that won the cup two years in a row. When she thought about it, that was the only time she'd seen any aggression in Richard. He was always just so laid back, with a great nature, a fund of funny stories, and hugely popular in his social circle. He was the epitome of the boy born with a silver spoon, and the last person she could think of who would plan to kill someone.

He'd been so helpful since the funeral, above all over the Christmas and New Year period. And on VE Day, May 8, she'd joined him and hundreds of others celebrating the end of the war. They laughed, cheered, and waved flags, with tears of joy, but for her mixed with tears of sadness. How she wished Harry had lived to see it. And Richard had arranged her move from Myrtle Avenue. He was just such a close friend. Adam's remark *couldn't* be right. Just *couldn't* be.

Now she'd become even more entwined with Richard. She thought back to mid-August, when she'd headed to yet another of Richard's dinner parties, and this time arrived first.

'Wow,' he said, 'you look great. Better than for a long time.'

'Thanks. I do feel better this week. I feel as though I've emerged from a long dark tunnel somehow, and it feels good.'

'That's great news. What will you do now?'

She shrugged. 'Don't know yet. I'll need to try and work something out.'

'Well, maybe I can help with that. What if I come round to your place tomorrow about ten?'

That was a surprise. Richard coming to see her?
'Okay, let's do that.'

'Good.' The doorbell rang. 'We'll talk then.' He went off to greet his next guests.

Next morning he arrived on time and kissed her cheek. Then came to the point. 'Look, Janet, you're more than a friend – more like a sister, in fact – and I'd like to try and help you – and help us at the same time.'

'What do you have in mind?'

'A couple of years ago at a dinner party, I moaned to you about my people, and you said, "What gets measured gets managed." I think it was Lord Kelvin you quoted. And that phrase has stuck with me ever since.

'There wasn't much I could do about it then. For the last six years we've just kept the business ticking over. But now the war's over, we've got a chance to move forward. And I'd like you to come and help me do that. Help me measure my people, and manage them. I'd give you a good salary and a bonus on top. What do you say, Janet? I'd love to have you with me.'

She tried to stay calm. She liked Richard a lot, but could she work with him every day? 'But Richard, I don't know anything about retail.'

'That's the whole point. We need to think in a different way now, and you've got loads of abilities we just don't have. Matt Lawson still raves about the work Harry and you did in his company ten years ago.'

'Well, that was manufacturing.'

'Don't do yourself down. Retail's a lot simpler than that. You're a talented woman, with a very sharp intellect. I think you'd be brilliant.'

Wow, what an opportunity. But could she *really* do something like that after such a long break? In the last year she'd lost her husband, her daughter (to a young man in London), and sold her house in Myrtle Avenue. But she felt she did need a challenge again. *What the hell, the war's over. Everything's up for grabs.* She'd make it work. *Let's go for it.*

'You know what? I'd like to try it.'

He clapped his hands, and stood up. 'That's great!'

'However, let's test the waters first. What if we give it six months to see if it'll work for both of us?'

'Sounds good to me.'

She held out her hand. 'Thank you, Richard. I'm very grateful.'

'It'll be a great partnership. Just like when we won the cup all these years ago.'

She laughed. 'Just like that.'

***

Next morning, she went to meet Richard at his store. She'd been there many times, but never in the executive suite on the fourth floor. Sara, his secretary, showed her into what would be her office to leave her hat and coat. Then into Richard's airy corner office, with great views across to the hills of Arran. She took a deep breath as she entered his office.

He stood up, very well dressed as usual, with a fresh flower in his buttonhole, and put her at ease. 'Come in, Janet. Have a seat, and welcome on board. I think together we can make this business great again. Let me tell you about it.'

She sat at his conference table, and tried to relax. He was impressive here. Master of all he surveyed.

He told her how his grandfather had started the business in 1887, then how his father had taken over in 1910 and had expanded the business into the present building. In the 1930s, his father had bought the *Gazette* to save it for the town, and the Egerton Hotel on Racecourse Road. But the department store was their main business.

Richard had taken control in 1940 with his father's passing, and had kept the business steady since then. But, with the war over, it was time to plan for the future.

'We need to take a hard look at the business from top to bottom, and change things to get it back on track. That's just too much for me alone. We've interviewed people from other stores, but they just didn't fit. You're almost like one of the family, Janet, and we think you'd be a great fit.

'We're aware of your lack of retail knowledge, so I've arranged a radio telephone call for you with Brad Marshall, a close friend of ours in the USA. He's an expert in retail operations, and has forgotten more than I've ever learned. That should be at four o'clock.'

'Do I have to prepare for that?' she asked, with a sense of unease.

'No, no. By then you'll have got a feel of how we work here, and you just need to listen and absorb what he says. He knows your background.'

'Okay, good.'

'Other than that, I'll show you around, and introduce you to Neil Hendry, my Finance Director. He's a bit old school. Been here thirty years, and thinks the right way to do things is the way my father did them, which irritates me at times. However, he only has a few more years to go now.'

Janet thought there didn't seem to be much love lost between Richard and Neil, at least on Richard's side.

'I'd also like you to meet the five floor managers and the stock control manager. They're the people who'll report to you.'

People reporting to me again? She'd need to prepare for that.

'Three of the floor managers have been in the services. Two have come back changed and may not stay, and the other one hasn't turned up yet. The only ones that have been here through the war are Peggy, who runs first-floor ladies' wear, and Connie, who runs this floor, household and furniture.'

'What did you do when the others were away?'

'I promoted senior associates from the floor on a temporary basis, and, on the whole, they did okay.'

'What do floor managers do then?'

'Oh, they . . .,' he waved, 'run the floor, deal with problems from customers or staff, make sure the floor is clean, clear, and well laid out, and meet sales targets.'

'And do they meet their sales targets?'

He screwed up his face. 'Well, kind of. In the last few years we haven't had targets as such. There was just too much going on with our people and with the products – or with rationing. But it's a good question. You should ask them what they think their targets are.'

'Okay, I will.' But she thought he sounded vague on details. Why mention sales targets if they didn't have any? Was he really on top of this business, driving its success, or was it his usual laid-back manner coming through? 'And you see my role as . . . what exactly?'

'Operations Director. Run the floors, put in your performance measures, take the tough decisions on staff, and help me run the business. You think with great clarity, and have great people skills. Okay, you've got to learn how the business works, but it's not that difficult.'

Janet pursed her lips. He'd lost some of his poise as the chat had gone on, almost as though he wasn't sure of his ground now. Yet he wanted her to commit to this role, which sounded like she had to take some nasty actions he knew were necessary, but didn't want to do himself. She was still intrigued, though. 'Okay, shall we have a quick look round?'

He smiled, and stood up. 'Fine, let's do that.'

They did a quick tour of each sales floor. Richard pointed out particular displays that had generated extra sales, and Janet began to see the store from a different point of view.

Richard introduced her to each floor manager. To her surprise, none of them impressed her. They seemed overawed by Richard, and hesitant to talk in his presence. She told each one she'd see them again later.

In the basement, she met the stock control manager, who showed her the stock rooms, packed full of products. She asked why there was so much stock.

'Some of it is new stock on the way in, waiting for space on the sales floor. The rest is last season's unsold goods held for the next sale in January.' He also looked nervous in Richard's presence.

Richard snorted. 'Oh, all the sales stuff will disappear in January.' Janet noted the stock control manager didn't comment on that.

They went back to the fourth floor and into Neil Hendry's office. Richard introduced her, and then left.

Neil was a silver-haired man with glasses and a slight stoop. He waved to a chair on Janet's side of the desk. 'Please, sit down, Mrs Barbour.'

'Oh, please call me Janet.' She looked around. Lots of neat piles of papers on the conference table, but his desk was almost clear. He seemed a very precise man.

He settled himself behind the desk. 'It's good to meet you at last,' he said, with a smile. 'I knew your husband through masonic links. He was such a great man, and a huge loss when he passed on.'

Her breath caught at his mention of Harry. He seemed so sincere too. 'Thank you,' she murmured.

'I understand Richard wants you to introduce measures of performance, and I agree with that, of course. However, in my view, measures are only part of the story. We need to act on them, if they're to be of any use. And we don't do that at all.'

Janet was surprised at his vehemence. 'Do you have an example?'

'Yes, I do. This should be a simple business to run. We buy products from a range of suppliers that we think our customers will want to buy. We sell in a comfortable shop at RPM prices that give us a good gross margin. If we keep our costs in line, we make good profits. Simple, except it doesn't quite work like that here.'

Janet raised an eyebrow in surprise. 'RPM prices?'

'Sorry, that's resale price maintenance. All retailers must sell products at prices set by the manufacturer. It avoids unfair competition.'

'Oh, of course.'

'So, take the first of these – buying in the right products. I think our buyers are okay on the whole. However, Richard continually interferes with their choices. He thinks he has "the eye", but he doesn't. We now sell less than half our products at full price because of the amount we have to offload at sale time. And that's a problem. Did you meet our stock control manager on your travels?'

'I did. He showed me the stock in the basement.'

'Uh-huh. Well, when you next meet him, ask to see Walker Street. It's a warehouse we rent to store even more products we can't sell. We should dump them on to specialists that sell surplus stock, but Richard won't allow it. We spend lots of money to keep them. And it's got to stop.'

'Have you talked to Richard about this?'

'Oh, yes.' He snorted. 'At every board meeting. And his mother tells him too. But I'm afraid Richard won't take tough decisions that might reflect on him. And you can't run a business like that.'

This doesn't sound good. 'So, do you make money or not?'

'Well, we scrape by. We make a small net profit, but it should be a great deal more. It's the net profit that allows us to reinvest in the business, and we don't do that well enough.'

Janet took a deep breath. It sounded like there were lots of problems under the surface. 'What measures of performance do you use?'

'It's mostly all sales related. We track overall sales by floor and by department, but I'd really like to know the sales by associate. However, the associates resist this, and so far, Richard has backed off. He won't confront them. But I think some of our associates are not that effective. We also track our costs so we know where we make money and where we don't. And that's it.'

Janet sat and thought for a moment. He'd been very open with her and seemed to talk a lot of sense. But she needed time to think about what he'd said. And Richard's hands-off approach bothered her. She stood and shook his hand. 'Thank you so much, Neil. I'd like to come back and talk to you again if I may?'

'Of course. Any time. My door's always open. I'm here to help. I just hope you can pull it all together, and help us turn the corner. You seem to get on well with Richard and the family, so that's a great start.'

She went back to Richard's office. He looked up as she knocked and opened the door. 'How did it go with Neil, then?'

'Went well. He has some measures in place for sales and products, but none for people. We need to fix that.'

'Sounds good. So, what about this afternoon?'

'I'll talk with the floor managers again. I want to know more about what they do.'

'That's fine. And we've had a telegram from the States. Brad will take a call from us at four o'clock. So you should be back here then. And my mother would like to see you at the end of the day – say around five thirty – at Laurel Avenue, if that's okay?'

'Yes, of course.'

'Good. Let's go for lunch.'

They ate in a private dining room adjacent to the main restaurant. Janet looked around. 'Very nice.'

Richard smiled. 'Yes, it's for directors and VIPs. You should eat here when you're around. Just let Sara know, and she'll organise it.'

After lunch, Janet met with each floor manager again. They began to relax with her one-to-one. Each of them had a fount of knowledge on how the business really operated, warts and all. The stock control manager took her to Walker Street, and showed her the stock held there. By four o'clock she was back in the boardroom for the call to Brad.

He came on the line. 'Welcome to the toughest business in the world.'

'That's not what I want to hear, Brad.'

He laughed. 'I know, but it's true. It sounds simple. You get as many folks as you can into your store, and then get them to buy as much as possible when they're in there. A zillion experts will tell you how to do it, but you've just got to figure out what works for you, and stick with it.'

'Right. Where do I start?'

'Okay. Let me go through my three pillars of retail management – give the customer value; give him a great shopping experience; and train and incentivise your people to deliver. Since you've never worked in retail before, can I cover some basics first?'

'Yes, please do.' She got ready to take notes.

During the next hour, he took her through the details of his three pillars. His approach was clear and logical, and gave her a route map to deliver a successful retail operation. He agreed to send his write-ups on each element so she could train her staff.

He finished off. 'Hope it all makes sense, Janet.'

She now needed time to absorb it all. 'It certainly does, Brad, and thank you for sharing it with me. Once I work out how I apply it here, maybe we can talk again?'

'Sure. Any time. Just set it up with a telegram.'

She read through her notes. Both Neil Hendry and Brad had similar views on how to run a successful retail business. The knowledge was already here. Richard just didn't apply it. So, with her knowledge of business, and support from Neil and Brad, it might not be so tough.

She now also saw Richard in a different light. He had such an enviable position, yet didn't seem in control. *Just what really motivated him?*

It was now after five o'clock, and Richard wasn't in his office. She put on her hat and coat, and headed off to see Richard's mother, Eleanor, at Laurel Avenue. Maybe *she'd* cast more light on the situation.

***

Janet walked from the town centre, out along the esplanade, and then turned onto Laurel Avenue. The hedge on her left shielded the Preston house, but through slight gaps, she glimpsed the lawn and gardens. The Prestons still had full-time staff to help.

The housekeeper, Meg, showed her through to the large garden room, with its semi-circular window that looked out over the garden to the sea beyond. Mrs Preston rose from her seat at the window. 'My dear Janet. Good to see you again.' She waved to a chair beside her. 'Please, sit here.'

Mrs Preston was always immaculate, her tall figure enhanced by long dresses, her once blonde hair now largely grey. She was still a very elegant woman. 'And how are you today, Mrs Preston? Keeping well?'

'Yes, I'm fine, thanks.'

'Richard said you wanted to see me.'

'That's right. I wanted to talk to you about the opportunity at the shop, and perhaps help you make up your mind one way or the other.'

'Okay.' Janet settled herself into her chair.

'Have you ever heard the phrase, *rags to rags in three generations?*'

Janet shook her head.

'It's a Yorkshire phrase. Charles and I first heard it before the war at a business dinner in Glasgow, from a couple who owned a large department store in Leeds. The phrase meant the founder of a business started poor – in rags – and built the business up. It then was well run by the next generation, because they picked up knowledge from the founder. But then the third generation didn't have the talent, and enjoyed the perks too much, and the business folded – back to rags.

'The phrase bothered Charles because he'd begun to have doubts over Richard's ability to run the business. In the end, he concluded that, when he retired, he'd move Richard up to chairman, and bring in someone from outside the family as managing director.

'However, then the war came and . . . well . . . Charles passed in 1940. We've more or less just kept the business ticking over since then. I have to be honest with you. Neither Neil Hendry nor I have been impressed with how Richard has performed over these years. So, just after VE day, I sat Richard down, and told him the plan for the future.'

'And how did he take it?'

'To my surprise, he took it well. He has great strengths, of course, but he's not a detail man, and avoids conflict. As MD, you have to be hard at times, and take tough decisions. He just can't seem to do that.

'So we put a discreet advert in the *Glasgow Herald* for an MD, and got a number of replies. Richard and I did joint interviews with the best candidates, but were shocked at the poor quality. And we weren't looking for a world-class expert either – you know, like Brad Marshall. We just wanted someone competent we could rely on. But he wasn't there.

'That's why we changed direction and looked internally. We think we've some bright people, and we also have time. We reckon rationing will go on for another few years. Neil thinks it might even last another five years, my goodness. But it gives us time to develop our bright people.

'Then, of course, when we heard you wanted to start work again, it seemed like a golden opportunity for us and for you. I've always been a great admirer of you, Janet, and that's why we wanted to offer you a senior position with us. We're well aware you have no retail background, but we think you can learn that. Then set your performance standards, run the floors, and do a great job for us. And, if it all works out, you could then take over as MD, and let Richard prosper as chairman.'

Janet was stunned. *Managing Director?* That was way beyond what Richard had said. Yet he must have known. Maybe they'd planned it this way. *This put a very different angle on the opportunity.*

'I . . . I don't know what to say,' she stammered. 'I'm speechless.'

'Yes, I'm sure you're surprised. But we think it's a risk worth taking, if you're willing to give it a go. After all, we've known you for years – you're like one of the family, for heaven's sake. And that would give Richard the chance to expand the business. We're lucky enough to still have good cash reserves, and I think Richard's shrewd enough to assess other business opportunities. He has good contacts, you know, although I'm a bit concerned about his current involvement with the Economic League.'

Janet hadn't heard of it. 'What's that?'

'Oh, it's typical Richard. It looks after the interests of businesses around the country. Most medium and large companies are members. Among other things, it maintains a list of left-wing activists and communists that might harm a business. We check potential employees against it before they're hired.

'Richard has got himself elected as a regional rep. But he's also joined a spin-off group called Triumph, which meets once a month in Manchester. It lobbies for businesses in a more direct way. That's as much as I know. Richard seems keen, and thinks it can help us in the long run. So I'm going along with it for now.'

Janet only half listened to Mrs Preston. Her mind raced with thoughts of being MD of Preston's department store, and all that entailed.

Then Richard arrived home. 'Has mother given you the grand plan, Janet? What do you think?'

'I'm a bit stunned, but excited too.'

'Well, it would be good for us all. And as I said, we make a great team.'

Janet told him about her discussion with Brad. They then chatted for a while, with Richard in full entertainment mode, with plenty of smiles and laughter all round, until Janet excused herself and headed home.

She was confused by the events of the day. Was she really better than the people the Prestons interviewed? They must think so, but what was the basis of that decision? She had to trust that the Prestons – or at least Mrs Preston – knew what they were doing. It was their business, after all, so they wouldn't take such a decision lightly. They must expect her to work her way into the job – to direct the operations first, and then move up from there. *Okay, then that's just what she'd do.*

***

Over the next couple of weeks, Janet talked at length with Neil Hendry, the floor managers, the stock control manager, and with Brad in the US on the detail of his pillars, and pulled together her plans for the future.

She presented them at the September board meeting. They were in three parts: get rid of surplus stock to stem the bleeding of cash; improve the customer experience to bring more people into the store and have them buy more; and train the staff and introduce new measures of performance, which in turn would drive an incentive scheme for all staff except directors. Her approach mirrored Brad's in the US, adapted to Ayr.

She gave her key figures. 'With these plans, we should improve our sales by a third. I think that's achievable.'

Richard cut in. 'Are these figures right?' He looked at Neil.

'Yep, they're correct. And our profits would return to where they should be, which we would all welcome.'

'You can say that again,' Richard mused.

Mrs Preston just sat quietly with a smile on her face.

They discussed the incentive scheme in detail, but in the end, the board approved Janet's plans. Mrs Preston said before she left, 'That's what we've needed for a long time now. Well done, Janet.'

Afterwards, Janet called her best friend, Helen. They'd talked at length on the phone about Helen's son, Adam, a bright lad, who found it hard to get and hold a job, just because he was partly deaf. Janet confirmed to Helen that the position at Preston's as her aide was now Adam's. He should start on Monday.

And so here she was, in the darkness of her bedroom, still awake, worried about Adam's message. *What should she do?*

As she worked more closely with Richard, she'd seen some traits that troubled her. But this new issue was much more serious. In a way, she'd prefer to ignore it, and let events take their course. But that was impossible now. Adam looked up to her, and would expect some moral guidance. After all, she was his godmother. She needed advice, and remembered Harry's brother's wife had a relative, Sandra Maxwell, who was a senior police officer in Glasgow. Maybe she could help.

Chapter 4. Sandra Maxwell

Superintendent Sandra Maxwell, head of Special Branch for the West of Scotland, enjoyed her Sunday mornings. They were her 'me time', when she relaxed her long limbs in a languorous bath, and then savoured breakfast with the Sunday papers.

Her mother went off to church, and she relished the silence of the big house in Hyndland, in the West End of Glasgow. She herself had given up on the church years ago, long before the war, when the love of her life had been killed in an RAF flying accident. Her local church minister had tried to comfort her. 'It's God's will,' he said, a phrase she thought was really stupid, because it implied life was pre-ordained.

In her grief, she'd snapped back, 'Nonsense! It was a maintenance error, and avoidable. That's not pre-ordained,' and walked out of the room in anger. In her job, she saw daily examples of lowlifes doing nasty things to innocent people. To think of all that as pre-ordained was just absurd. People were responsible for their own actions.

Then the phone rang. She picked up the receiver. 'Two-five-six-seven?'

'Is that Sandra?' A woman, sounding hesitant.

'It is.'

'Hello, Sandra. This is Janet Barbour here. I was married to Harry, Fred's brother. We've met several times at family parties.'

Sandra remembered her. 'Are you the business expert?' She always admired women who had prospered in a man's world.

'That's right.'

'Oh, hello. What can I do for you?'

'Well, I have a bit of a problem here in Ayr that might be a police matter. I'd like some advice, please.'

Sandra's professional brain kicked in and she pulled a pad and pencil towards her. 'Okay, tell me about it.'

'My young nephew, Adam, is with me at the moment. He's partially deaf and has a talent for lip-reading. Last night, at the local tennis club, Adam lip-read a conversation between two men – both close friends of mine – that has given us cause for concern. Hence why I called.'

'Okay, what was the conversation?'

'Here it is.' She read it, giving Sandra time to note it.

When she finished, Sandra sat back. *Could be something sinister.*

'How accurate is Adam's lip-reading?'

'Well, I did a test with him, and he got my words a hundred percent.'

'You say you know these men? Who's saying he'll *kill the captain*?'

'That's Richard Preston, owner of the large department store here in town, and various other businesses. Probably the richest man in the area. He's also my boss, as it happens.'

'Do you think he's capable of killing someone?'

Janet snorted. 'Not at all. It's a ridiculous thought.'

'But he could pay someone else to do it?'

There was a pause. 'I suppose he could.'

'And the other man? Who's he?'

'That's Daniel Bloomfield, his very sharp lawyer.'

'And will they meet this morning?'

'Yes. They and two others meet every Sunday to play golf. It's said that during their game, they sort out everything to do with money and business in this town.'

'And who are the two others?'

'One is Johno Houston, who's a top accountant with a firm in Glasgow. The other is Matt Lawson, who runs a large engineering company here in town.' Janet hesitated. 'You know, Sandra, this is . . . nonsense. I've known these men all my adult life. There's no way they'd get involved in anything like this. I'm sorry, I shouldn't have bothered you.'

'Oh, it's no bother.' Sandra wished she had a pound for every time a family member said that about a businessman she'd arrested. 'Do you know why Preston was in Manchester?'

'Yes. On Thursday, he had a meeting with his accountants to do with expanding our business. On the Friday he had another business meeting, but I don't know the details. His mother mentioned it a few weeks ago. If you give me time, I might remember.'

'Okay. Does Preston travel much?'

'Not really. He's at the shop most days, but goes to Manchester or London – maybe once a month?'

'By car or train?'

'Train.'

'Have you heard him refer to anyone as captain?'

'I haven't. I mean, there are the obvious ones – at the tennis club or golf club. But they don't fit. I can't think of anyone else.'

'Do you have any idea why Glasgow?'

'I'm sorry, I don't.'

Sandra thought for a moment. 'I'd like you to have a think on the Manchester meeting, and any reference to a captain. I'll come down and talk with you and Adam later today. Would that be okay?'

'Yes, of course.'

'Good. I'll be there around three o'clock. And neither of you should talk to anyone about this, okay? Now, what's your address?' Sandra took a note of it and ended the call.

Lip-reading evidence could be a problem in court. She'd had a case a year ago when they had secretly filmed a man suspected of stealing war equipment. He met another man and the film showed him speaking. She brought in an expert lip-reader to transcribe what the man said. His words named yet another man, unknown to her team, and that led to evidence of further collusion, from which they built a watertight case.

But the lawyers were reluctant to use lip-reading as part of their case. They put its accuracy between thirty and seventy percent. Thus, the defence could challenge it as unreliable 'hearsay' if there was no confirming evidence. Because of this, some judges wouldn't accept lip-reading evidence, so the lawyers preferred not to use it at all if they didn't have to. But Sandra herself believed lip-reading could often provide a lead to other evidence. She saw it as a useful tool in the fight against crime.

She called one of her team, Inspector Tom Hamilton, who lived in Ayr, and asked him to meet her at Ayr Police HQ around four o'clock. She then called Colonel Charles 'Chuck' Campbell of the US Army Air Force, based at Prestwick Airport, and asked to see him around five o'clock. 'Think it might be important.'

'That means it *is* important, Sandra. No problem, see you then.'

***

Her driver dropped her at the block of flats. Sandra pressed the 'Barbour' button and the door buzzed open. She took the lift to the top floor.

'Thanks for coming,' Janet said, and shook hands.

Sandra smiled. 'Good to see you again.' She looked out of the windows to the sea and the hills beyond. 'Magnificent view.'

Janet guided her into the apartment. 'Yes, it is. I'm very pleased with it. Gives me all I need now.'

'Oh, of course. I was sorry to hear about Harry. Sorry for your loss.'

'Thanks.' They entered the lounge. 'This is Adam.'

Sandra shook his hand. He was a fine young man, she thought, and noted his hearing aid in place.

While Janet made tea, Sandra talked with Adam about what he planned to do in Ayr. She was surprised to learn he was starting at the Preston department store the next day. But he then explained the circumstances. She realised how conflicted Janet must feel in this situation.

Once seated, Sandra pulled out her notebook. 'I'd like to check on our discussion earlier. Is that okay?'

They both nodded.

'Good. First of all, I'd like to test your lip-reading, Adam. How far away from Mr Preston were you?'

'About six yards or so.'

Sandra asked him to go to the end of the room and then stood six yards from him. 'I'll speak to you, Adam. Would you take off your hearing aid, and repeat my words back to me please?'

He pulled out the aid and switched it off.

As she turned away to get her notebook, she said, 'Oh, would you just move your cup please, Adam?' She turned back and Adam still stood in the same position, waiting to start.

Janet stepped forward. 'I'll move it.'

Sandra waved. 'No, it's okay. Forget it.' Janet seemed very nervous.

She checked her notebook and faced Adam. 'Yesterday, I met a Captain Wyper from Manchester, but he just spoke a lot of nonsense.'

He repeated her words exactly.

'Okay, thank you.'

They resumed their seats and Adam put his hearing aid back in.

'Very impressive.' Sandra turned to Janet. 'Now, Manchester. Have you remembered anything about Preston's Friday meeting?'

'Yes. His mother mentioned a meeting of the Economy League, or something like that?'

'Do you mean the Economic League?'

'Yes, that's it. Have you heard of it?'

'It's to do with businesses, I think.'

'Richard's a regional rep and meets with a spin-off group called Triumph in Manchester. I think that was his meeting on Friday.'

Sandra took notes. 'Do you know where they meet?'

'It's a hotel in the centre. The Midland.'

'Okay. So, the meeting referred to would have taken place on the twenty-eighth?'

'That's correct.'

'Does he keep a diary or notes on his meetings?'

'He keeps a notebook with his decisions and actions from meetings every day. He uses it to organise his time and thoughts.'

'Uh-huh. Is there any chance you could see his entry for Friday?'

Janet blushed and shuffled in her seat. She seemed uncomfortable at the question. 'He keeps it in his desk, so I think it's unlikely.'

Sandra tried to calm her. 'Well, if you could, it would be helpful. After all, Adam might have got his words wrong, or there might be an innocent explanation. We should try to find out, shouldn't we?'

Sandra thought both of them were now uneasy with her. Maybe they now realised the implications of getting her involved.

'Why don't you just ask him?' Adam asked.

Sandra pursed her lips. 'Well, that's not a good idea for two reasons. First, if he *is* planning something sinister, he'd simply deny it, and we'd lose the chance to catch a potential criminal. Second, it would destroy the rapport you both need to have with this man in future, probably to your disadvantage.'

Janet and Adam digested this. Janet blurted out, 'He's not a criminal. He's just not the type.'

Sandra thought for a moment. 'Can I tell you a true story? Two years ago, we knew there was a group of German spies in the country, but we didn't know who or where they were. Then, one day, one of the group made an error. And that single mistake allowed us to identify them, arrest them, and put a stop to their activities. Now, one man was a lecturer at Glasgow University. When we convicted him, it stunned his colleagues. They had no idea such a fine man could do that. So, you never know what truly motivates other people, even people you know well.'

'Everyone has a secret,' Adam murmured.

Sandra glanced over at him. 'Pardon?'

'Oh, sorry. Someone said that to me last night, and I scoffed at the time.'

Janet cleared her throat. 'If this *did* turn out to be some sort of crime, could you keep us out of it?'

Sandra hesitated. The point was important for them, but she had to be honest. 'Well, I can't give a guarantee, but we'd always try to protect your identity. You would also probably not be called as witnesses. Evidence of a crime would have to come from other sources.'

There was silence again in the room.

Sandra checked her notebook again. 'Have you had any further thoughts on this captain Preston mentioned?'

Janet shook her head. 'I've never heard him refer to anyone as captain, other than those at the golf club or tennis club. I've just no idea.'

'Okay. Not to worry.' Sandra closed her notebook. 'So, you asked me here to give you advice. I think you should behave just as normal. Don't upset the relationships you have with Mr Preston. But if you can find any info from Friday, or hear him refer to anyone as "captain", please let me know.' She gave each of them a card. 'That number should get through to me at any time.' She stood up. 'Oh, and if he has a meeting out of town, would you also let me know? And I *will* do my best to keep you out of it. But please don't talk to anyone else about this. Agreed?'

They nodded, stood and shook hands. 'Thank you,' Janet said, with a weak smile.

Sandra left them to their thoughts. She felt that if Janet, earlier in the day, had thought her way through what they'd just discussed, there was a strong possibility she wouldn't have called her. It wasn't easy to report friend or family to the police, and she sympathised with Janet's position. She'd probably felt obliged to act because of Adam. *But,* she told herself, *you've a job to do – catch the bad guys without fear or favour.*

***

The police HQ was in an old building, just off the High Street. Tom Hamilton was already there. 'Got a problem, ma'am?' he asked.

She waved him to sit. 'Could be. Do you know a man called Preston? He runs the department store here.'

'I know *of* him, but I've never met him.'

Sandra summarised the call from Janet, and her discussion. 'There may be nothing in it, of course, but we're better safe than sorry. So, let's do the obvious. Put a tap on his home and office phones. My authority. And put a tail on him. Let's build up a picture of this guy.

Let's get to know him better. But keep the tail well out of sight.'

'Sure. What about the golf game on Sunday? If the others are part of the plot, do we follow them too?'

Sandra thought for a moment. 'Well, we can't put a tail on them all. And we'll never pick up what they say on a golf course. If Preston's the leader, let's just find out more about him first, and then follow the others if we need to. One of them's a sharp lawyer, so he'll know all the tricks. Is that okay with you?'

'Yes, fine. Leave it with me.'

'We also have to work out why Glasgow? They seem to know a particular sniper that can do a job for them. I haven't heard of anyone recently, but let's put out feelers and see what we can find. Keep in mind the story from Birmingham last week of the ex-soldier who shot a pub landlord after an argument. Tragic. But we could have damaged ex-soldiers with guns in Glasgow too. So keep your eyes and ears open. I'll talk to the chief about it tomorrow. Give me an update every day.'

'Okay. Will do, ma'am.'

***

Back in the car for the few miles' drive to Prestwick Airport, Sandra thought about her next meeting. She enjoyed working with the Americans. They were so relaxed compared with her colleagues in Scotland. She was by far the highest ranked woman in the Scottish police force, yet some of her colleagues seemed to regard her as an alien. The Americans just accepted her. Very refreshing.

An airman showed her into a conference room in a low building marked with a USAAF plaque, on the far side of the runway. Chuck and another man stood as she entered. Both were dressed in sweaters and slacks. The other man seemed familiar, sturdy with a big smile, though she was sure she hadn't met him before.

Chuck came forward and shook her hand. 'Sandra, great to see you again. Let me introduce you.' He turned to his colleague. 'General, this is Superintendent Sandra Maxwell of the Scottish Police. She looks after us real well over here.' He turned to her. 'Sandra, this is our commander-in-chief, General Eisenhower.'

She almost dropped on the spot. *Of course it was.* The last time she'd seen him was on a cinema newsreel standing next to Churchill. The general came over and shook her hand. 'Pleased to meet you, ma'am. Thanks for looking after Chuck and the boys.'

She recovered quickly. 'Oh, it's a pleasure, sir. Is this your first visit to Scotland?'

'It is. And I should just say it's a little bit of heaven on earth you have here. We took some time off yesterday and played some golf at . . . where was it, Chuck?'

'Turnberry, sir.'

'Yeah, Turnberry. Beautiful golf course, with the water and the hills, and that special rock in the water. What's it called again, Chuck?'

'Ailsa Craig, sir.'

'Yeah, that's it. Just beautiful. Then we went on to Culzean Castle. Do you know it?'

'I know *of* it, but I've never been there.'

'Oh, it's very special. I'll be back with Mamie next time. Let her see this wonderful country of yours.'

'Well, anything I can do to help, just call me, sir.'

'Will do, ma'am. Well, you guys are here to talk, so let me go grab a cup of coffee, and leave you to it. Nice meeting you, Sandra.'

'And you, General.' They shook hands again, and he left the room. Sandra turned to Chuck. 'Wow. What a man. He just oozes charisma.'

'He sure does. And you'll see more of him. He's just been gifted the top apartment at Culzean Castle, so he expects to be over here more often. Wants to just play golf and relax.'

'Really? How did he get that?'

'Oh, the family who owned the castle wanted to sell, but would be hit with a huge tax bill. So, to avoid that, they gifted it to your National Trust, on condition the general had the exclusive use of the top apartment for life in recognition of his leadership during the war. And everyone agreed, so here we are. He's on his way back to Washington, and took the opportunity to see Culzean. It's magnificent, Sandra. They say it's the finest work of a Scottish architect, Robert Adam. The general's thrilled with it.' He waved to Sandra to take a seat. 'Anyway, you wanted to see me.'

'I do, Chuck. Thanks for your time. We've picked up signals of a possible assassination on someone referred to as the captain. Now, we've no idea who that may be. But one thought I had was your Captain Akers. He's the front man for your deep-water submarine base study. Since it leaked a few weeks ago, and with atom bombs dropped on Japan, there's some anti-American feeling around. So can you double up on security for Captain Akers, and keep him out of Glasgow.'

Chuck pursed his lips. 'So, let me check this. You don't know Akers is the target, but it's a possibility?'

'That's correct.'

'How real is the threat?'

'I don't know, Chuck. The people behind it are rich enough to pay someone to do it. And we've a lot of men back from the war, damaged beyond repair, their moral compass shot to hell, and some have held on to their guns. We've got all sorts of problems around the country with these guys, so I don't want to take any chances. Better safe than sorry.'

'Sure, I agree. We'll increase security for Akers. Is there any other help we can give you on this?'

She thought for a moment. 'I don't think so. But if we find we're up against trained military, then I may come back to you.'

'Please do. We're always happy to help.' He stood up. 'Well, thanks for the warning. I'll see you out.'

As they emerged from the building, there was the loud clattering noise of an aircraft engine.

Sandra watched an aircraft hover, and then slowly descend and land nearby. 'Wow. What's that?'

Chuck smiled. 'That's a brilliant new type of aircraft. One of our new Sikorsky R-4B helicopters, otherwise known as a "whirlybird" or "eggbeater". It flies – and it hovers. It's a brilliant machine. We've got it fitted out with cameras to take both still and moving pictures. It's transformed our survey work. The general and I flew over the Clyde this morning, and had a look at potential sites for the new base. Because we can hover, it gives us time to study the details from a new angle, and take pictures and movies of the area. We think the Holy Loch looks interesting, so we'll see what happens once he gets back to Washington.'

'Wow. It's fantastic.'

'Once it settles in, I'll take you up, and give you the full experience.'

'That would be great.'

'And maybe we could have dinner afterwards.'

She hesitated. *Was he flirting with her?* She hadn't thought of him in that way. She saw him as tall, rugged, capable – and now, interesting. 'Well, let's see.'

They shook hands and she got back in the car. On the way back to Glasgow, she planned out her talk with the chief the next day, and sketched an outline plan to find potential snipers in the Glasgow area. She also planned to talk with her opposite number in Manchester,

Frank Parker, to see if he could dig up some info on this Triumph group that met there. She *had* to find evidence that led back to Preston.

Chapter 5. Strang

After the war, Strang had two jobs. One, a self-employed plumber in London. The other, killing people for money. Lots of money.

He'd killed his first man just before the war started, when he was eighteen, and sill known as Ricky.

The man was the son of George Cornish, who had abused Ricky two or three times a week from the age of eleven. Ricky remembered that first time as though it was yesterday.

George was a coach at the football team, and had singled Ricky out for one-to-one training. 'You're a good lad, Ricky. Got a great future in the game. And I can get you into United when the time is right. Would you like that? It's how you get on in football. You look after me, and I look after you. But you don't tell anyone. This is just between us. You're special, Ricky. Okay? Spit and shake and hope to die?' He spat into his hand, and held it out.

There were just the two of them in the dressing room. Ricky wasn't sure, but he would love to play for United. George had a friendly smile. *Nice guy.* Ricky spat into his hand and shook George's.

'That's great, Ricky. Now, if you just do me a special favour, it'd be a great start.' He dropped his shorts. Ricky couldn't help but look at his big prick. George took Ricky's hand. 'Just fold your fingers round it and pull it. Nice and firm. That's it. You see how quickly it stiffens. That's because you're so good. Oh, God, it feels great. Keep going. A little bit faster now. That's it. Oh, my God.' George closed his eyes and clenched his jaw as he spurted. 'Oh, God, that was great.

You're a special lad, and I promise you'll go far in this game. But remember, not a word to anyone. Okay?'

Ricky nodded, not sure what had just happened. But George seemed happy. 'Okay, George.'

He lived with his mother, and told her George said he could have a great future with United. 'Oh, that's good,' she said.

***

The abuse continued for years, with mutual sessions once Ricky could get an erection. He wondered if this meant he secretly enjoyed the experience, even though he felt nothing – no elation – no joy – nothing. It only stopped when Ricky was fourteen, and refused to take George up his bottom. George lost interest and moved on to other lads.

To try and blot out that experience, Ricky joined a local gym that focused on weights and judo training. He built up his upper body strength and ability in hand-to-hand combat. He was proud of the strength in his arms and hands, but didn't smile much.

Two incidents combined on that fateful evening just after his eighteenth birthday. Ricky had just heard that George's son, John, had got a trial for United. He felt duped. John Cornish was nowhere near as good a player as he was.

And his girlfriend, Emma, had broken off their relationship, such as it was. He knew they had problems, and that it was his fault. He really liked her, and they often petted. When he fondled her breasts, he got an erection. But when she put her hand down to play with him, it subsided. He knew it had something to do with the Cornish experience, but didn't know how to fix it.

That night, anger welled up inside him like a volcano. He cursed Cornish and his whole bloody family. He ended up in a pub, and had a couple of large whiskies to drown his sorrows. This was unusual, since Ricky prided himself on his fitness. He noticed John Cornish on the other side of the pub having an argument with a group of lads.

Cornish then stormed out. Ricky slipped out a side door and followed him. Light rain made the darkness even more oppressive. Cornish walked for a bit and then turned into a narrow side street. Ricky looked around. It was all quiet. Cornish had stopped for a pee. Ricky walked towards him. 'Need a hand with that, mate?'

Cornish glanced up as he fastened his fly. 'No. I'm okay. Not into that.'

'But I know someone who is. Your father.'

Cornish shook his head. 'No way, mate,' he replied with a smirk.

The pompous bastard. He deserved to die. It took just a second for Ricky to use a judo move and get Cornish on his back in a choke-hold. He squeezed harder, and watched Cornish's eyes change from wonderment to fear, and then to realise that Ricky's face was the last thing he'd see. A train passed at the end of the street. Its lights flashed on them. Ricky held his hands in position until Cornish lay still.

Ricky lifted Cornish, and carried him through a break in the fence onto the rail track. He reckoned this must be the main line into King's Cross. He put Cornish face down with his neck and hands on the nearest rail. He took a finger of one hand, and wrote 'SORRY' in the dirt beside the track, then put the hand back on to the rail. He turned Cornish's head to the left, then stepped back towards the fence. A few minutes later, a train came round the far bend towards him and passed over the body. The eight fingers and severed head rolled into the space between the rails. The body rolled a couple of times along the side of the track.

Ricky peered at the blood oozing from the neck wounds, and checked the area. There wasn't too much soft ground, so there were no footprints. All seemed fine. Everyone would just assume the lad had committed suicide. He made his way back through the fence, up the street, and home.

***

The local newspaper was full of young Cornish's suicide. The lad had personal problems, and had threatened suicide before.

Ricky went to the cemetery on the day of the funeral. He stood well back, behind a wall and a hedge, but could see a stunned George Cornish leading the group of mourners. A young lad came along the side of the wall and stopped. 'You're Ricky, aren't you?'

'Yeah.'

'I'm Donny. A couple of years behind you at school. Were you raped by that big bastard too?'

Ricky shook his head. 'No.'

'He raped me for three years. Full of great promises.' Donny stared through the hedge. 'I should be happy to see him so unhappy. But I'm not. The only happy day I'll have is when *he's* in the ground.'

At that moment, Ricky decided George Cornish deserved to die too.

***

He planned it in detail this time. He bought a pair of flesh-coloured unlined rubber gloves from Boots, and wore them each time he prepared something.

He took a couple of sheets of 'Notice' paper and a pencil from the dressing room, and copied George's handwriting for the 'suicide note'.

Can't live without John. Need to join him. Sorry.

He stalked George for a few weeks and found he visited a pub on a Wednesday night, then left on his own to drive home in his van.

The next Wednesday, Ricky 'just happened to pass' as George left the pub. 'Hi, George. How're you doing?'

The rain teemed down, and George peered at him in the darkness.

'Any chance of a lift, mate?' Ricky asked.

George seemed to recognise him. 'Okay, jump in.'

As he drove, George asked, 'You play for anyone these days?'

'Yeah, Enfield.'

'Not a bad team. How're you getting on with them?'

'Oh, I think my claim to fame is I have the biggest prick in the team.'

George guffawed. 'Biggest prick in the team? I'd like to see that.'

'Well, if you're up for a mutual, take one of these side streets. It's quiet enough here.'

George glanced at him. 'Serious?'

'Sure. No problem.'

'Okay, you're on.' George turned off the main road into a quiet side street lined with factories, all locked up at this time of night. Ricky thought the rail line at the end of the street must be the same line he'd used before, but a few hundred yards further along. George drove to the end of the street and switched off the engine. 'Okay. Show me this big prick, then.'

Ricky leaned back as though to unfasten his fly. As George leaned over towards him, Ricky grabbed his neck in a choke-hold and squeezed tighter and tighter. George struggled to get out of the hold, but slowly lost consciousness. Ricky enjoyed the changes in his eyes, just as before with John. Within a few minutes, George was still.

Ricky pulled on the rubber gloves. Then took a sheet of blank paper and the pencil he'd taken from the dressing room, covered them with George's fingerprints, and placed them on the pile of papers on the dashboard. He then took out the 'suicide message', placed George's fingerprints on it, and put it in George's pocket.

He got out of the van, went round to the driver's side, lifted George out, and carried him to a break in the fence at the end of the street. He came back, locked the van, and put the keys in George's coat pocket. He made sure no footprints showed from the passenger side.

He then lifted George onto the rail track and positioned him as he'd done before with John. Then he moved back to the fence. Within a few minutes, a train came and decapitated George. Ricky made his way through the fence, past the parked van, and home.

***

A week later, he was back at the cemetery behind the wall, and watched the cortege arrive. Donny sidled up to him. 'Didn't think I'd see you again so soon.'

They watched the ceremony in silence.

Donny glanced at him. 'See the papers say he was to be questioned about child abuse. They say that's what drove him to suicide.'

'So they say.'

They stood in silence again.

Ricky glanced at Donny. 'You happy now?'

Donny frowned. 'Happy?'

'Last time you told me it would be the happiest day of your life when you saw that big bastard in the ground. So is this your happiest day?'

'Yeah, probably.'

'So what will you do now?'

Donny shrugged. 'Don't know.'

Ricky turned to him. 'Listen, Donny. Don't let him ruin your life, even after he's dead. In an ideal world, what would you like to do?'

'Be a mechanic. For cars.'

'Okay, that's good. Go and get a trade. Or join the army. You'll get great training in the army.'

Donny looked down. Ricky grabbed his upper arm. 'Donny. Will you do it? For me?'

'Okay, Ricky.'

Ricky patted his arm. 'Go for it, man. Don't let anyone put you off.'

Donny gave a wry smile. 'Okay.'

'I need to go now. See you around.'

'Yeah, see you.'

***

Three weeks later, Ricky's life changed. He was now clear to kill as many people as he wanted. The more the better. As soon as possible. Provided they were Germans. On Sunday, September 3, 1939, Chamberlain announced Britain was at war with Germany. Ricky could now kill Germans – legally. Bloody brilliant that.

On the Monday morning he went to the army recruiting office. There was already a small crowd there. Ricky told them he wanted to join up, and kill Germans in hand-to-hand combat. The officer listened, took notes, and passed him through for a medical check. Within two days he started basic training, and very quickly learned how to succeed in the army. Get super-fit; if anyone more senior asked you to do something, say 'Yes, sir' and do it; and, at all times, protect your mates.

Six weeks later, Ricky was told to go and see a Captain (Snuff) Evans at a location near Kilburn tube station in London. He joined a handful of others outside the hall. When Ricky's turn came, he thought Evans looked as tough as old boots. The man was well-built, with a square weather-beaten face and cropped-hair, and a strong Welsh accent. He also had an almost permanent smile, more sinister than friendly.

Evans explained he wanted to form a special unit of fifteen men aimed at 'target acquisition'. That was a fancy name for raiding and capturing German installations well behind enemy lines to allow the main army to forge forward. He'd been intrigued at the comment on Ricky's notes that he wanted to kill Germans with hand-to-hand combat. 'Are you that good?' he asked.

'Yes, sir. Been London Counties judo champion for the last two years.'

Evans pursed his lips. 'Ever killed a man?'

Ricky hesitated. How the hell should he answer that one? He wondered what to say.

Evans cut in after a few moments. 'I'll take that as a yes. Those who haven't would have said no by now. I don't want to know the details.'

Ricky sighed with relief.

'What's your favourite weapon for close combat? Knife? Gun?'

Ricky held out his hands. 'These, sir. They're powerful and silent.'

'Well, we sure want silence. We'll do lots of silent killing.' He checked Ricky's notes again. 'You've got a great report from basic training. Done very well.' He thought for a moment. 'Tell you what, I'll have you if you want to join me. But it'll be dangerous. So you've got to volunteer.'

Ricky stood to attention. 'I volunteer, sir.'

Evans shook his hand. 'Welcome aboard. Go next door and see Corporal Titch. He'll sort you out.' He indicated a door on the far side of the room. 'Anything else you want to know?'

'What happens now, sir?'

'You'll have eight weeks intensive training in Scotland, and then we'll go get 'em. Ready for that?'

'Yes, sir.'

'Anything else?'

He seemed approachable. 'Can I ask, sir, why you're called Snuff?'

Evans smiled. 'Oh, we all have nicknames in this unit. And I have a saying: We'll snuff the Germans out like candles.' He put his thumb and two fingers together pointing downwards, and flicked them like he was snuffing a candle out. 'Surprise 'em, kill 'em, just snuff 'em out like candles, boyo. That's why I got called Snuff and the name's stuck.'

'Thank you, sir.' Ricky saluted.

Next door, he found Titch. Ricky assumed his nickname was because of his small stature. Titch took his papers, and sat Ricky at a table to complete the paperwork. There were another six soldiers already there. They all looked real tough nuts.

Ricky signed the papers, and Titch asked him his weapon of choice.

'Just these.' He showed Titch his hands like he'd done with Snuff.

'Strangler, huh? Hey guys, meet Strang, short for strangler.' He pointed at the others in turn. 'Blade, Foxy, Hammer, Badger, Chiv and Spike.' They each waved back in turn. From that moment, Ricky became Strang for the rest of his army career, and beyond.

The group sat around a large table. Strang sat next to Spike. 'Did he say your name was Spike?'

'Yeah. That's what Titch called me when he heard my weapon of choice,' he said, with a Glasgow accent.

'A spike?'

'Yeah. Ram it hard up their arsehole. Destroys their insides, but doesn't leave a mark on the outside.'

'Blimey.'

Strang joined in with the group chat and laughter, and it became clear, as others joined the group, that Titch allocated nicknames that referred to looks or weapons – and the names all stuck.

Spike fascinated him. The lad was good-looking, with wide dark eyes and a full mouth. When he smiled, his whole face lit up, and he showed perfect teeth. Strang just had to smile back. The lad was a real charm merchant, thought Strang, and yet he was a killer too. *They sure were a mixed bunch.*

After another hour or so, Snuff came into the room and told them he'd interviewed twenty-four people, and selected these eighteen. He wanted a final fifteen. So, after the training sessions, three wouldn't make it. Strang sensed an immediate mood among the men that each of them would be one of that final fifteen. It was a shrewd move by Snuff.

They were loaded onto a bus, and set off for Euston Station to catch a train to Fort William, then on by bus to Achnacarry, in the remote Highlands of Scotland.

For the next eight weeks, Snuff put them through an intensive physical and mental training programme that improved their fitness and stamina. It included weapons and close-combat training, map-reading, small boat and underwater training, demolition and survival techniques, and basic French and German. He told them they'd be the Germans' nightmare attackers – silent killers striking from nowhere, playing by their own rules.

They had to give up smoking. 'Tobacco smoke clings to you,' Snuff said. 'It's a big giveaway of your position.' They also had to give up shaving for similar reasons. Strang had no problem with any of that.

They were issued with special rubber-soled boots that made minimal noise, and perfected Snuff's 'triangle' technique, where they operated in threes with only one of them moving, covered by the other two. Strang, Titch and Spike became one of these 'triangles'. They saved each other's lives countless times.

Strang loved it. The unit, led by Snuff, and known as 'The Panthers', operated behind enemy lines, with big successes and few casualties. Snuff would analyse a German asset, work out how they would defend it, and use his lads to silently take possession. They killed hundreds of enemy soldiers. Twelve of the original group survived through to demob.

They were initially part of the regular army, but became part of the Commandos that were set up in 1940, and then part of the Special Boat Squadron set up a year later. But they always remained a separate unit.

Strang was one of the few people who didn't celebrate VE day. He hated the thought his killing days might be over.

***

On their demob day in 1945, Strang joined Titch and Spike in a pub in Camden Town, in North London. This was Titch's old stomping ground. They chatted about their wartime experience, and their regret it was now over. They agreed they'd built up rare skills during the war – killing skills – which *had* to be worth something.

Strang said, 'There's lots of nasty buggers out there who deserve to die. And we can help them on their way – for a price.'

Titch asked, 'But how do you avoid getting caught?'

'We make it look like suicide. Did you see the bit in the paper this morning that the suicide rate is now ten times the murder rate, and set to increase further? If it looks like a suicide, the cops will just assume that's what it is. And there's lots of ways you can do it – tall building or cliff, underwater, by train, poison, car exhaust. It's endless.'

'But what if they *do* think it's murder. Then they'll come after us.'

'No, they won't. Because the first thing they'll look for is who of the guy's contacts had a motive for killing him. We'll have no contact with the guy, and no motive. They'll never trace us.'

Spike pursed his lips. 'How would you do it then?'

They clustered close around the table. 'Let's say I strangle someone, If I just leave the body, the cops will work out he's been strangled, and they'll chase it as a murder. But if I put a suicide note in his pocket, written on his notepaper, in his handwriting, with his pencil, and with his fingerprints all over it, and I leave the body with the neck on a rail line, where a train decapitates him, they'll just assume it's another suicide. We pick up our money, split it three ways, and leave no trace.'

Titch thought for a moment. 'How much are we talking about?'

'I'd say a thousand each per hit. Let's say four thousand in total, including expenses.'

'Christ! That's a lot of dosh.'

Strang leaned forward. 'We've got all the skills, guys. Nobody else can do it like us. We've been killing at close quarters for years.' He looked at Titch. 'And you used to be an expert forger.' Then he turned to Spike. 'And you can charm your way in anywhere, and get through any lock undetected. It's perfect for us.'

They all leaned back. 'That money sounds good, for sure,' Titch mused. He turned to Strang. 'You seem to have worked it all out. Have you done this before?'

Strang shrugged. 'Well, not for money.'

'What? You did it for free?'

'Well, not exactly. Just helped society by getting rid of a couple of very nasty buggers.'

Titch pondered this. 'How would we get paid, then?'

Strang leaned forward again. 'Remember the night we got stuck in that barn in France? You told me about your gaff here in Camden. You said it looked like an ordinary newspaper shop run by your Uncle Albert, but at the back it connected with other houses and alleyways your family used for smuggling, running a bookie's, and various other iffy businesses. You reckoned there were fifteen different exits, and no one knew. Get our money through that. Half up front, half on delivery. Slip Albert a few quid for his help.'

'You really *have* thought it through. What if we didn't get the second half?'

Strang smiled and snorted. 'We'd get it. We'd kill the bastard if he reneged on that.'

Spike nodded. 'Yeah, kill the bastard.'

Titch scratched his head. 'So, if we decide to go with it, how do we drum up business?'

'You told me once you knew a bunch of gangsters here in North London. They always need people bumped off. That would be a start. And if we're good, which we will be, the word will spread.'

Titch leaned forward. 'There's maybe a better way. These gangsters all have shady lawyers that they go to for advice. These lawyers are a real closed shop. If it works for them, they keep it to themselves and charge a fee. They'd be a better group to get in with. And they wouldn't talk about it either.'

'Sounds good.'

Titch pulled out a piece of paper. 'Right, what info do we need from these guys on a potential target?' He took notes. 'Name and address and contact number for the person calling. Name and address of the target. Instructions on how to get access to him. A photo to make sure we get the right guy. Any distinguishing features. Some of his notepaper and a pencil. A sample of his handwriting. Oh, and whether he's right or left-handed. That would be a basic error if we missed it. Anything else?'

'When they're likely to be on their own,' Spike said. 'And how well they're protected.'

Strang cut in. 'Whether they've got a car and its number plate.'

'What they're into sexually, if we need to entice them somewhere.'

Titch laughed. 'That's a good one, Spike. We could do with a woman in the team, to lure them.'

Spike pursed his lips. 'Well, if we need a woman, I know who might help.'

Titch gulped. 'Is she safe?'

'Sure. She's my sister.'

'Would she really be up for this?'

'Yeah, she's kind of done it before.'

Strang realised he didn't know Spike that well. They'd saved each other's lives lots of times, yet he didn't know anything about Spike's family or life outside the army.

'Just let me check. Do you want us to cut her in?'

'That's up to you guys. I'll go along with whatever you decide.'

'What do you think, Strang?'

'It would be good to have a woman as a lure. I think if she helps us with the job, we cut her in. Put the price up to cover it, Titch. It's still worth it.'

'Is that okay with you, Spike?'

'Of course. If you guys are happy, then I'm happy.'

'Could we meet her? Is that possible?'

'Sure, Titch. She's in the café two doors down. We're going up the West End after this to celebrate. Have hardly seen her in six years.'

'Do you want to go and get her?'

'Okay.' Spike got up and left the pub.

Titch glanced at Strang. 'Could work well. Let's see what she's like.'

A few minutes later, Spike came back holding a young woman by the hand. There was a wolf whistle from the other side of the bar.

Spike introduced her. 'This is Margaret, Maggie for short. Strang and Titch.' He gestured to the others.

They both stood and shook hands. Strang thought she was beautiful. Long dark hair, the same dark eyes as Spike, the same mouth, teeth and smile. She wore a white sweater and grey skirt, with the grey jacket hung over her shoulders. She was slim, with a great shape, and maybe a couple of years younger than Spike. It reminded him of the first time he'd met Spike. She had the same warmth in the smile, yet there was that same hint of darkness behind it. But there was no doubt she could entice any man anywhere.

They all sat down. 'These are the guys I told you about. Saved my life a hundred times.'

She smiled at them. 'Thanks for looking after him.' She spoke with a Glasgow accent. Strang wondered why she was in London, but he *had* to respond to that smile.

'Well, he did the same for us,' he said. Titch nodded in agreement, clearly just as enthralled with her.

Spike got them to huddle closer together, then spoke quietly to her. 'We've been killing bad guys now for six years, and we're . . . very good at it. We want to do it for money now, and would like you to help us.'

Her expression didn't change. 'What would I do?'

'Just lure the targets to a quiet place where we can take care of them.'

'What? Are you going to rob them?'

'No, no. We get paid for doing it.'

'Who pays you?'

'The guy who wants the target bumped off.'

She thought for a moment. 'And would I get a cut?'

Strang realised that underneath the veneer, she was a hard case.

'Yeah, of course,' Titch said
'How much?'
'A thousand each.'

She pursed her lips. 'I take it you guys have done this before?'

They nodded. Strang said, 'It would look like a suicide or an unfortunate accident.'

She looked around them again, her expression still the same. 'Okay, I'll do it.'

'That's great,' said Titch, and checked his notes. 'Okay, I think I've got it all. I'll act as the middle man to start with, and see how it goes. Okay?'

'Okay.' Strang was impressed with Titch. The years working with Snuff had paid off. They all sat in silence.

After a few minutes, Strang said, 'So, is it a goer?'

'Bugger it. I'm already bored now the war's over. I'm for it, provided we always double check our tracks.'

Titch glanced at the others. 'Okay. I agree with Spike. I'm in.'

Strang put his hand flat on the table. 'Welcome on board.'

The others put their hands on top of his and smiled. Then Strang got another round in.

***

Strang met with his partners every Monday morning in a makeshift conference room in Titch's extensive gaff in Camden. They each used a separate entrance.

Titch called it Camden Vermin Control, and set it up with a phone line to another of the houses. He then altered it to ring a special phone behind the counter in Uncle Albert's newspaper shop. Callers had to leave a phone number and time, and someone (Titch) would call them back.

Titch would then detail all the info they had to provide, and make it clear that unless they provided it in full, he wouldn't do the job. They should deliver it, addressed to 'Uncle Albert' at the newspaper shop. If the job was accepted, they should then deliver half the fee within three days, with the other half on completion.

For every 'hit', the partners agreed they'd each get £1000, with the other £1000 in a pot to cover expenses.

Strang was impressed with how Titch had arranged it all. He couldn't wait to get started.

After a couple of weeks, they got their first call – to take out a man called Billy Perkins. He lived just off the Whitechapel Road, in the East End of London. His photo showed a thin-faced man with a pencil-thin moustache and black slicked-back wavy hair. He was a ladies' man, who hung out in the saloon bar at the Blind Beggar pub.

They pored over a street map. When Strang saw the main rail line out of Liverpool Street passed close by, they drove to the area to see whether he could use the same technique he'd used before. They found a side street with access to the rail line, and accepted the job.

Over the next few days, they pulled a plan together. Maggie would be the lure in a fair-haired wig. For her cover story, she'd stay at a local hotel while her 'aunt' was in the Royal London Hospital nearby. Spike visited the hospital, and came back with the name of a likely 'aunt' and her ward number. Titch booked a hotel room using a false ID, for three days, paid in advance.

The Blind Beggar offered food in the evening. Maggie would go there, engage with the staff, and try to catch the eye of the target, Billy. Spike would also be in the pub to keep an eye on her, and protect her if something went wrong. Her aim was to get Billy out of the pub to take her back to her hotel. There was a dark alley off the Whitechapel Road at that point, and they'd nip into it for a quick kiss and cuddle on the way.

Strang would wait in the alley and do the deed. Then he and Spike would load Billy into the car, which Titch would have nearby, with false plates, just in case. Maggie would head back to her hotel on her own. The lads would drive to their chosen side street, place Billy on the rail line with his suicide note (written by Titch) in his pocket. They would then head back and pick up Maggie. If anyone ever questioned her, she'd say Billy had gone up the alley to have a pee. She'd waited, but he never came back. She just assumed he'd bottled it, and headed back to the hotel.

Strang was amazed at how relaxed she was, and concluded it was not her first time in a similar role. He'd love to know more about her.

The 'hit' went off much as they planned, though Strang had to wait in the alley longer than he wanted before the couple arrived.

Titch got a copy of the local newspaper, which carried a story on Billy Perkins' suicide. He'd had money worries, and his friends said he'd become anxious. He'd also been in the company of an unknown blonde woman earlier in the evening. The police wanted her to come forward, and give them details of his state of mind that night.

So, Camden Vermin Control was now up and running, and within a few weeks, they could select jobs from those that applied. They limited themselves to two 'hits' a month, which gave them time to make detailed plans before each job.

Strang was happy. The money rolled in. They each earned more in a week than most people earned in a year. And the team worked well together. Titch was an excellent organiser and forger; Spike demanded detailed cover stories for all possibilities; and Maggie went along with whatever they wanted. She performed her role with confidence and skill. And Strang got a thrill each time his victims' eyes changed as they expired. He loved that. Life was good.

Chapter 6. Katy

Katy Young loved stories. She loved to get them, write them, put her quirky stamp on them and, most of all, see them in print. She'd learned so much from her shrewd editor, Kenny. He didn't change much of her work now.

She met the others outside the sports hall for the Tuesday night five-a-side training session. It was the Saturday night crowd plus two others, Gav and Les, the goalkeeper. She smiled at Adam. 'How's it going at Preston's then?'

'Fine, though it's only been two days.'

'What is it you're doing exactly?'

'Oh, I'm helping to develop a new initiative.'

'That's interesting. What's the initiative?'

He grinned at her. 'I can't talk about it now. It's still subject to final approval. But I'll let you know as soon as we launch it.'

'Okay, you're on.'

She liked this young man. He was bright and intelligent, could think on his feet, and was mature for his age too, compared with the other lads here. Then she thought back to Saturday night. What *had* he written in his notebook when she returned to the table? He'd been very guarded about it. She was too much of a nosy parker at times. It was her biggest fault – or maybe her biggest strength – in this job.

They got on to the pitch at seven o'clock. Pip had persuaded a group of young lads to stay on and act as an opposing team by paying them each a sixpence. Katy took off her long gabardine coat, and put it on an adjacent chair just inside the door. The others dumped their jackets and ran on to the court, where Adam began to use his special training method.

Katy watched as he got them to play. Then, when he blew his whistle, they had to stop with their eyes closed, and tell him where each of their teammates were, and where they were moving to. They also practiced the two-touch method. Gav, who was new to this, seemed the most resistant, but the others tried their best.

Katy pulled out her notebook from her satchel, wrote a reminder to check back with Adam on his Preston initiative, and noted how he was training the team.

She jumped when the ball struck a couple of adjacent chairs and knocked them over. One of the young opposing lads ran over, grabbed the ball, and resumed the game.

Katy got up to lift the chairs and the jackets, and noticed Adam's jacket was one of them. It lay on the floor with his notebook almost out of the pocket. She glanced up. They were all at the far end of the court.

She lifted the chairs and sat on one to collect the jackets. She leaned over and coaxed Adam's notebook from the pocket. She turned back a page and noted the contents on her pad.

28/9
T Targets
CA (PT)
HD
EB
HM
SC
AB

She then turned over another page and read his neat handwritten conversation dated 29/9. That must be what he'd written on Saturday night. She read it through and winced. *Where had it come from?* She noted it in her pad in shorthand.

The next page just had a list of random words, so she turned the pages back, and pushed the notebook into his pocket. She lifted all the jackets and put them on the seats again, then sat and watched them train. Pip marched up and down like a team manager, and Adam shouted at the players, and tried to get them to play his way. But all the time, her mind raced with the conversation she'd read. *What the hell was it all about?*

After the session, they all agreed to meet again for the league game on Thursday. Pip and the boys all went their separate ways, and within moments, Katy was alone with Adam.

'I'll walk you home,' he said.

'No, you don't have to. I'll be fine.'

'Hold on a sec.' He pulled his hearing aid box from his top pocket and adjusted it. 'I had to turn this down because there was too much of an echo in there.'

'How do you think it went with the team?'

'Fine. Gav was a bit cynical at the start. He called me a nasty name at one point. But he came round in the end, and was quite enthusiastic.'

'I didn't hear that. What did he say?'

'Oh, it doesn't matter now. And I don't know how loud he said it. He was talking to Les at the time. But I'm a very good lip-reader, so I knew what he said.'

It was like a light going on in her head. *Of course. That's how he did it.* And his notes must be a conversation he had lip-read between Richard Preston and Daniel Bloomfield. *That's* what he'd noted when she returned to the table, and why he'd asked who they were. She couldn't wait to read her notes again.

They strolled towards her home, talking about the team and how they should play the match on Thursday. She waved him goodbye at her gate, and dashed inside.

She pulled out her notebook, and re-read the conversation. *Jesus!* Preston was going to kill someone? The captain, whoever *he* was. And then there was the second page, dated a day earlier, but written in Adam's notebook after the conversation. The initials meant nothing to her, but the first name on the target list read like a captain. She needed help, but couldn't go to Kenny. He was too close to Richard Preston. She'd call her colleague Archie for advice.

On her way over to Archie's, she worked out what to say. Archie now operated freelance, but had been a crime reporter on the big Glasgow dailies for years. He was streetwise, and seemed to have 'pals' everywhere – in the police, and even among the criminal classes. He used a private detective called Davie Watson, who lived in the town, to gather information on targets. She'd seen Kenny pass cash to Archie on occasion, and concluded there was a slush fund to bung sources. She dreamed of being like Archie. He could smell a story, and write it for Joe Public. He'd know how to handle this.

He opened the door, the usual bags under his eyes, hair going grey at the temples, a careworn expression on his face. 'Come on in.' They went into the front room.

She explained a friend had overheard a conversation between Preston and Bloomfield, and took him through it. She also showed him the list of targets she'd obtained.

Archie sat in silence for a few minutes. 'First things first. Is your source reliable?'

'I believe he is.'

'And why did he tell you about it?'

She was stumped. She hadn't expected that one. 'Well, he . . . he knows I'm a reporter,' she stuttered.

He stared straight at her. 'Uh-huh. And what does he expect you to do? Write it up, go to the police, or what?'

She shrugged, but could feel her face burning. 'I don't know.'

'Or will he go to the police himself?'

She knew she was in trouble. 'I don't know.'

He pursed his lips and studied her for several minutes. She felt guilty, and knew it showed in her eyes.

'Do you want to tell me the real story? I'd guess your source doesn't know you've got this. Correct?'

'You're right. I copied it from his notebook without him knowing.'

'Uh-huh. And why do you think it's genuine, and not the first lines of a novel, for example?'

'Because I was with him when he wrote it, and he asked me who the men were. I didn't realise it at the time, but I found out tonight he's an expert lip-reader.'

'Ah. Now I get it.' He paused. 'Do you think he'll go to the police?'

'I don't know.'

He thought for a moment. 'It's almost certain he will. And the last thing they'll want, or your source will want, is for you to trample all over it.' He rubbed his face. 'And Kenny would *never* run a story against his friend, boss, and owner of the newspaper, without a hell of a lot more evidence of collusion than a conversation lip-read at a dance. I don't think you can use it, Katy, and you shouldn't tell Kenny. You'd get into all sorts of trouble there. And it would also destroy any relationship you have with your source forever. Oh, I'm not saying there isn't a story, maybe even a big one, but in my opinion, you just can't use it.'

'Mmm, I think you're right.'

He leaned forward in his seat. 'Having said that, there's still the question of who the captain is. The initials mean nothing to me, but the obvious link would be a competitor or a supplier that's giving him trouble over a deal. And businessmen can get very nasty with each other.

'Then there's the Glasgow link. Why Glasgow? Lots of streets are like canyons, with tenements along each side. Ideal for a sniper hit. Or maybe they know a killer there. I'll talk to a few pals tomorrow.'

She got to her feet. 'I appreciate it, Archie. And thanks for your advice.'

'No problem. Always glad to help.'

On her way home, she thought about the discussion, and Archie's advice. It had saved her from a mauling by Kenny. But she still thought it was a good story.

***

Janet sat in her darkened lounge with only the standard lamp lit above her chair. She sipped a glass of white wine, and watched the sun set.

She picked up the list of initials, and read it for the tenth time. *What did it mean?* Adam had got it from Richard's notebook. He'd gone to deliver the draft cards for the new corporate image. Sara, the secretary, had been on the phone, and just waved him into Richard's office. Richard was away somewhere, so Adam left the cards and a note seeking approval. He'd seen Richard's notebook on the desk, opened it, found the page for last Friday, and copied the contents. It had only taken a few seconds, and he'd waved to Sara on the way out.

Janet and Adam had talked about the list over tea. It didn't mean anything to either of them, though the first line might refer to the 'captain'. Adam asked whether they should contact Sandra Maxwell, and Janet agreed she would call her after Adam left for the sports hall.

Once he'd gone, she studied the list, but it still didn't make any sense. She felt caught in a dilemma. Now much closer to Richard, but with a moral bond to Adam. In the end, though, she had a duty to report it.

***

In the gathering gloom, Sandra sat at her desk and studied the list of initials, with the 'captain' apparently referred to at the top. She assumed the 'T' in 'T Targets' referred to the Triumph group.

Over the last couple of days, apart from her initial link to the US Air Force, she'd concluded the next most likely link would be to a business relationship that had gone sour. After all, it was within an Economic League business meeting. She'd researched the organisation and found it was well-established, with reputable and eminent leaders, and supported industrialists and businessmen. Frank Parker in Manchester was trying to find out more about the Triumph group, and she'd a call arranged with him for tomorrow morning.

She picked up the phone and called Chuck Campbell in Prestwick. 'I've got more info on what we talked about on Sunday, Chuck. I'd like to know Captain Akers' first name, please?'

'It's Steve. Stephen C Akers.'

'What's his middle name?'

'Hold on and I'll check.' She heard him opening a cabinet. 'It's Carlsson. He's from Swedish stock.'

'Does he ever use that middle name as a first name – like Carl, for example?'

'Never. In fact, I had to look it up. I didn't know it offhand. No, he's always known as Steve Akers.'

'Well, I think in that case, this problem I've got doesn't apply to him.'

'Hey, good news. Right?'

'Well, it's good news for you, Chuck. But I've still got the problem of who the target is.'

'Oh, of course. Sorry about that.'

'At least it's one less thing I need to worry about.'

'Yeah, though after your visit, we've doubled up on security anyway.'

'That's a wise move right now, Chuck.'

'Hey, when will you come for your helicopter ride?'

She laughed. 'I'll give you a call.'

'Okay – and don't forget.'

'I won't.' She rang off.

She read the list again. It held the secret of the target, but how could she find it? She'd need to know if Preston had had a bust-up with another company to the point where he'd take direct and drastic action. And she'd have to check back with Janet and Adam on that. Otherwise, it looked impossible. She decided to sleep on it, and start again in the morning. She went home, listened to the Light Programme on the radio, and read that day's paper.

***

At four o'clock, Sandra woke with a start. She sat upright, wide awake, her brain racing. She jumped out of bed, went downstairs, and found the *Glasgow Herald* she'd read earlier. She looked up the parliamentary report, and checked the names against the list from Janet.

CA – Clement Attlee – Prime Minister
HD – Hugh Dalton – Chancellor of the Exchequer
EB – Ernest Bevin – Foreign Secretary
HM – Herbert Morrison – Deputy PM
SC – Stafford Cripps – President, Board of Trade
AB – Aneurin Bevan – Minister of Health.

The list matched. *It was the bloody cabinet, for God's sake.* And Attlee was the prime target. Her heart raced. How the hell had her brain worked that out while she slept? And more importantly, how did a man like

Preston think he could kill the prime minister? Wow, this was serious. Her new problem had now risen to the top of the pile. She sat and planned the steps she needed to take. It wasn't just Preston. There were others behind this plot, and she wanted them all.

***

Sandra arrived in her office early on Wednesday morning, and called her new boss, Commander Dave Burnett, Head of Special Branch in the UK. She liked working with him. He let his people do their job, but to keep him informed of anything that affected national security. She hadn't talked with him about the Preston case, since up to now she hadn't been sure it was a Special Branch job. But it sure as hell was now.

'I need to brief you on developments up here, sir.' She told him the background of the threat, what she'd done so far, and the revelation last night that the target was the PM. 'I need to know my timing, sir. Can you find out when the PM is next in Glasgow, or Scotland, so I know how long I've got to find the killer?'

'Right, Sandra. I'll call the Parliamentary Protection Squad and get back to you.'

'Thank you, sir.'

Sandra also reported to the chief constable of Glasgow on local matters, and called his secretary. She'd see him in an hour.

While she waited, she asked her secretary, Gillian, to have all her senior staff meet with her in two hours' time. Then she thought through her steps again.

Her phone rang. 'Commander Burnett, ma'am.'

'Right, Sandra, I've spoken to PP and the PM has only two appointments scheduled in Scotland. The first is on Saturday, October 20, in Musselburgh. Do you know it?'

'Yes, it's near Edinburgh, sir.'

'And the other is on Sunday, May 5, next year, when he attends the May Day march through Glasgow. There are no other appointments in Scotland, though that might change if there's an emergency of course.'

'Okay. So he's in Musselburgh two weeks on Saturday. Do you know his appointments that day?'

'Yep. He's got a civic reception at the town hall in the morning. He then goes to the local Labour Party hall across the street to address the annual conference of the Scottish Council of the Labour Party. Then in the afternoon he has a private meeting at a local nursing home with his colleague, Mr Westwood, Secretary of State for Scotland, who's recovering from an operation.'

'That's great, sir. I'll call Ted in Edinburgh, and bring him up to speed.'

'Okay, Sandra. The PP group tells me the PM gets an average of three death threats a week. Most of them from sad little men in sad little bedrooms who are all talk and no action. But this sounds different. Keep me posted, and tell Ted and Frank to call me if they need any support. If Preston has paid someone to do the deed, we've got to find him and stamp on him.'

'Yes, sir. What about Preston? I don't have enough to get a warrant and bring him in. Everything I've got is legally hearsay, even though I believe it.'

'Oh, he'll have covered his tracks, Sandra, and used a shady lawyer as a middle man. I think we should try and find the sniper, and work back through the money trail. Or, if Frank finds out about this Triumph group, we see if we can nail Preston that way. But if we're not getting anywhere a couple of days before the PM's visit, pull Preston in. He's supposed to be a respectable businessman, so that should scare the shit out of him and frighten him off. Let me know how you get on.'

'Will do, sir.'

Sandra then went to see the chief constable and briefed him too. 'I've got my people trying to pick up any info on a sniper in the area, but we really need the force as a whole to help. We have to find this guy and we've only got a couple of weeks. Can you ask the divisions to help, sir?'

'Yes, happy to do that. Leave it with me.'

She called her opposite number, Ted Wishart, in Edinburgh, and explained the situation. Between them, they ran all Special Branch operations in Scotland. 'Dave wants us to treat this as a top priority, Ted. I've got teams out in the west to try and ID a sniper. Can you do the same in the East?'

'Will do. We have all our plans in place already for the PM's visit, but I'll review them again today. We'll put a double cordon around the PM to prevent the public getting too close, but a distance shooter would be more difficult to protect against. The town hall at Musselburgh has a belfry that we've already blocked off, but we'll check it again. There are no other high buildings around the area, so we'll do another check on each house that looks on to the main street. Thanks for the warning.'

Finally, she called Frank Parker in Manchester. 'Any joy on this Triumph group, Frank? The whole thing has escalated, and Dave wants us to focus on it. He asks you to call him if you need any help from London.'

'We haven't got very far with the Triumph group, Sandra. They booked the meeting room at the Midland through the secretary to Sir Anthony Hewlett-Burke, who's a big noise in the City, and chairman of a couple of huge industrial companies. He was one of the men at the Triumph meeting last Friday, according to a waiter that served tea partway through. He said there were eight of them in total. But at this point we don't know any of the others, except for Preston, of course, whom the waiter also served at dinner the previous evening. We're still checking the hotel bookings for the Thursday night to see if we can link any other guests to Triumph, but so far without success. Some of the attendees could be local, of course, and would not have stayed there. But not much to go on so far.'

'Okay. Thanks, Frank. We'll keep in touch.'

Sandra's senior team had already assembled in the conference room by the time she got there. She had four inspectors, and each covered a different area.

She got straight to the point after bringing them all up to speed. 'We've got a couple of weeks to identify the sniper. We need to put a lot of resources on this. The chief has alerted the divisions, so we should begin to hear back soon. It's top priority, lads. Have any of you heard anything so far?'

Tom Hamilton cleared his throat. 'Yes, ma'am. One of my guys got one of his snouts last night. The snout said he overheard a lad in a pub in Springburn last week say he'd a great sniper for hire. The snout only knows the lad by sight, but he could probably find out more.'

Sandra snarled. 'If he gets a bung.'

'That's the way it is with these guys, ma'am.'

'Oh, I know. Okay, bung him. We need to know more, and quickly.'

'Right, ma'am. Will do.'

'Keep your eyes and ears open, everyone, and let's find the hitter.'

'Yes, ma'am.' They all got up and left the room.

Sandra had taken as much action as she could for the moment. Now she just had to wait for the info to start coming back to her. But it wasn't easy to wait. She went back to her office to check on her other projects.

***

Katy met the group at the sports hall on Thursday evening for the five-a-side league match. She watched from the side as the team won their game, seven goals to two. They were ecstatic. Their first win, and by such a big margin. They went off to a local café to celebrate.

Afterwards, Katy agreed to let Adam walk her home. For the last two days she'd worried about the story, but had concluded she had to let it go.

'Just to let you know, I've got a note to get the story on your new initiative at Preston's. How's it going?'

'Fine. And I *will* let you know about it when I can.'

'Thanks. And what else is happening in your life?'

He looked puzzled. 'You mean apart from the team winning their first ever league game tonight? I thought Pip would wet herself.'

She laughed. 'It's been a long-running sore with them that they always lose.'

'Well, it's all changed now.'

'Anything else of note?'

'Nothing. All just routine.'

He was so relaxed and sanguine. Maybe she'd got it all wrong.

***

The following morning, Katy found a note on her desk. Archie wanted her to call him. She went to a phone box near the post office.

'Just to let you know, Katy, the word on the street is the police are searching for ex-soldiers still holding their guns, and a sniper, who's lined up for a big hit soon. So it looks like your man has talked to the police after all.'

Dammit. A major story brewing and she couldn't use it. *Shit.*

Chapter 7. Richard

Richard came out of the shower room with a bath towel wrapped round him, still drying his hair with a hand towel. He glanced out the bedroom window. A beautiful Monday morning. The start of an eventful week that would end with a bang, if all went to plan.

There was a knock at the door. 'Mister Richard?' It was Meg, the housekeeper.

'Just a minute, Meg.'

'It's Mister Bloomfield on the phone for you.'

'Oh, okay. I'll be right out.'

Bit early for Daniel to call. Must be important. He slipped on a pair of underpants, wrapped the bath towel around his waist and went out to the upper hall. He picked up the phone. 'Yes, Daniel?'

'Hi Richard. Can you call me back in private asap?'

He hesitated, wanting to know more, but realised it was not the time to talk. 'Okay, about half an hour?'

'Right, I'm in the office. Bye.'

Richard walked back into his bedroom. *Shit. Must be really serious.*

He got dressed, told Meg he'd get breakfast at the shop, and left the house. Instead of his usual route onto the esplanade, he went the other way across into the estate on the other side of Racecourse Road, and into a public phone box.

'What's wrong?'

'I've just heard Stewart and Kincaid were lifted by the police last night. They raided Stewart's house with armed police, and lifted Stewart and his brother – and a sniper rifle. They also lifted Kincaid from his house at the same time.'

'Shit. Anything likely to come back to us?'

'Don't think so. We've used a false ID throughout, and left the money in a secret drop for them to collect. I've also heard the cops are all over the city like a rash on the hunt for shooters. Probably after that incident in Birmingham. So it's maybe coming from that. Though I did hear there was a rumour among the police of a planned sniper attack, which is not so good.'

'Well, there's only you and me, and your contact man, knew about it. And we haven't talked. Right?'

'Right.'

'What should I do?'

'Just stay calm. Check any notes you have about Triumph that you wouldn't want the police to see. Make sure you have your story straight about Triumph – lobbying organisation, or whatever. If the police do approach you, answer their questions, but deny all knowledge of any shooting plans. And, as your lawyer, get me involved.'

'Bloody hell, the police? I don't like the sound of that. And what do I tell Sir Anthony? He needs to know what's happened.'

'Well, call him and let him know the job's off this weekend. And agree with him what to say about Triumph if asked.'

'Shit. He won't be happy. Do we know of anyone else for the job?'

'At this late stage? No chance.'

'Okay, thanks. Talk to you later.' Richard rang off, and stood for a moment, his brain numbed. Then he asked the long-distance operator for Sir Anthony's number. His hand shook as he waited for an answer.

'Anthony,' said the familiar voice.

'Morning, Sir Anthony, Richard Preston here.'

'Oh yes. Bit early for you. What do you want?'

'Just to let you know our plans for the weekend have changed. Our . . . operator was lifted by the police last night. I'm told they're rounding up ex-soldiers with weapons after the recent incident in Birmingham.'

'Oh? What was that?'

'An ex-soldier still had his gun and shot a pub landlord in a dispute.'

'I see. Do you have an alternative for the operation?'

'No, it's too late now. I'm afraid the job's off.'

'That's too bad. We'll cover it at our next meeting.'

'Fine. One last thing, I just wanted to ask how we describe the Triumph group, if I'm asked by the police.'

There was a long silence. 'The police? Why would they ask you that? Have you been blabbing?' Sir Anthony's tone had now become much more menacing.

'No, of course not. Well, only to my lawyer, who organised it.'

'Well, why would the police be interested in Triumph, or you?'

Richard stuttered through his answer. 'Th-there was apparently a rumour among the local police of a planned sniper attack.'

'Well, they'd get that from the . . . operator, surely.'

'No, I mean *before* they lifted him.'

'Jesus, man. If that's the case, they could only get it from you or your lawyer. Shit! How stupid can you be?'

'No, no. We haven't talked to anybody. I mean, it's possible it could have leaked from someone at the Manchester meeting.'

'Not at all. Apart from you, I've been doing business with all these guys for years. There's no chance they would talk. It has to be at your end. How otherwise would they link the job to you and to Triumph, you provincial cretin? Jesus Christ, I don't believe this. Well, I'll tell you, my friend, if the police come knocking at my door, then you're in big trouble. In fact, you're already more trouble than you're worth. I don't want to see you again. And as for this matter – you got yourself into it, and you can bloody well get yourself out of it. You're on your own. Don't expect any support from us!' He rang off.

Richard's mind was in a whirl as he walked to the shop. He went up to his office, and asked the restaurant team for tea and toast. He looked out the window, but saw nothing. He now regretted joining the Triumph group, and was annoyed at himself for blurting out about the police to Sir Anthony. *Shit.*

***

Richard sat with his head in his hands. The whole thing had blown up in his face, with less than a week to go. He tried to stay calm, but Sir Anthony had chided him like a schoolboy, just as his father used to do. His stomach churned, and he rushed to the bathroom.

Afterwards, he began to think through what Daniel had said. He pulled the notebook from his desk, and checked his entry for last week's Triumph meeting. It was damning. But he couldn't just tear the page out and burn it, otherwise that would leave a trace if the book was examined. He had to take a new notebook and copy out all the entries, but change the damning one.

He took a new notebook from his cupboard, and soon arrived at the Triumph meeting. He avoided all mention of targets and wrote:

'28/9 Triumph
Lobby on electric power supply issues.
Presentation on hydraulics. Good, but not relevant.'

He went on to insert the subsequent entries from his old notebook and finished a few minutes later. His gardener, Ben, always had a fire going in the garden for burning rubbish, and Richard had used it before for burning old papers. He'd burn the old notebook later, and no one would ever see that damning entry.

***

Sandra Maxwell sat with Tom and her senior team, and discussed the initial interviews Tom had had with Kincaid and Stewart. She'd sat behind the one-way mirror in the next room, and listened to each of them.

She shook her head. 'I'm disgusted the army have let Stewart out like that. He should be in a mental hospital. He doesn't even know what day it is. He only wants to shoot things. Anything. And we have to pick up the pieces. I'll talk to the chief and to the commander. It's just not acceptable.'

'What can they do now, ma'am?' Tom asked. 'Most of the guys have been demobbed. It's probably too late.'

Sandra sighed. 'Yeah, you're right. But better late than never. Anyway, let's talk about Kincaid. Did he start blubbing at one point?'

'He did, ma'am. I think he realised he'd got himself into a situation he hadn't planned for. He's a pal of Stewart's brother, and when they saw Stewart shooting in the Campsies, they realised he was exceptional, and thought they could make money out of it. But Kincaid's a car salesman, and didn't think it through. Though, having said that, I've seen his notes for the planned shoot on Saturday, and they're pretty detailed. He had diagrams of the belfry at Musselburgh Town Hall, and details of a house on the main street occupied by a single old lady, with access from the back for a getaway. So, he put a bit of effort into it.'

'What about this guy, John Clark, who commissioned and paid for the shoot? Do we know anything about him?'

'We've tried to check him out, ma'am, but we didn't get far. The name's probably false. After the initial meeting, he always contacted Kincaid by phone, and passed the money over using a bin at Mugdock Country Park. If Kincaid wanted to contact him, he left a message in the classified column of the *Evening Times*. We just can't trace Clark at all.'

She shook her head in frustration. 'We need to get a link back to Preston. Why don't you have one last go at Kincaid, and see if he can remember anything else about Clark? Tell him we could charge him under the Treachery Act, 1940, that's still in place. Could mean twenty years, or even execution. Scare the shit out of him, and see if he remembers anything that might help.'

'Okay, ma'am. Will do.'

The meeting broke up, and Sandra sat thinking what else she could do to find the people behind the plot. Not much, she concluded. Unless they got an unlikely break, the John Clark lead was probably a dead end. It had all the signs of a smart lawyer behind it, and Preston had a smart lawyer pal. She checked her notes. His name was Daniel Bloomfield. Maybe worth a look. But right now, she had no hard evidence on either of them.

The best she could do, if the commander agreed, would be to haul Preston in to 'help with their enquiries'. She knew Bloomfield would see it as a fishing expedition. But she began to form a plan that just might give them a fright, and get them to back off from any other stupid ideas they might have. *After all, we have a duty to prevent crime, not just detect it.*

***

By the Wednesday, the latest interview with Kincaid had thrown up no new information, so Sandra called Commander Burnett.

'We've got a rock-solid case against Kincaid and Stewart, sir. The prosecutors are happy with it, though I'm going to write to you about Stewart. The man is severely war-damaged, bordering on criminally insane, and should never have been demobbed in that state.'

'Well, I'm not sure we can do much about it now.'

'I know, sir. But at least it records our concerns.'

'Okay. What else have you got?'

'I see this from two points of view, sir. The first is we have a duty to prevent crime where we can, and second, we should always protect our informants.'

'I agree, Sandra. Is your informant vulnerable?'

'Could be, sir. So I want to suggest we bend the rules a bit to achieve both of these objectives.'

'Well, you know me. I'm happy to bend the rules provided it doesn't result in the wrong type of action.'

'Right, sir. So, at this point, I've got no link back to Preston. None at all. The man who contracted the hit, John Clark, is a false ID. But it has the smell of a smart lawyer, and Preston has a pal who's a smart lawyer.

'I want to bring in Preston to help with our enquiries, but not as a suspect. I think he'll bring his lawyer pal with him. I'll explain that, as a result of the recent incident in Birmingham, we had a major trawl to identify any similar cases here, during which we uncovered Kincaid and Stewart, who planned to kill a major political figure.

'We'll tell him there were no links back to who organised this, except that the man who commissioned the hit, according to Kincaid, said something like, 'It would be a triumph for Triumph.' Kincaid didn't know what that meant, but we'll say it set us off on a search for an organisation called Triumph.

'Through my opposite number in Manchester, we discovered a Triumph group that met in a hotel there a few weeks ago, and Preston was identified by a waiter as one of the attendees. We therefore talk to him about this group to see if it had any link to our shooters.

'Now, of course, he'll deny all knowledge of that, but I believe it will stop them in their tracks. When the lawyer goes back to his man who paid Kincaid and asks him why he mentioned Triumph, the man will deny saying it, and the lawyer will realise we have duped him. But he can't come back to us and say we lied because that would expose him as knowing who paid for the shooting. And I think we would achieve our two objectives – to prevent any further crime along the same lines and protect our informants.

'Frank in Manchester has managed to identify only two members of the group – Preston and Sir Anthony. I think you should do the same with Sir Anthony, who seems to be the leader, and stop him in his tracks too. What do you think, sir?'

There was a pause. 'Very clever, Sandra. I think it would work, though we should make the phrase referring to Triumph a bit more vague – as though Kincaid kind of remembers it, but can't be sure. Leave a shred of doubt in Preston's mind. Let's do it.'

'Good, sir. I thought I'd pull Preston in tomorrow morning. Could you do Sir Anthony at the same time?'

'Yes, go for it. And let's talk tomorrow afternoon.'

Sandra thought about the conversation. She liked Burnett. He was keen, supportive, and took decisions quickly. She couldn't ask for more.

She picked up the phone and asked Gillian to get her a Mr Preston, who owned a department store in Ayr.

'Mr Preston, this is Superintendent Maxwell of the Special Branch based in Glasgow.'

'Oh, yes?' He sounded nervous.

'As part of a major investigation, we've tripped over an organisation called Triumph, and we believe you're a member. Is that correct?'

He hesitated. 'Well, yes. How did you know that?'

'Oh, we got it from contacts in Manchester, and we'd like to know more about this group. Would you help us with our enquiries, please? Come to my office, say tomorrow morning at ten o'clock?'

There was silence on the line.

'Or I can come to you, if it suits you better.'

'No, no. I'm happy to come to Glasgow. What's your address?'

She gave it to him. 'So, ten o'clock tomorrow? Could you also bring any relevant notes or minutes of meetings, please?'

There was silence again. 'Should I bring my lawyer with me?'

'Well, we don't regard you as any sort of suspect, so it's not necessary from that point of view. But it's not a problem if you want to do so.'

'Okay, see you tomorrow, then. Bye.'

'Goodbye, and thanks.'

***

Gillian buzzed through just before ten o'clock. 'That's Mr Preston and his lawyer, Mr Bloomfield, in Interview Room One now, ma'am.'

'Thanks, Gillian.' She turned to Tom Hamilton and Bill Jamieson. 'Okay, let's go see.'

She'd told Tom earlier that she didn't want Preston to meet him at this stage, so that he could still be used for observations in Ayr if necessary. He'd watch the interview from behind the one-way glass.

She entered the room and held out her hand in greeting. 'Good morning, I'm Superintendent Maxwell and this is Inspector Jamieson.'

The two guests murmured 'Richard Preston' and 'Daniel Bloomfield' as they shook hands. Sandra thought Preston looked nervous, though, in fairness, most people were nervous faced with a police interview. Bloomfield seemed more relaxed. They sat down on opposite sides of the table.

'We'd like to record this interview for our records, if you don't mind. Is that okay?'

Bloomfield asked, 'I assume if we want it, we can have a copy?'

'Of course,' Sandra nodded over to Bill.

Bill started the recording machine. 'Informal interview with Mr Richard Preston and Mr Daniel Bloomfield at Glasgow Police HQ, Thursday the eighteenth of October, 1945. Time 10.05 a.m. Superintendent Maxwell leading, with Inspector Jamieson attending.'

Sandra opened. 'Thank you for coming here this morning, gentlemen, to help us with our enquiries. You're not suspects, and not interviewed under caution, and you're free to leave at any time. Is that clear?'

'Happy to help,' Preston murmured.

'We will be talking about sensitive matters here. I'd therefore like you to hold what we discuss as strictly confidential. Is that agreed?'

They both spoke their agreement.

'Fine. So let me give you the background. A few weeks ago, there was an incident in Birmingham, where an ex-soldier, still retaining his gun, shot and killed a pub manager in a dispute. You may have read about it in the press.

'Now, part of our duties as police officers is to prevent crime where we can, and so this incident set alarm bells ringing in most police forces around the country. In our area, we launched a major trawl to identify any similar ex-soldiers, and to date we've arrested ten people holding illegal weapons.

'Now, two of these people – we'll call them Mr A and Mr B – had a sniper rifle, and during their arrest, we discovered they had a plan to assassinate a major political figure, who shall remain nameless. Hence how we in Special Branch got involved.'

Sandra thought both Preston and Bloomfield now looked a bit shifty.

'These two men admitted they were hired and paid by a Mr X – who at this stage is still unknown to us – to carry out the act. However, they also revealed Mr X, among other things, had stated it would be a great *triumph* for them. We thought that an unusual phrase, and wondered if it was a play on words.'

Bloomfield scrawled some notes on his pad.

'So we then did a trawl of our Special Branch operations around the country to see if the word "triumph" rang a bell with anyone. Manchester SB found a group with that name held a monthly meeting in a hotel there. The last meeting took place on the twenty-eighth of September.

'Now, we know you were one of the attendees at that meeting, Mr Preston. A waiter who served tea part way through the meeting had also served you at dinner the previous evening, and knew your room number from the chit.

'That's why I called you. We'd very much like to know more about Triumph, its aims and objectives, who its members are, and whether it had anything to do with our shooters? Could you tell us more about it, please?'

Preston cleared his throat. 'Well, I can tell you straight off. The Triumph group I know in Manchester has nothing to do with your shooters. I mean, there must be dozens of groups called Triumph in the country. It's a common name.'

'That's true, of course. But perhaps you'd tell me about *your* Triumph group? It would be helpful, if only to eliminate them.'

He hesitated for a moment. 'It's a group formed to lobby the government on behalf of businesses. I was invited to join it a month ago.'

'Who invited you to join?'

'Sir Anthony Hewlett-Burke, a very eminent man. He's the leader of the group. He heard a speech I gave to the Economic League, and invited me to join.'

'So this group is part of the Economic League?'

'Well, not really. Business is the only way to create wealth in this country. Triumph focuses on that. The EL deals with wider issues.'

'Do you have a list of Triumph members?'

'I don't, though I could ask Sir Anthony if he has one, and pass it on.'

'Well, we can ask him ourselves. My colleague's interviewing him at this moment.'

Preston started coughing, and took a drink from his glass of water.

'Are you all right?'

He recovered. 'Yes, I'm fine. Sorry about that.'

'So, Triumph is a group that lobbies government on behalf of businesses. Do you lobby Conservative and Labour parties, or just whoever's in power?'

'We lobby both government and opposition parties.'

'And do you favour one over the other?'

'Well, it's fair to say we prefer a Conservative government. They're much more business-friendly.'

'So you'd be upset at the last election result then?'

'Yes, we were. There's no denying that.'

'And how far would you take that?'

Preston looked puzzled. 'How do you mean?'

'Well, would you be prepared to take direct action against the Labour government in any way?'

'Certainly not! We're respectable businessmen. That choice is made at the ballot box for good or ill.'

'Uh-huh.' She checked her notes. 'What form do your meetings take?'

'It's a morning meeting on the last Friday of the month, and in two halves. The first half is a debate among ourselves on the issues facing businesses today. We agree which one we'll lobby the government on. We then each contact our local MP and one member of the relevant committee during the next few weeks.

'In the second half, we have a guest speaker from one of the main universities telling us about the future of modern technology.'

'I see. And do you take notes or have minutes?'

'Yes, of course. Here are my notes of the meeting in September, with the guest speaker slides, and the minutes that arrived the following week.' He passed the items over to Sandra.

She thumbed through them. The notes in his book did not mention anything about targets. Had Adam got it wrong, or had Preston rewritten his notes?

She pursed her lips. 'The waiter who replaced water jugs half way through told us he saw someone's notes on the table.' She opened her file. 'This is what he saw.'

She passed a paper to him on which was typed,

'Targets
CA (PT)
HD'

'He said there was a list of initials, but that's all he could remember. It's not clear from the minutes. What had you discussed?'

Preston swallowed. He stared at the paper. 'Erm. I think it was a list of cabinet members we would lobby in the following weeks.'

'On what?'

'Improving electric power supply.'

'I see. But your notes don't mention any targets. I'd have thought that was an important action for you from the meeting.'

'Well, I had to lobby Herbert Morrison. It's not something you forget.'

'And have you done so?'

'Not yet. I've been too busy with the business.'

'What does PT mean beside the first name?'

'Erm. That's the prime target. We would always have one on any list.'

'And, in this case, that's Clement Attlee, right?'

He paused. 'Yes. That's correct.'

'Fine, thank you. I think that's as far as we need to go today. May I come back to you and talk again?'

'Of course. Always happy to help.' He forced a grin.

'Is there anything you want to ask me?'

Bloomfield sat back. 'What happens now?'

Sandra looked them straight in the eye, one after the other. 'Well, we continue to try to find the people behind this plot, and throw them in jail. Or even execute them under the Treachery Act.'

There was silence in the room. Both men dropped their gaze.

Sandra stood and extended her hand. 'Thank you for coming in. We appreciate it.'

'That's okay,' Preston said, and shook hands.

Bill showed them out, and then came back into the room. Tom came in from next door.

Sandra smiled. 'What do you think of that?'

Tom shook his head. 'Guilty as hell. No doubt about it. We just can't prove it.'

'I agree,' Bill said. 'Preston was really upset to hear we were interviewing Sir Anthony. He didn't feign that.'

'Well, that's his problem. I'll talk to the boss later and hear how he got on. But we can't take it any further at the moment, unless there's a breakthrough. Thanks, lads. Let's get back to work.'

***

As they left the building and walked towards their car, Richard turned to Daniel, desperate to get his thoughts. 'How do you think it went?'

Bloomfield seemed lost in thought, and stopped walking. 'I think it went okay. But what gets me is Norrie talking about "a great triumph" to Kincaid. Why would he say that? Maybe it was just a poor choice of words. We've never mentioned Triumph to him. I'll check with him and get back to you. But don't worry, that was just a fishing expedition. They've nothing on you, otherwise they'd have charged you on the spot.'

'Good to know.'

They walked on to where the driver waited in the car, and headed back to Ayr.

***

In mid-afternoon, Commander Burnett called. 'How did it go with Preston, Sandra?'

'Went fine, sir. My team think they're guilty as hell. They're dead against the Labour government, but said they wouldn't take any direct action. They're "respectable businessmen" after all. We can't prove anything, but I think we've given them a fright, sir. Let's hope that's the end of their nonsense.'

'Yes, we had much the same this end with Sir Anthony. Lots of bluster and outrage. Let's hope we've stamped on it. What about Saturday? Have you checked with Ted? Does he need any help?'

'Well, I've offered anything he needs, but he said he's got it all in hand. It's going to be pretty much an exclusion zone for a couple of hundred yards around. But I'm ready to help if he needs it.'

'Okay, that's fine. I'll have a word with him later. And Preston? Are you keeping the watch on him?'

'We'll keep it going until the PM's visit at the weekend, just in case. If we're all clear after that, we'll pack it in. According to our tail, he uses public phone boxes for private calls anyway. We don't have enough to lift him, but I'm hoping after today, he'll crawl back into his box.'

***

Richard's phone buzzed. 'Mr Bloomfield, sir.'
'Yes, Daniel?'
'Call me back when you've a minute.'
'Okay, five minutes.'

Richard put on his jacket, coat and hat, took the service lift to the ground floor, and left the store. He went to one of the phone boxes near the post office.

'What's wrong?'
'I think the police might be playing games with us.'
'In what way?'
'Norrie's pretty sure he didn't say "a great triumph" to Kincaid, although he admits he had to do a lot of persuading. But as I thought, he's never heard of the Triumph group.'

'So, why do you think they're playing games?'

'If Norrie *did* say that, then what Maxwell says is fair enough. But he's pretty reliable, and if he *didn't* say it, then it means she's making it up.'

'Jesus. Why would she do that?'

'It could be a big fat message. We know you're behind this plot, but we can't prove it, so back off.'

'Can she do that?'

'Of course. She sets the rules. And she knows we can't go back and accuse her of lying. She's a smart cookie and no mistake. But if that's the case, it leaves us with one almighty problem.'

'What's that?'

'Who *did* tell her about you, Triumph and the plot? If it wasn't Norrie, then it must be someone else up here. So who knew?'

'There's only you, me or Norrie. We talked on the Sunday morning, three weeks ago, after the golf. I haven't talked to anyone else since then.'

'Well, it wasn't me or Norrie. You didn't mention it to Johno or Matt?'

'Definitely not.'

'Well, she must be right. Maybe Norrie did give a hint, though he says he didn't. In the meantime, it's probably better if you end your links with Triumph.'

'Well, that's already taken care of. I've been fired by Sir Anthony.'

'Really? Why?'

'Because he thought the only way the police could know of a link between me, Triumph and the plot was if someone had blabbed. So, he doesn't want to see me again. I said the leak could be from Manchester, but he poo-pooed that.'

'Oh well. You're probably better out of it.'

'Yeah. See you Sunday.'

Richard walked slowly back to the shop. It looked like he was now clear of the mess he had got himself into. He just had to steer clear of any further trouble. Just get back to normal. *Shit*, it was a close call, though. He'd never do that again.

***

Richard enjoyed the golf game on Sunday morning, and the usual banter amongst the four of them. But he couldn't wait for his 'me time'.

By two o'clock, he was on the *Lady E*, the family's one big indulgence. He fired up the diesel engines, headed out of Ayr harbour, and turned south towards his special spot in Culzean Bay. This is what he looked forward to all week. Being on his own. Away from everyone. He loved driving the motor yacht his father had bought before the war. He relaxed at the wheel, the trauma of the past week now a distant memory.

Just north of Culzean Castle, he stopped and deployed the sea anchor, and let the boat settle. He then went down into the saloon, and unlocked his private store. It had two shelves and two drawers, each stacked with these gorgeous special garments. Which should he choose today?

Sometimes he'd strip naked, and wear them to enhance his pleasure. But today he needed to be quicker. He chose a special favourite – a fabulous pale blue item. Then he poured two tots of Glenmorangie. One for before and one after.

He pulled down his trousers and pants, and stretched out on the sofa, already semi-erect. He drank the first tot of malt whisky, savouring the mellow flavours. He then took the magic garment, and rubbed it against his naked body. The smooth touch felt exquisite against his skin, now even more sensitive. He fell into an aura of joy. To him, this was pure love. Perfect love. His body trembled with a wave of bliss as he climaxed, and then he slowly sank into an invisible blanket of calm.

He relished the silence for several minutes. Then rose, carefully folded the garment, and locked it away until next week. He drank his second tot of whisky. Then he cleared up, hauled in the sea anchor, fired up the engines, and guided the boat out of the bay.

He followed much the same route every week if the weather held. Southwest from Culzean Bay around Ailsa Craig and back to Ayr harbour. Three to four hours depending on his mood. Sheer love and pleasure on board. Nothing else could give him that intense euphoria. Nothing.

Chapter 8. Ayr

Monday, October 22, dawned bright and beautiful in London. The sun shone as hordes hurried to their offices, and traffic moved more freely than usual. It was almost like a spring day. However, in contrast, the Northern Line was having one of its sick days, with stuttering trains, and packed passengers frustrated as hell. By the time he got to Camden, the others had already arrived. Strang hated being late.

Titch opened the meeting with the overall financial report. 'We're four months in, and we've done eight 'hits'. The expense money has stacked up. It's got almost six thousand in it, since all but one of the 'hits' has been in London.'

Strang was happy with the money he earned, and the others seemed happy too. And what pleased him most was none of them had spent crazy amounts. They maybe dressed and ate better, but so far they hadn't spent big on cars, for example. They were all very sensible, and that was good.

Titch glanced at Strang and Spike in turn. 'I met an old friend of ours last week.' He paused. 'Snuff.'

Strang thought that *was* a surprise. 'Jesus. What did *he* want?'

'He made me an offer. To join him in killing people for money. To look like suicide.'

Strang and Spike exchanged glances. 'Genuine?'

'Seemed to be. He said all the right words. Said he had a problem settling back into civvy life. Wanted to use his skills.'

Strang pursed his lips. 'What did *you* say?'

'Told him I wasn't interested. I'd re-integrated into the family business. He then asked if I'd kept in touch with you guys. I said I hadn't seen you since demob.'

Spike asked, 'What do you think?'

'I couldn't shake off the feeling that, if the authorities were searching for anyone doing that type of thing, he'd be the ideal guy to dig them out.'

'Where did you leave it?'

'I've got his details here.' He put them in a desk drawer. 'For me, it's no action. I hope you agree.'

Strang and Spike agreed. Maggie asked, 'Is someone going to tell me about Snuff?'

Spike glanced over. 'Yeah, I'll tell you later. He was our captain during the war. A bloody good leader. This is just a bit of a surprise to us.'

She shrugged. 'Okay.'

Titch leaned forward. 'Back to business. I also had another problem last week, which I think I've dealt with, but I need your approval. You've heard me talk about Monty. He's a kind of lawyer/fixer, with great contacts. He's given us half our business so far, and I've tipped him a few hundred from the expense account. But he now wants a commission.

'He reckons he can get us lots of work. But he wants ten percent for each job we accept. I've told him the fees on each job are £4000, with £1000 for expenses, so ten percent would be £400. And he's happy with that. We could easily pay it out of expenses. Working with a guy we know is a big plus for us. What do you say?'

There was silence as everyone looked at each other.

'Is ten percent reasonable?' Spike asked.

'He's kind of our sales guy, and ten percent sales commission is okay. I'd recommend we accept it. I think it's a good deal for us.'

Strang shrugged. 'Okay. I'll go along with it.'

Spike nodded. 'Yeah, me too.'

Maggie raised a hand. 'And me.'

'Great. I'll let him know today.' Everyone smiled. Strang liked another positive decision by the group. 'I assumed you'd agree, so on that basis, he's asked us to do an urgent job for his best client. He'll bung us an extra couple of thousand if we do it next.'

Strang snorted. 'Blimey. Sounds like someone's been *very* naughty.'

'Right, I've got the details here. The target's a businessman in Ayr, Scotland, called Richard Preston. Here's his photo. He owns and runs a department store in the town, together with a hotel and various other businesses. Do you know the place, Spike? You're Scotch, aren't you?'

'No, Scotch is what you drink. I'm Scottish, the same as my sister.'

'Oh, sorry, mate. Right, are you okay with going back to Scotland?'

Spike and Maggie exchanged glances. 'Yeah, it should be okay.'

'Good. This guy Preston seems to spend most days at his shop, but plays golf every Sunday morning, and then goes out in his boat – the *Lady E* – alone on Sunday afternoons. Looks like that's the time to get him. What do you think, Spike?'

'It'll be good to brush up our boating skills again.'

Strang smiled. 'Yeah, and have a holiday in Scotland at the same time. What's Ayr like?'

'It's a nice seaside town. Good beach. Good sailing too on the Clyde.'

'Sounds great.'

Titch cut in. 'I've thought about it over the weekend. The target's single, and we don't know what he's into sexually. But I'm sure you'll find out, Maggie. I suggest we put you up in the hotel he owns, which should give you the best chance to get to know him and his weaknesses. Is that okay?'

'Yeah. Where will you be?'

'I thought if we need a lot of gear, like yachting stuff, we'd better rent a house. The three of us would stay there. And we'll also have to hire a car and a boat. Expenses are going to be high on this one.'

'Sounds fine.'

'Okay, we've a job to complete this week. What if we go up to Scotland next weekend and take it from there? I'll book you into the hotel, Maggie. What ID do you want to use?'

She shuffled in her handbag and pulled out an ID card. 'Use this one.'

Titch took a note of it, and handed it back. 'Okay, I'll get busy on that. Look forward to whisky and porridge next week.'

They all laughed.

***

On Saturday afternoon, they picked up their rental car near Glasgow's Central Station, and headed south out of the city. The rows of black tenements changed to red sandstone tenements, then to terrace houses, then semi-detached, until, by the outer suburbs, rows of detached bungalows. Strang had passed through Glasgow years ago going to the training camp with Snuff, but hadn't realised the city was so big.

They drove south across the moors to Kilmarnock, then through the rolling fields of Ayrshire. As they breasted the hill a few miles further south, the Clyde estuary opened up ahead of them.

'Wow,' said Titch, who was driving, 'that's impressive. What's the big rock in the middle of the water, Spike?'

Spike looked up from the back seat. 'Ailsa Craig.'

'So, what is it? Can you go there?'

'I think so. It has a special rock that makes the best curling stones in the world, so there must be access. It's about ten miles out from Girvan, so I assume you can get a boat from there.'

'How big is it? Do you know?'

'From memory I think it's about a thousand feet high, and about a mile in diameter. Most of the cliffs go straight down into the water.'

'Impressive.'

They dropped Maggie at Ayr Railway Station for her to catch a taxi to make her arrival at the hotel more natural. Titch said, 'We'll pick you up outside the hotel every night at ten to swap notes until you meet Preston. Then we'll stay separate. Here's the number of the house if you need to reach us.' Maggie got out, and Titch lifted her case from the boot. She joined the taxi queue outside the station.

Titch drove off to the house he'd rented. It was a semi-detached villa in a quiet street, not far from the town centre. Nice house, Strang thought. Titch signed all the forms for the agent, paid him and got the keys. The agent gave them a quick tour, and left them to it. 'I'm happy with this,' Titch said. 'You okay, lads?'

'Yeah, it's fine.'

They settled into their separate rooms, and then went out to find a grocery store. Their ration books didn't give them much, but it was enough to get by. They picked up a map of the town and the area, and walked over to the harbour. Strang pointed out the *Lady E* moored on the opposite side of the harbour.

Titch gawped. 'Jesus, it's a forty foot motor yacht. What do you think? Four berth?'

Spike whistled. 'Maybe more. It's a beauty.'

'We need to have a look on board,' Strang said.

Titch pointed the way. 'Right. Let's check the access.' They crossed the bridge over the harbour, and came down the other side to the *Lady E*. The cabin windows above the deck had their curtains closed. 'What about the locks, Spike? Can we get in okay?'

Spike studied the boat. 'I think the main access is through these doors from the lower side decks, so that's not a problem. And we can use the walkway below us here to shield us from the other side. Let's see how we get down there.' He walked towards the end of the dock and peered over the side. 'There's a stair here with a chain, so it's not a problem.'

Strang liked working with these guys. They were so calm and careful. Real professionals.

Titch looked around. 'Okay, what do you think? Come back tonight, or early tomorrow morning?'

Strang glanced over at the other side of the harbour. 'Couple of pubs over there. Might be busy tonight. Let's do it early tomorrow.'

The others agreed. Decision made. Now they had to find the best place to leave the car. They walked round the dock and found an ideal place between two sheds. Then headed back to the house.

Titch outlined their options. 'I assumed he had a sailboat. I did some research and found that one of the biggest causes of fatal accidents on sailboats is getting your head bumped by the boom when drunk. So, I had been working along these lines. We could do something similar with a motor yacht – like he slips on deck while drunk, and bangs his head.

'My original idea was to pretend I was in distress and ask him for help, but that's maybe not so easy now with him on a motor yacht. Let me have a think.'

'When should we do it?' Spike asked.

'How about a week tomorrow? It'll take us a few days to organise.'

'Makes sense.'

'How about the aunt in the nursing home?'

'Fine. St Joseph's is the biggest in the area, but they can't see me till Monday. I'll do my stuff then.'

Strang smiled. Spike had perfected an approach with nursing homes, where he represented a trust interested in taking patients who were active, but had no visitors, on a free bus tour. He'd hire a minibus for a Wednesday to take half a dozen patients, with a couple of staff, wherever they wanted to go. During his initial visit on Monday, he'd identify a patient as a likely 'distant aunt' for Maggie. Spike could talk his way in anywhere.

They went out to a pub for a meal. Titch was his usual cheerful self, and chatted with locals. Strang and Spike just left him to it, and sat quietly at the side.

After a while, Titch joined them again. 'Got it sussed, lads. That Ailsa Craig is the place to do it. There are only a couple of lighthouse men there at the weekend. The quarry men all go home. It'll take the cops at least an hour to get over there. By the time they've figured out what happened, we'll be long gone.'

Strang was duly impressed. They walked back to the house and Titch went off in the car to collect Maggie.

'How's the hotel?' Spike asked her.

'It's fine. Nice room and good food. No sign of Preston, though. I chatted with one of the waitresses. They don't often see him, and she couldn't tell me much about him. So, how did you get on?'

'It's coming together,' Titch said. 'The broad plan is you hook Preston quickly, and get him to take you to Ailsa Craig on his boat next Sunday. You soften him up, and get him very drunk.'

Maggie nodded. 'Okay.'

'Spike and Strang will appear from hiding and arrange the "accident". I'll come alongside and collect you. We'll crash his boat onto the island. By the time anyone gets there from the mainland, we'll be back in the car and on our way south. Does that make sense?'

Strang thought it sounded fine, though he didn't fancy a long wait on board the boat. He liked action.

They agreed to meet next day at the harbour around lunchtime to see Preston on his boat. They needed to make sure they had the right target.

***

At six o'clock on the Sunday morning, the three of them, dressed in black sweaters and slacks, with black balaclavas and gloves, listened for any sounds. The harbour had only a few pockets of feeble light cast on the decking. It brought back memories for Strang of their exploits in enemy territory, blending into the shadows.

Spike crouched, ran over to the end of the wharf, and disappeared down the stairway. Strang and Titch waited and watched, then Spike signalled, and one by one they joined him on the stairway below the harbour deck. They approached the *Lady E* along the lower walkway in the same manner. Strang and Titch waited in the shadows while Spike climbed on board. Within seconds, he had the door open. Each of them put on black overshoes before they stepped on board. Titch really thought of everything.

Strang joined Spike inside the lower wheelhouse. Titch hid on deck beside the entrance. He would tap twice on the bodywork if anyone approached. Strang admired the brass instruments, and the high-quality wood finish. A plaque said 'Saunders Roe Limited, 1937'. Strang had never heard of them, but they sure made a nice boat.

Strang and Spike tiptoed down into the saloon behind the wheelhouse. They used pencil torches that reflected off the varnished deck and shiny wood panels.

The saloon had plush sofa style seats along both sides. Spike tried to open a cabinet, but found it locked. He pulled out his bunch of keys, and opened it within seconds. It was a well-appointed drinks store, with full bottles of whisky, gin and brandy, and with rows of crystal glasses, all held safely in wooden holders. They nodded to each other, impressed.

Spike locked the cabinet, and went to the next one. He unlocked it with a different key, and this time they smiled at each other in surprise. The trays and drawers held a selection of ladies' underwear – bras and panties, stockings and suspender belts, slips and nighties – all in pure silk, and in large sizes. Spike grinned. 'Gotcha! That's Maggie's bait,' and locked the cabinet.

They moved through the rest of the boat, checking out the large two-berth cabin to the rear. Beyond the galley at the front was another small two-berth cabin with a concealed water closet. Ideal for a hiding place, Strang mused.

They went back out onto the deck, locked the access door, and gave Titch a thumbs-up. The three of them stepped onto the lower walkway in turn, took off their overshoes, and worked their way back to the car.

'How did it go?' Titch asked.

'It's a beauty. Worth a bundle.' Spike turned to Strang. 'Will you tell him, or shall I?'

Strang waved for him to go on.

Titch turned. 'Tell me what?'

'Our Mr Preston's into pure silk ladies' underwear.'

'Blimey, Maggie will make good use of that.'

'You can say that again.'

Strang sat in the back and wondered what Preston did with the underwear. Did he go out in the boat wearing it? Seemed very odd. But he agreed. Maggie would be happy.

***

Just after half past twelve, the three of them strolled along the harbour. Strang glanced across at the *Lady E. How much would that cost?*

To his surprise, Strang noticed the Harbour Hotel was open and serving drinks in the bar. He'd just assumed there would be no strong drink sold in Scotland on a Sunday. 'Do you fancy a beer while we wait?' he asked the others.

'Yeah, sounds good,' Titch said, and entered the hotel. Strang went to the bar, and asked for three beers.

'You've got to sign the register first,' the barman said. He pointed to a list lying on the bar and then walked away.

Strang turned to a man. 'What's this register?'

'Oh, that? Are you a bona fide traveller?'

'I don't even know what that means.'

'Well, you've got to be a bona fide traveller to buy a drink on a Sunday. It's nonsense, but you have to sign in. You need to have come more than three miles, and be going more than three miles.' He pulled the register over towards him. 'Just sign whatever you like. No one ever checks it. I mean, look at the names here.' He leaned over with a smile and pointed to the list. 'There you go. M Mouse going from Hollywood to Girvan. And here's R Hood, from Sherwood Forest, going to Maybole, with his companion M Marion.'

'I'm from London.'

'That's more than three miles, so you're sorted.'

Strang shook his head in amazement. What a country. The politicians here must be nuts, he thought, though probably no worse than anywhere else. He signed the first three names he could think of, all going from London to Glasgow, and then ordered his three beers again.

They stood at a window, and watched the *Lady E*. Strang spotted Maggie on a bench outside, talking to a woman with a pram. He nudged the others and pointed.

***

Maggie leaned over and touched the pram cover. 'Oh my, she's beautiful. How old is she?'

The woman beamed. 'Just over six months now.'

Maggie cooed at the baby. 'She's so gorgeous. You must be very proud.'

'Well, surprised more like. I mean, that's my eldest for you. Opens her legs for a young soldier home on leave. I warned her too. They're like bloody rabbits when they're on leave. But not her. She says she's in love, whatever that means. He's just back from the Far East now and demobbed. Says he'll look after her and the baby. I'll believe that when I see a ring on her finger. So stupid. But I couldn't put her in a mother and baby home, or one of them convent places. They're horrible. No, she might be stupid, but she's mine. And I'll make sure she's okay, one way or another.'

Maggie smiled. 'I'm sure it'll all work out.'

'I hope so. Anyway, you've just got to get on with it, haven't you?'

'You're right.' Maggie looked across at the *Lady E*. A car had just pulled up beside it. A man got out and boarded the boat. He went to the upper wheelhouse, and began to get it ready. He then climbed back down onto the deck, gathered the ropes that another man on the harbour had loosened from their supports, and went back up to the wheelhouse again.

'There's a man getting on with it in fine style, huh?' she said to the woman, and nodded over to the *Lady E*.

The woman glanced over. 'That's Richard Preston. Fine style all right.'

'I'm a visitor here. Who's he?'

'Oh, he owns the big department store in town. Very rich, I'm told.'

'Rich, huh? That sounds interesting. Is he married?'

The woman laughed. 'Oh, I don't think you'd get far with him, dear. I think he might be one of those – what do you call them – you know, men that don't like women. He's definitely not married.'

'Have you ever met him?'

The woman shook her head. 'No, dear. He's not interested in the likes of me. He's only interested in those that splash lots of cash. He's all over *them* like a rash. No, he lives in a different world, he does.'

'Oh well. You can always hope.'

The woman smiled. 'Best of luck, dear. Nice to talk to you. But I need to go now and get her fed.' She stood up. 'Bye for now.' She walked off with the pram.

Maggie heard the burr as the diesel engines started. She watched Preston in the wheelhouse. He looked over and held her gaze as the boat slowly moved out of the harbour. Well, he'd certainly know her again if they met, she thought. Preston looked okay. Early forties, maybe. Let's see what happened once she splashed some cash.

She turned around to see where her colleagues were just as they emerged from the hotel. Titch moved his head to indicate she should follow them, and she got up and strolled after them at a distance.

***

Strang stretched out on a sofa, and watched Maggie take off her coat and hat. No matter what she wore, she always looked stunning.

'What do you think?' she asked him.

'About what?'

'About Preston. Can you take him okay?'

Strang glanced across at Spike and shrugged. 'Don't see a problem.'

'That's good.'

Spike cleared his throat, and smiled at Strang and Titch. 'We've got news for you.'

'Great. What is it?'

'Our Mr Preston's into ladies' underwear. Big style. He has a cupboard on board filled with pure silk ladies' underwear and nightwear. All in larger sizes.'

She smiled. 'Wow. A man with a fetish. Lovely.'

Strang had never heard the word. 'A what?'

'A fetish. It's an object that stimulates a man sexually. Usually ladies' clothing of some kind.'

Strang frowned. 'How does that work then?'

Maggie sighed. 'Well, my next door neighbour, Tamsin . . . how do I put it . . . caters for such men. She says lots of men have a fetish, but they never talk about it. Other than to women like her. It's all kept hidden in the closet. Women's underwear is a very common fetish. But it can be any item of women's clothing. Skirts, blouses, shoes, boots, gloves, hats, coats, capes, anything really. And then it has to be a specific material. Silk or satin, cotton, lace, rubber, leather, plastic, fur. It just goes on and on.

'And the special fetish garment affects almost all the man's senses. The sight of shimmering silk, for example, will turn him on. The whisper of satin as it swishes. The smell of plastic, leather or rubber. And most important of all, the touch that can send a man crazy with desire. It becomes an obsession. Some men will do anything, even petty crime, to get hold of a fetish object. Tamsin's got a whole room full of stuff she uses to satisfy her clients' desires. Mostly they just want to make love to the garment. Easy money, huh?'

The three men looked at each other in shock. Strang splayed his hands. 'How the hell can that happen?'

'I don't think anyone knows. Tamsin thinks, when they were babies, their mothers cuddled them, while wearing that garment. They then associate the garment with love and affection, which gets triggered at puberty into a sexual desire.'

'Never heard of such a thing. Is it very common?'

'Tamsin thinks it is. She says there are more fetishists than men who like other men. And there are lots of them.'

'Jesus. So what does that mean for Preston?'

'Well, he obviously gets turned on by wearing, touching or stroking himself with pure silk garments. And I can use that, lads.'

'Thought you could,' Spike said, with a smile.

Strang thought about what Maggie had said. His mother had never cuddled him. So he didn't have a fetish. But he *had* become addicted in a different way by that big bastard Cornish. It had left him with a desire for . . . well, killing. He didn't know which was worse – to want to make love to silk panties or kill someone. Well, he *did* know, really. Ultimately, both obsessions had much the same effect – driving the sub-conscious to act. And Maggie was right. You couldn't talk about it.

Since he met Maggie, he'd had a recurring dream. He stood alone by the side of a road in the middle of a forest. A car came along and stopped. The driver was a very attractive older woman – not Maggie – who leaned over, smiled, and waved for him to join her in the car. But his body had frozen. He couldn't lean forward and open the car door. He couldn't speak. After a few moments, she smiled at him, waved, and drove off.

He knew what it meant, of course, but didn't know what to do about it. Preston and he were probably alike in being trapped in some sort of addiction, but at opposite ends of a spectrum from soft to hard. There must be a 'normal' point between the two, but he didn't know what that was or how to get there.

Titch interrupted his thoughts. 'Tell you what. Why don't we go down the coast to see where Preston goes?'

They all agreed and piled into the car. They followed the coast road south, and navigator Spike took them off on a side road towards the sea near Dunure. They parked the car, walked over towards the cliffs, and watched Preston's boat as it sailed slowly into the bay below them. Preston launched the sea anchor, and then went back into the cabin. Strang exchanged glances with the others. They all knew what he was doing.

After half an hour, Preston reappeared, raised the sea anchor, and sailed off towards Ailsa Craig, which sat proud and clear in the distance.

They got back on the coast road, and passed a sign – 'Electric Brae'.

'What the hell's an electric brae, Spike?'

'As I recall, it makes you think you're going uphill when you're going downhill.'

Titch pulled onto the side of the road and stopped. 'So, are we going uphill or downhill right now?'

They all looked around them. 'We're going downhill,' they all agreed.

Titch let off the hand-brake and the car began to roll backwards. 'There you go, you're all wrong. We're going uphill.'

Strang cleared his throat. 'That's electric?'

They all laughed, and continued their way south to Turnberry. They walked over to the lighthouse at the edge of the golf course. Titch raised his binoculars, and pointed out Preston's boat in the distance well on its way to Ailsa Craig.

They enjoyed the scenery and fresh air, then headed back to Ayr. They dropped Maggie off near her hotel, and headed for the house.

The three men wandered down to the harbour around half past five and sat on a bench. The *Lady E* arrived just after six o'clock, and reversed slowly into its berth. A man came out of a Jaguar car and caught the mooring ropes. Preston locked up and joined the man in the car. Within a few minutes, they were gone.

Strang turned to Titch. 'What do you think, then? Will your plan work?'

'Yeah, I think so. Still a few details to work out, but I think we can make it look like an accident. And that's what we want.'

Strang had every confidence in Titch.

Chapter 9. Jean Munro

Richard arrived early, and waved to Janet, already in her office. He set his desk calendar to Monday, October 29, and thought about Janet. She'd made such a difference over the past few weeks, with detailed plans for her new training, measures of performance, and an incentive scheme, all of which would go live on Thursday.

That would allow the business to take full advantage of Christmas trading, and set the financial targets for next year. He liked the way she handled staff meetings, with crisp, clear answers to all questions. Even Neil Hendry seemed like a new man with her around.

And young Adam had settled in too. Richard had got used to his hearing aid now, and the lad seemed to communicate well. Richard's mother had also taken to Adam, and had set up a meeting with him at Laurel Avenue each morning at eleven to discuss performance figures. Adam seemed to handle that well too.

The first item on the agenda for the day was to finalise and approve the *Gazette* article that would announce the new image for the business. So, once the store was up and running, Janet, Adam, and Neil Hendry, gathered in Richard's office.

They all had copies of the mock-up article Katy had delivered last Friday. The article was entitled 'Now for the Future', and Richard asked Adam what he thought.

'I like the headline,' Adam replied. 'It's clear and punchy. And Katy tells me she used only one three syllable word – "customer" – which makes it very easy to read. The only issue I have is with the last sentence, where she says the store will become the new status symbol for the town. I think that's the wrong emphasis, and I'd change it.'

'To what?'

'I think it should be more customer-focused, like "Now for the future – clear customer care!" so the emphasis is on the customer, and everyone realises it.'

'I like that. What about you, Janet?'

'I agree with Adam. The article is well written, but I'd be happier with Adam's suggestion.'

Neil cut in. 'I agree with that too.'

'Good. Mother gave me her comments last night, and made much the same point.' He looked around the group. 'Are we all agreed, then?'

Everyone nodded.

'Okay, Adam. Go back to Katy with your suggestion. And let's build that phrase into our promotional literature. Thank you. Let's get on with the rest of the day.'

As the meeting broke up, Sara came in with a note for Richard. It was from Peggy in ladies' wear. 'Big spender in lingerie.'

He stood and put on his jacket. Floor managers had to let him know when they identified a big spender, someone buying several items from the goods on show, or an item from the separate luxury selection.

In 1941, as part of wartime austerity, the government had brought in utility ranges, with a CC41 mark, for footwear, furniture, textiles and clothing, and these were the main ranges he displayed in these departments. However, there was still a demand for luxury items alongside these ranges, so he had discreet signs put up that referred to them.

Customers didn't need clothing coupons to buy luxury items, but since the war started, their prices had soared, and the government had added purchase tax, so they were now very expensive. Richard held these items in separate, closed-off display areas to emphasise the discreet nature of such purchases.

When he arrived at the lingerie department, he glanced over to the displays. Before the war, they'd always included luxury silk items that he desperately wanted to go over and touch. But never did, of course. Now it was only utility ranges on show. Still attractive, but they didn't have the magic of pure silk.

Peggy, the floor manager, together with a sales associate, talked with a fair-haired woman at the service desk. The woman was dressed in a tailored grey suit, with matching hat, shoes, gloves, and handbag, which all shouted 'money'. As he approached, he realised she was the woman he had seen at the harbour yesterday. She'd looked stunning from a distance. Close up, she was even more stunning.

She was in her late-twenties, with an oval face, clear dark eyes, gorgeous lips, and perfect teeth that showed when she smiled. She also had a very shapely figure. He smiled. 'Hello, I'm Richard Preston, and I'd like to welcome you to our store. Can I help you?' He extended his hand.

She held the direct look, the smile and the handshake as she studied him. Then said, 'Thank you, Mr Preston. I'm Jean Munro. Nice to meet you. I noticed the sign up there that luxury silk items might be available. Now, I just *love* pure silk, but I haven't seen it for years, so...' – she waved her left hand – '... I asked your assistant.' She smiled again.

He noted she wore wedding and engagement rings. *Dammit, she's married.* He found his voice. 'Of course. Peggy, do you have the key?'

'Got it here,' she said, and walked over to a curtained section nearby.

As they followed, the woman seemed to glide along beside him. He turned to her. 'We've had very few new pure silk garments since the war started, so the range is a little limited. But most of them are classic designs that just don't date. Let's see what you think.'

They went into the enclosed display area, and Peggy put the lights on. Spotlights shone on mannequins on one side of the room wearing pure silk underwear and nightwear. On the other side, they wore fur coats. The group moved over to the silk side.

The woman went to a long, pale gold nightdress. She turned to Richard. 'May I touch it?'

He nodded.

She put her hand behind the garment and held it up. 'Oh, my God. It's beautiful. So smooth. And see how it shimmers and reflects the light. Isn't that fabulous?' She looked directly at him.

He felt almost hypnotised. He wanted to go over and touch the garment, but he just stood and watched her, his body tense like a spring. 'It certainly is,' he stammered.

She checked the price ticket, and then held the garment up to the side and tilted her head in admiration. She turned to him and smiled. 'I think I must have this, you know. And it's in my size. May I just check it?'

He couldn't speak for a moment. His throat tightened. 'Of course,' he blurted, and turned to Peggy.

Peggy stepped forward, gently took the nightdress off the mannequin, and held it towards the woman by the shoulders. She took it, held it against herself, and looked in the full-length mirror. 'Oh my, it's so beautiful. What do you think?'

'It certainly is,' Peggy said, 'and that colour suits you so well.'

Richard just stood and admired the beautiful woman swaying with the beautiful garment. That vision would stay with him forever. He wanted to know *much* more about this woman, married or not.

'I'll take it,' the woman said, and passed the garment back to Peggy.

They left the enclosed area, and went back to the service desk. Peggy prepared the paperwork. 'That's twelve guineas plus tax, madam.'

Richard wanted to make a gesture to keep her interest. 'Give Mrs Munro ten percent off, Peggy, since it's a special purchase. Use my staff discount number.'

Peggy recalculated. 'Eleven pounds, eighteen shillings, madam.'

The woman opened her purse and picked out three five-pound notes.

'Thank you, madam. I'll just send this to the cash desk. Won't be a moment.' She put the cash and paperwork into a metal cylinder, and sent it through a pneumatic tube. Within a few moments, it came back with the paperwork stamped, and the change enclosed.

Peggy handed over the receipt and change. 'It's so beautiful, madam, and I hope you get great joy from it.' The assistant at the desk wrapped the nightdress carefully, and put it into a soft bag.

The woman smiled at Peggy and the assistant. 'Thank you, I'm sure I will. Would you deliver it to my hotel, please?'

'Certainly, madam. Which hotel?'

'The Egerton.'

Richard stepped forward. 'Oh, that's part of our group. It's not a problem. Leave that with you, Peggy?'

'Yes, Mr Preston.'

Richard thought how he might keep this woman in the store a little longer. 'Do you have any more shopping to do?'

'Not really. I was just browsing.' She turned to Peggy and the assistant. 'Thank you so much for your help,' and moved away from the desk.

Richard moved with her. 'We appreciate your business. Have you time to join me for a sherry?'

She looked up at him, and smiled. 'It's maybe a bit early for that, but tea would be nice.' She put her hand lightly on his arm.

'Certainly, it would be my pleasure.'

Richard guided her over to the lifts, and they went up to the fourth floor. He showed her into his office, and ordered tea for two from the restaurant. They stood together, and looked over to the hills of Arran.

'It's a wonderful view from here, Mr Preston.'

'Oh please, it's Richard.'

She smiled, and it took his breath away. 'Richard, I'm Jean.'

He tried to relax. 'I think I saw you at the harbour yesterday, when I was taking the boat out. Are you here on holiday?'

'Oh. That was you? My goodness. Yes, just a week's break. Back home next week.'

'And where's home?'

'Perth.'

'Nice city. I know McEwens of Perth, of course.'

'Yes, it's a nice store, though I think yours is better.'

He laughed. 'That's good to know.'

A waitress came in with the tea and laid it on the table. He poured and they sat down.

'So, is Mr Munro with you too?'

She looked him straight in the eyes, and smiled wanly. 'I'm afraid not. My husband died some years ago. Fell off a mountain in the Cairngorms just before the war.'

'Oh, I'm sorry to hear that.' Inwardly he rejoiced.

'I came here on holiday once as a young girl, and thought it would be nice to come back for a break. I might also have a distant aunt in a nursing home here, and I could look her up, if she's still around.'

'So, what are your plans, then?'

'Nothing special. In fact, if I'm honest, I'm here to work out my plans.'

'Oh? In what way?'

'Well, when I lost James, my husband, I was devastated. I just didn't know what to do. Then war broke out, and everything went crazy. Even in Perth. I couldn't stand it there, and decided to go back to London, where I had lived before I met James. I picked up on my old life again, and one day, on a whim, replied to an advert for a secretary to a senior army officer, and got it. I had been a secretary before I married.

'The job was with Brigadier Paterson, who was an expert in logistics, and helped to plan our invasion strategy. I found it really exciting, and gradually got drawn into yet another crazy life in London.'

He laughed. 'Crazy? How was it crazy?'

'Oh, it was like we were all on a giant carousel, with bankers, lawyers, businessmen and army officers all riding their own horses, with the carousel getting faster as the war went on, the fairground music getting louder, working twelve-hour days, partying for four to six hours a night, and sleeping when we could. All in darkness, of course, with lightning flashes, not knowing if the next doodlebug had our names on it.

'And people kept falling off the carousel. Killed or maimed by the flying bombs. Even a close friend of the Brigadier unmasked as a top German spy. And others jumped aboard as it sped on and on. And during the final invasion, the carousel got even faster, the music louder, the lightning stronger, until one day . . . one day . . . ' She had tears in her eyes. 'One day it was like someone had pulled out the plug. It all just stopped. And the lights came on, and we cheered, and looked around at each other, got off our horses, hugged and exchanged addresses – "must keep in touch" – and went home.'

She still had tears in her eyes. He wanted to go over beside her and give her a hug, but managed to stay seated in silence.

'So, I went back to Perth, where people lived as though nothing much had happened. I couldn't get my head round that. I needed to sort out in my own mind what I should do. Stay, or go back to London. And so I decided to go to a neutral place, near the sea, and try to work out what I should do.' She shrugged. 'I feel a bit lost just now, so I'm here to try to sort out my future.' She pulled a handkerchief from her bag, and dabbed her eyes. 'I'm sorry, I didn't mean to go on as much.'

He leaned over and touched her arm. He didn't know what to do, but said, 'Well, if there's anything I can do to help while you're here, I'll be happy to do it.'

She smiled. 'Thank you, Richard. That's very kind of you. But I don't want to take up your time. You're a busy man.'

'Oh, it's no problem,' he said, and patted her arm again. He didn't want to lose this woman. He wanted to stay with her, comfort her, and help her. He'd never felt this way about a woman before. 'Tell you what. Why don't we have a quick lunch, then I'll take you out in the car. We can visit somewhere nice, like down the coast, or a walk in the park, or visit Burns' Cottage, if you'd like some local history.' He felt awkward suggesting these, when he really just wanted to be with her and hold and caress her. But how could he do that? He felt, though, after her initial impact, he was getting back his normal 'mine host' persona.

She smiled again. 'That would be nice. Do you have a ladies' room handy?'

'Of course.' He stood and went to the door. 'There, on the left.'

She went off to the ladies' room, and he popped into Sara's office. 'Tell Neil and Janet I'm entertaining a VIP customer for lunch. Ask them to eat in the main restaurant today, please? And call Ben. Ask him to have the car over in say an hour or so. I'll be out for the rest of the day.'

She looked up with surprise. 'Oh? What about your meeting at two?'

'What's that again?'

'It's to finalise all the arrangements for Thursday. For the launch.'

'Oh, right. Janet knows what needs done. We've decided it all, more or less. Tell Janet just to take any final decisions necessary.'

'Yes, Mr Preston. Will do.'

He went back into his office as Jean Munro returned. He was confident he could cheer up this woman, and help sort out her future.

***

Richard lay on his bed, his hands behind his head, reflecting on the day. Jean captivated him. He wanted to be with her all the time, for ever. Was this love?

After lunch they'd gone to Burns' Cottage, and spent a couple of hours together, she with her arm through his. They admired the incredible, evocative poetry of Robert Burns. In the late afternoon sunshine, they then went to the Heads of Ayr, and looked down on the town as dusk began to creep in.

He dropped her at the hotel and went home to change. They met again in the bar of the hotel an hour later. During that hour, he felt a gap in his life. Such was the impact Jean had had on him.

They dined at his favourite table over by the picture window. The room was half full – not bad for a Monday night, he thought – but he only had eyes for her. She talked about her life in London. She had even met

Churchill once, when he came to the War Office for a meeting, and she had to organise it. He was fascinated to hear about his hero, and as the evening wore on, he felt a warmth and desire for her that he'd never had before with anyone.

He'd suggested he pick her up on Tuesday morning, and take her for lunch at the luxury Turnberry Hotel down the coast. And she agreed. She'd asked him about Arran, and he offered to take her over there on his yacht on Wednesday. They'd tour the island to let her see the beautiful scenery. She'd also asked him about Ailsa Craig, and he suggested that, if the weather held, they could sail down to it on Sunday. She smiled and agreed. That was a first for him. Sunday afternoon was his precious 'me' time. He never shared it with anyone. Now he thought about it more as 'our' time.

He wanted to show her off to others, assuming she agreed. They could have dinner on Thursday with Matt Lawson and his wife. They were always good company. And he should take her to meet his mother on Friday evening. A big step, but he felt his life had changed since this woman had arrived, and the change just might be for the long term. So his mother should meet her. And then there was the tennis club dance on Saturday night. All his friends would be there. Sunday on the boat. And then Monday, the day she had to go home. Could he sweep her off her feet before then? How would he face Monday without her? He was already annoyed he had to be at the shop on Thursday, Friday and Saturday. When had his business ever intruded into his personal life?

But while he had all these plans in his mind, he still wasn't confident about going further with her physically. When they'd parted earlier, he didn't know whether to shake hands or kiss her cheek, or even her gorgeous lips, which he so wanted to do. He'd stood and held both her hands, and looked in her eyes, not wanting to part. She'd waited and then smiled that fantastic smile, leaned up and kissed him on the cheek. 'Thank you so much, Richard, for a wonderful day. I really enjoyed it, and look forward to seeing you tomorrow.' She then glided off to her room. He'd walked on air all the way home.

He worried though about what he'd do if the relationship *did* become physical. He'd never been intimate with a woman. He was still a virgin at the age of forty-two. Not that he hadn't tried.

He thought back to his first attempt, when still at school. His father had sent him to a private boys' boarding school in Edinburgh. It had a reputation as one of the top schools in the country. And he'd hated it.

There seemed to be a pecking order among the boys based around their fathers' wealth and position. His father was quite wealthy, but as a businessman with a department store, he didn't compare well to the bankers, lawyers and diplomat fathers of the others in his year. Richard offset this with a joky personality, and a natural talent in golf and tennis, where he was always in the top three, and became accepted into the inner group.

The boys talked nonstop about women and girls, and there was the usual crop of pin-up magazines that were taken avidly to the toilets. But the inner group had access to 'Bigsby's book', which was a porn magazine at a different level, printed in Denmark. Bigsby's diplomat father travelled a lot, and Bigsby claimed he'd filched the book from his father's stash of porn. He rented it out for a penny a night or tuppence for a weekend. The book showed a series of black and white pictures of a couple as they met, kissed, caressed, stripped and played with each other, and then became fully intimate. Comments attached to each picture were in Danish, German, French and English. They were all very exciting, but Richard thought the sexiest picture was one where the lad stroked the girl's silk panties. That turned him on the most.

A rite of passage of the group was to lose your virginity as soon as possible after your sixteenth birthday. This was organised for Richard by his friend Simon, who had lost his to a woman called Crystal, whom he now visited regularly, and who plied her trade from a house in a quiet street off Leith Walk.

Richard went in first, and it was a disaster. Crystal tried hard, and had Richard strip her and stroke her, but he found the smelly, sticky, reality of her body off-putting compared with the easy stimulation of stroking his mother's silk panties or gawping at Bigsby's book, and he couldn't sustain his erection.

While he waited in a side room for Simon, the lady's maid came in and spoke to him. 'Don't worry about it, dear. It's normal for your first time. The problem is you boys spend too much time with dirty pictures, which are fantasy. They don't show you how to treat a real live woman. You need to give them up for a month and come back. You'll be fine. Crystal will look after you okay.'

Richard did exactly that, but the second visit was no more successful. Now he had a sense of failure that dominated any approach to intimacy with a woman, and he'd just avoided it. But now, with Jean, he so wanted to caress and love her, but was scared to start. She also had been active in that sense, at least with her husband, if not with others in London. He'd have to overcome that fear if he was to have any future with her. He put out the light and tried to sleep.

***

Janet waved to Richard as he arrived on the Tuesday morning. But instead of carrying on to his office, he came in and sat opposite her. 'How did it go yesterday?' he asked. 'All okay?'

'Yes, everything went fine. No problems.'

'Good,' he murmured.

She waited for him to go on, but he just sat, lost in thought. After a long pause, she said. 'She must be quite a woman, this Jean Munro. Peggy told me about her.'

He glanced at her. 'I think she is, Janet. She's a widow from Perth spending a few days here to work out her future. She's been in a high-powered job in London for the last few years, and now needs to decide whether to come back to live in Perth, or stay in London. Maybe I can help her decide.'

'Do you mean offer her Ayr as an alternative?'

He stared out the window. 'Mmm. We're not at that stage yet. But I'd like to think it's possible.'

Janet felt a twinge of regret. Over the years, their relationship had become like brother and sister. But someone else sharing his life would alter that. 'I hope you get what you're looking for then.'

He pursed his lips. 'Thanks.' He stood up. 'I'll be out today and tomorrow. Is that okay with you?'

'Of course. If it's okay with you, it's okay with me.'

He stood at the window. 'I'm taking her down to Turnberry for lunch today, and then over to Arran on the boat tomorrow. But I'll be back Thursday, Friday and Saturday.'

'That's good. You'll remember we have the full staff meeting at nine o'clock on Thursday to launch the new incentive scheme?'

He turned and leaned back on the windowsill. 'Look, could you do me a favour, Janet?'

'Of course.'

'Could you write me out a speech to give to the staff on Thursday? Five minutes max? I just can't think about it at the moment.'

'No problem.'

'Do you need me to call in?'

'Well, I think you *should* call in a couple of times. We'll leave any messages for you with Sara.'

'Right.'

He still stood as though he was thinking what to say, then glanced at her. 'Can I talk to you in confidence?'

'It won't be the first time.'

He leaned over and closed the door. 'I've never felt this way before, Janet, and I'm a bit old for the dating game. I'm scared I'll make a mistake and lose her. What should I do?'

She thought for a moment. 'Well, it's not always easy once you have established lifestyles. But if she's interested, and you stay polite and considerate, you should be okay. Just take it easy, don't push it too quickly, and let it take its course. Just try to be your natural self.'

'Thanks. That's good advice.' He looked at his watch. 'Well, I need to go, so talk to you later.'

'Have a nice day,' she shouted as he left her office.

She sat for a moment, then went through to see Neil Hendry. 'Got a minute?'

He spread his hands in front of him.

She sat down opposite him. 'Richard's just told me he won't be in today or tomorrow. He's entertaining the new lady in his life.'

'Yes. I heard about her.'

'She's a widow from Perth visiting the area. From what Peggy says, she's probably a *rich* widow. Very well dressed, and carrying lots of cash.'

'Well, good luck to him. I hope it's not just another of his daft impulses.'

'Not this time. I think he's smitten.'

'I hope it works out for him. In the meantime, should we run the business the way we want then?'

'I think so, Neil. We've a lot to do before Thursday. I think we just carry on the way we've planned, Richard or no Richard.'

'I'll go along with that.'

She stood up. 'I think we can make this work.'

'I agree. It's just what we need.'

'Good. Leave any messages for Richard with Sara. He'll call in a couple of times a day.'

She left and went back to her office. With Richard's attention diverted, she needed to take more control, and Neil seemed happy with that. It would be an interesting few days.

***

Katy sat and watched Adam as he put the team through their paces at Tuesday night training. They seemed to respond well to his commands. He got them to do the two-touch approach, but quicker. He wanted them to just glance at where their teammates were, rather than look. It seemed to her, even though she didn't know much about football, that he'd developed a sort of sixth sense in them as to where each of their teammates were. Pip still marched up and down the side as though she was their manager. Katy pulled out her notebook and jotted down a few notes.

At the end of the session, they all went their separate ways, and she and Adam headed for their usual café. 'Are you happy with the team?'

'Yeah, I think they're doing okay. We'll see how it goes on Thursday when we play the second top team. That'll be a good test for them. Anyway, how're you doing? What's happening with all your stories?'

'Oh, they're fine. Just put my gossip column to bed before I left tonight.'

'Gossip column? I didn't know you did that.'

'Yes. It's called "Clayrissa". Clever name, huh? Another of Kenny's bright ideas.'

'Clayrissa? Didn't realise that was you. How do you get the stories?'

'Most of them come to me. I get about a dozen letters a week. I just select the best and write them up. The problem is, Kenny demands proof if we name names. And that's not always easy to get. Hence why it's mostly anonymous.'

He smiled at her. 'I'd love to follow a story through with you, and see how you write it.'

'What? Learn all my insider secrets? It would spoil the illusion. Anyway, it's all just a grind to get the detail. The writing's the easy bit.'

'I'd still like to see how you do it.'

'Well, give me a story and we'll see.'

'I gave you a story last week – on our new image.'

'Adam, that wasn't a story. It was an advert. Preston owns the newspaper, for God's sake.'

He looked downcast, and she touched his arm. 'I'm sorry, I didn't mean to be so sharp. It was a good story, but not a *story* story. It was a story about a "thing" whereas a *story* story is about a person, with something happening that's interesting or newsworthy.'

He thought for a moment. 'Tell you what. I've got a *story* story for you.'

'Really?' She got her notebook out. 'Tell me then.'

'Richard Preston has a new lady friend.'

She couldn't help herself. Her jaw dropped in astonishment. 'What? You're joking.'

He sat back with a smile. 'No, it's true. For the first time in history, he's taking time off from the shop to be with this woman, and show her the sights. He's smitten. It's the talk of the steamie.'

Her pencil hovered. 'Talk of the what?'

'Oh, sorry. That's a Glasgow expression. The steamie is a public washhouse in Glasgow, where all the women take their household wash, and have a good chat and gossip while they're doing it. The talk of the steamie just means everyone's talking about it.'

'I see. Right, who is she then?'

'Well, her name's Jean Munro. She's a widow from Perth visiting the town for a week's holiday, staying at the Egerton. He took her down the coast today, and they're going over to Arran tomorrow on his boat.'

She wrote the details in shorthand as he spoke. 'Wow. That *is* a *story* story. How did they meet?'

'She came into the shop, and bought some expensive nightwear. The manager who served her said her clothes were super expensive, so she's probably a rich widow.'

'I need to know more. What does she look like? Does she have a family? Or a job? Anything more?'

'So, what will you do with it?'

'As I say, I'd like to know more. It would be ideal for my Clayrissa column. You know, along the lines of "You've missed out, girls of Ayr. The fair maid of Perth has bagged the county's most eligible bachelor".'

'The fair maid of Perth?'

She rolled her eyes. 'It's a literary allusion, dummy. It's a novel written by Sir Walter Scott.' She leaned over and playfully slapped his cheek.

He laughed. 'Oh. So, how do you find out more?'

'I'll get Archie's team onto it.'

'Tonight? Can I come with you?'

She thought for a moment. 'I'll need to check if he's in. Give me a minute. I'll use the phone box over there.' She left the café and asked for Archie's number.

'Hi, it's me. Just checking if I can come round and see you?'

'Sure.'

'It's complicated, though, Archie. It's another Preston story, and my source wants to come with me. If he's there, we can't mention the previous Preston story.'

'Right, I get you. No problem. Come on round.'

'Okay. See you in ten minutes.'

She went back into the café. Adam looked up as she approached the table. 'Right, he's in. Let's go.'

They walked through the town, and then diverted off into a housing estate. 'This is it,' she said. They walked up the path and she rang the bell.

Archie opened the door. 'Come in.'

'This is Adam. And this is the famous Archie.'

They shook hands and went into the front room.

'I guess you want help,' Archie said, when they'd all sat down. 'What's the story?'

'You won't believe this, but Preston's got himself a new lady friend, and this time it looks like it's serious. Good story for my Clayrissa column. But I need to know more about her. Can your team help?'

'That *is* a surprise. But you don't really need to know more for Clayrissa. You could embellish it from what you've got.'

'Oh, come on, Archie. Please,' she pleaded. 'I need to . . . flesh it out a bit. Please?'

'Okay, I'll see what I can do. Give me the details.'

'She's a Mrs Jean Munro, a widow from Perth, staying at the Egerton for a week.'

'And what does she look like?'

Katy looked over at Adam with eyebrows raised.

Adam shrugged. 'I don't know. I haven't seen her.'

Katy sighed. 'We don't know.'

'Okay, not to worry. We'll find out what we can. Come back on Thursday around the same time, and I should have some info for you.' He shook his head. 'Gossip column.'

'Archie!' Katy said indignantly. 'It's important!'

'You're right. Of course it is.'

Katy stood up. 'Right, we'll leave you to it. Thanks, Archie, as always.'

'Take care. See you Thursday.' Archie turned to Adam. 'Do you know what you're doing linking up with this one?' He indicated Katy.

Adam chuckled. 'I think so.'

'Best of luck, mate.'

They all laughed and Katy led the way out. As they walked towards her house, Adam said, 'Tell me about Archie again.'

'Oh, he's so experienced. He was a crime reporter on the *Record* for years, and has pals everywhere, in the police, among the crooks. He uses a private detective to dig out info on people. A guy called Davie, who used to be a cop. I'm amazed at what he finds sometimes.'

'Okay. Let's see what happens on Thursday.'

They stopped at her gate and she smiled up at him. Then she leaned up and kissed his cheek. 'Thanks. See you Thursday.'

That was the first time she'd shown Adam she liked him. She looked back, and blew him a kiss as she closed the door. She liked him a lot. He was kind of serious, but nice with it. And he seemed to like her too. She stood with her back to the door for a moment, and smiled to herself. He was a really nice guy.

***

Strang sat on one of the easy chairs, and read a newspaper. He didn't read very well, and struggled with some words. But he got the gist. He jumped as the phone rang in the hall.

Titch rose and left the room to answer it. There was a brief muttered conversation, and Strang looked up as Titch came back into the room.

'That was Maggie. She's hooked Preston big style. He's spending lots of time with her, and wants to introduce her to his friends and family. He's biting hard, and he'll take her to Ailsa Craig on Sunday, so we're all set. I checked the forecast today, and the weather will hold okay. She needs more cash to keep up the independent rich widow act, so we'll drop some in at the hotel tomorrow when Spike's away.' He clapped his hands. 'Looks like we're on for Sunday, guys.'

'Thank Christ for that,' Spike said.

'At least it's comfortable. Just think when we waited in the woods in France, sometimes for days, to get a target. We're good at this.'

Strang just smiled and went back to his paper. He could sit it out for weeks, if necessary, to get a target. Waiting didn't bother him.

Chapter 10. Tom

Sandra Maxwell enjoyed these quiet moments at the end of the day, when she could relax and savour what she'd achieved. She preferred to have just her desk lamp on to give the room a softer light.

There was a knock at the door. She looked up. Tom Hamilton stood silhouetted against the lights of the outer office. 'Got a minute, ma'am?'

She sat back and beckoned him to sit. 'Sure. Come in. What can I do for you?' She liked Tom. He was one of her best detectives, and still retained enough of his boyish good looks and charm to be popular.

'I've been doing some detective work.'

'That's good. It's what we pay you for.'

'Well. This is a bit different. Unpaid overtime.'

'Okay. Fire away.'

'When I was fourteen, I fell in love with this girl.'

She sat up in surprise. 'Is this a long story?'

He nodded. 'Could be.'

'In that case, would you like a snifter? The chief often stops by of an evening, and this is his favourite tipple.' She pulled a bottle of Black Label and a couple of glasses from her desk, and poured some whisky into each. She passed him one. 'Cheers.'

'Cheers.' He took a sip. 'Nice.'

'Back to your story. '

'I fell madly in love with this girl, as did every other guy in my year at school. Her name was Cathie McCabe. She was in the year ahead of us. You know the story of the ugly duckling? Well, this was it for real. She hadn't registered with anyone before. But one day she became this beautiful young woman every lad lusted after.'

Sandra settled in her chair, and took a sip of whisky.

'Cathie didn't walk anywhere. She kind of glided. Like a swan. I don't know whether she tried to walk like a model or something. But that was the way she moved.

'Anyway, that was thirteen years ago, and of course, once she left school she was soon forgotten, and we all got on with our lives.

'Except three days ago, on Monday evening, Diane and I were in the Egerton Hotel in Ayr, with my best mate and his wife, when in walked our old friend Richard Preston, who owns the place, of course, accompanied by this very attractive woman. I instantly thought it was Cathie McCabe. She kind of looked like her, and glided in the same way Cathie did all those years ago.

'So I left the table, found one of the managers I know, and asked her about the woman with Preston. She's a widow on holiday for a week, staying in the hotel, and has a distant aunt in a local nursing home. She's Mrs Jean Munro, 40 Atholl Gardens, Perth, according to her registration. She showed that ID on arrival, but I now know that ID is false.'

Sandra leaned forward. 'Really?'

'Yeah. That's the second time in my life I've seen that address. The first time was on my first case as a DC. The Goldman case, back in '39. Do you remember it?'

She shook her head. 'The name rings a bell, but I don't remember the details.'

'I've looked up the file to remind me. Mr Goldman had a pawnbroker's shop near St George's Cross. We got a call on Monday, 22 May 1939, from a member of the public concerned that the shop hadn't opened that day. On the Friday, Mr Goldman had asked him to come back on the Monday to conclude his deal.

'Anyway, we entered the shop and found the place empty. Goldman lived above the shop, and that was empty too. No trace of him. He had a book on his desk in the shop that listed all the items he'd valued. It's still in our file. The last item listed was a five-stone diamond necklace with sapphire settings he'd valued at £2000, which means it was probably worth £10,000. And the name and address of the customer was a Mr James Munro, of 40 Atholl Gardens, Perth. As a young lad brought up on the Maryhill Road, I thought it was a grand address to have, and it just stuck with me. This listing had a cross against it. That meant the deal had not completed. All the completed deals had a tick.'

Sandra sat up straighter in her chair.

'We questioned the member of the public who had reported the incident about his visit on the Friday evening. His statement is in the file. He says he arrived just before five o'clock. Goldman had a customer, and asked him to wait. However, after ten minutes Goldman came to him, and asked him to come back on the Monday. The man said he needed money now, and Goldman gave him a couple of pounds on account, showed him out, and locked the door. He didn't see what the other customer had with him, but it looked like a large heart-shaped box, and could have held a necklace. He described the customer as a well-dressed, pleasant young man in his twenties.

'We trawled the neighbours, and one of them reported Goldman had left his shop on the Saturday morning around ten o'clock with a young fair-haired woman, and got into a taxi. We traced the taxi driver, and he remembered them well. He said Goldman was very quiet and didn't say a word – in fact, he looked ill. And the young woman was very attractive. She said she was his niece. She spoke with a local accent, and said they were on their way to Antwerp to visit his brother. He dropped them at Central Station. They had a couple of small cases with them.'

'And could they get to Antwerp then?'

'Yes. Belgium wasn't cut off until mid-1940.'

'Okay. Sorry to interrupt. On you go.' She gave him another tot of whisky.

'We could find no trace of them from that point on. And they hadn't crossed from any channel port. They just disappeared.

'We also went up to Perth to check on James Munro. He was a bank manager, and had gone off on a walking holiday in the Cairngorms the week before with his girlfriend, a very attractive dark-haired girl called Janice. Munro was tall and bald, and in his early forties. He didn't match the description of the man seen with Goldman on Friday night. He also wasn't married at the time, nor had ever been married. There's nothing further on Munro in the file.

'So, I've now talked with a DI in Perth, who looked up their file for me. Munro never appeared back at the bank. His family listed him as a missing person just after that, and he's still a misper to this day.

'The DI checked with the bank. Because Munro went missing, and had access to all the accounts and safety deposits in the bank, they carried out a major audit. It took over four months to check all the safety deposit boxes, and one of them was missing a very expensive five-stone diamond and sapphire necklace. The owner could prove it had been in his safe deposit box, and as a result, the bank, or its insurers, paid out £14,000 in compensation.

'But the bank hushed up the whole thing. He said there's a note in the file – "Advise Glasgow Northern", but we have no record of receiving any info from them. And, of course, by then the war had started, and everything was going nuts. The house in Atholl Gardens reverted to the bank as the mortgage-holder, and they sold it to the executor of James Munro's estate – his younger brother, Hugh – who still lives there today.'

'And what about the girl? Janice? Was she also posted missing?'

'No, she wasn't, because according to the file, no one knew her surname. The Perth police at the time interviewed the B&B owners where she stayed, but they kept no records. They thought Janice was visiting Perth to see her brother, and to visit an aunt in a local nursing home, but they never saw the brother, and the police couldn't trace any aunt. The girl just disappeared.

'However, Hugh Munro's wife is also called Jean, and according to the Perth DI, she lives there with her family, and works as a clerkess in the town. I asked him to check, and she was at work as normal yesterday.

'Now, to me, it's not a big leap of imagination to think that the girl Janice could easily adopt the identity of James Munro's sister-in-law. And I wouldn't be surprised to find the date of birth of Mrs Jean Munro in Ayr is the same as that of Mrs Jean Munro in Perth. You can go a long way in a deception with a real name, address and date of birth.'

Sandra swallowed a mouthful of whisky. 'I like it.'

'Now, Cathie McCabe had a brother, Alex, who would be a couple of years older than her. I kind of knew *of* him. But you know what it's like in your teens – you really only know your own age group. So I asked my mother. She knew the McCabe family because she worked in a local newsagents' shop, and they were all regular customers. She describes Alex McCabe as a real charmer. "If he fell into the River Clyde, he'd come out with fish in his pockets," she said.'

Sandra smiled at the Glasgow expression. 'So where was he when Goldman left home?'

'Good question. We have no record of Alex McCabe, or his sister, in our files. My dad told me

McCabe was a pretty good football player, and played with a junior team called Rutherglen Glencairn. I checked with the Glencairn secretary, and on that day, McCabe played for them in the Scottish Junior Cup Final at Celtic Park, in front of twenty thousand people. He confirmed McCabe was with the team from the previous night in a local hotel. Rock-solid alibi.'

'Crikey. Can't get better than that. So, does he fit *anywhere* in this story?'

'I think he does, ma'am. My dad said McCabe worked with a company called Barton Construction, which at the time was quite big. The company folded a year ago, mainly because Mr Barton fell ill. But I've talked to him, and he confirmed that he employed Alex McCabe as a gang boss, which is a kind of working supervisor. He checked the jobs McCabe had worked on, and they included the reconstruction of Glasgow Central low-level station in late 1938, and an extension to Perth High School in the spring of 1939. He reckons McCabe then left to go to London, and heard he'd joined the army, though there's no trace of him in army records.

'Good place to hide at that time.'

'Yeah, right. Barton also mentioned they had to rebuild part of the low-level station after a bomb strike in '41, the same night as the Clydebank blitz. But they had to delay the job because they found a body in the rubble. I've checked our archives, and it was a man found in a wrecked store room at the end of a platform. The room wasn't on the plans, and no one knew it was there. Except, of course, the person that built it.

'The body had deteriorated, and couldn't be identified. They had no ID, though they found a note deep in his jacket pocket with an address in Antwerp. They checked the details against the misper register at the time, but there was no match. I believe that body was Mr Goldman, put there by his attractive niece. I also think Mr James Munro probably passed the missing necklace to his girlfriend during his walking tour of the Cairngorms, and was bumped off shortly afterwards.

'I also think all the "very attractive" women I've mentioned are the same person – Cathie McCabe – and her brother, Alex, controlled all of it. I took the winning Glencairn team picture to the member of the public who had raised the Goldman case, and asked him if the man in the picture – Alex McCabe – was the man with Goldman on the Friday night. But he couldn't be sure after all this time.

'I think these two – Cathie and Alex – are con merchants, who work together to rob wealthy men, and have several different identities. God knows what false identities they have now, except I'm pretty sure one of them is Mrs Jean Munro, currently in Ayr, and companion of her next victim, Mr Preston. And I'm also sure the brother won't be far away.

'Now I can't prove any of this, ma'am, and I don't know what to do about it. What do you think?'

Sandra drummed her fingers on the desk. 'Good piece of work, Tom. But how sure are you this woman in Ayr is Cathie McCabe? I mean, it would be ironic if we now had to protect Preston after the problems he's given us in the last few weeks.'

'You're right.' He sat and thought for a moment. 'I just feel *very* strongly the woman *is* Cathie McCabe, ma'am. But can I prove it? No. I could question her, of course, but if it *was* her, she'd just clam up and disappear again.

'We don't know where she lives. If we did, we could maybe find clues to her past. But how can we do that when we don't even know if there's a crime being committed, and it's not an SB job anyway?'

'Well, let's just take it one step at a time, Tom. I'm happy to go with your instincts. Put a tail on her, and see if she leads you to the brother. Then we'll take it from there. Okay?'

'Okay, ma'am, and thanks.'

'No problem. Keep me posted.'

'Will do, ma'am.' He stood up.

'By the way, Tom, I'm down your way on Sunday. Going back to see our original informant on Preston.'

'What's the word on that?'

'Well, we don't have enough evidence to charge Preston, or any other member of Triumph. The boss has questioned Sir Anthony again. There are only fourteen members in total. He wrote a personal letter to each of them, told them our investigation is complete, and no further action will be taken. The regional SB heads delivered the letters last week. I gave Preston his in a hotel near Kilmarnock.'

'What was his reaction?'

'He just read it and shrugged. He objected to us suspecting him because of a waiter's comment, but I'm sure he felt relieved. They seem to have learned a lesson. I understand the Triumph group has now broken up. And that's good. But we'll keep all their IDs on file.'

'Right, so what do you tell the informant?'

'I'll just tell her I can't go into details, but there seems to have been a misunderstanding, and the matter's now closed.'

'Well, if it keeps them in line, it'll be worth it.'

'And . . . I'm also doing something else that very few people in this country have ever done.'

He cocked his head. 'What's that?'

'I'm flying in one of these new American helicopters on Sunday afternoon.'

'You're kidding me! How did you manage that?'

'Well, you know we work with Colonel Campbell at the US Army Air Force base at Prestwick? The last time

I was there I saw it hover and then land, and Chuck invited me on board.'

'Brilliant. I'd love to do that.'

'I'll tell you all about it – if I survive.'

'Survive?'

'Well, to be honest, Tom, I'm shit scared of flying.'

'Why?'

She felt tears well up in her eyes. 'Not many people know this, but ten years ago, I lost the love of my life in a plane crash. He was in the RAF, and it was a maintenance error. I vowed then I would never fly. For years afterwards, my stomach churned when a plane passed overhead. I expected it to crash at any moment.

'Yet now we see on the newsreels all these foreign places – Paris, Berlin, Rome, Washington – and I think I'd like to go there. I told you I met General Eisenhower at Prestwick. I mean, the man's real, not just an image in a newsreel. And these places are real too. But I'll need to conquer my fear of flying to see them. So, this is a first step along the way, and I just hope it works.'

'Oh, I'm sure it will, ma'am. Look forward to hearing about it next week.'

She smiled. 'Thanks, Tom. Talk to you later.'

'Good night, ma'am.' He turned and left the room.

She sat and thought about their discussion. It was often these tiny fragments that uncovered major crimes. Tom's instincts were usually pretty good. His story sounded plausible. They should stick with it for the moment and see where it led.

***

They all left the sports hall with smiles on their faces. Kev punched the air and slapped Adam on the back. 'Great feeling, man. Bloody great!'

Katy laughed, and shared in their success. They'd just beaten the second top team in the league by eight goals to five. Everyone shouted their farewells, and Katy and Adam walked to their usual café.

'You must be really proud of them tonight. They did what you've trained them to do. Well done, you.'

He chuckled. 'Yeah, it was a good result. Should take us up to sixth place. If we keep this up, we could finish top of the league. Wouldn't that be exciting?'

'Wouldn't it just?'

They chatted on for a while, then she reminded him they had to go to Archie's to hear about Mrs Munro.

This time, an older man with grey hair was sitting in the front room. Archie said, 'This is Davie Watson, our favourite PD. I thought you'd like to hear his feedback for yourselves.'

Katy and Adam shook hands with Davie, and settled down on a sofa.

Davie cleared his throat. 'I've got news for you.'

Katy leaned forward, with her notebook on her lap.

'I don't know who your Mrs Jean Munro is,' he said to Katy. She felt a pang of disappointment. 'But I know who she *isn't*.' Katy waited for him to go on. 'She's *not* Mrs Jean Munro of 40 Atholl Gardens, Perth.'

Katy looked across at Archie. 'Wow, I didn't expect that. Well, that's my headline gone phut.' She turned to Davie. 'You've no idea who she is?'

He shook his head. 'No idea. There *is* a Mrs Jean Munro living at that address, but she works for a company in Perth, and she was at work as usual today.'

Katy pursed her lips. 'So, what do we do now?'

'Well, that's not the end of it,' Davie went on. Katy thought he seemed to be enjoying this. 'Yesterday afternoon, while Mrs Munro was away with Mr Preston on his motor yacht, I spoke to Ella, my favourite receptionist at the Egerton. While I was there, a man came in with a package for Mrs Munro. An envelope about this size, well bound up with tape, maybe with photographs? The receptionist said she'd make sure Mrs Munro got it when she returned, and the man left.

'I nipped out a side door, jumped on my motorbike, and followed this guy in his car – at a safe distance, of course. He's staying in a rented property in Bellevue Road. I bunged the letting agent, and he told me the man – a little tough-looking guy – had rented the property until Sunday with two mates. They're here to sail and fish. He showed me the letting agreement, and the little guy's name and address is William Garvie, 14 Rochester Road, Camden, in London.

'Now, I've checked this today with a mate in London, and guess what? He's definitely *not* the William Garvie that lives there. The *real* William Garvie works with London Transport as a bus driver, and was on duty today on the 134 route.'

Katy felt her jaw drop. 'What the hell's going on?'

Davie settled back in his chair. 'Well, the first thing is not to jump to conclusions. Lots of people come here and use false identities. It's not illegal. In my experience, they're usually trying to get away from domestic abuse.'

'What's that?' Adam asked.

'You know, domestic abuse! Husband bashes his wife. Sometimes the other way round. I was a cop in this town for over twenty years, and half our workload was domestics of some sort. In places like the Larkfield estate, probably half the husbands beat up their wives. But it goes on everywhere – even in Myrtle Avenue.'

Adam shook his head. 'I never knew that.'

'There are lots of reasons why people might want to hide their identity. But in this case, it's unusual to have two separate visitors to the town, both with false identities, somehow linked. That's intriguing.'

Katy scribbled in shorthand, and tried to capture exactly what Davie was saying.

'Young Danny, my nephew, kept an eye on Mrs Munro today. In the morning, she wandered round the shops and splashed some cash. Had everything she bought delivered to her hotel. In the afternoon, she took a taxi to St Joseph's Nursing Home, and visited an old lady there. Danny saw them walking round the garden at one point. And as we speak, she's dining with Mr Preston and Mr and Mrs Matt Lawson at the Egerton.

'However, being a nosy bugger, I thought I'd find out a bit more about Mr Garvie. He did something *very* different. He and his two pals drove up to a boatyard in Troon this morning, and hired a motorboat called the *Cassie*. Mr Garvie then sailed the boat south, down past Ayr to Girvan, while his two mates drove the car south. They all met at Girvan harbour, and came back to Ayr by car. They went out for an early meal at a café, and they're now back at Bellevue Road. Now, why would they do that?'

Katy looked around at Archie and Adam and shrugged. 'Okay, tell us why.'

'I don't know. I'm not aware the fishing is any better off Girvan than off Troon or Ayr, so I'll be interested to see what they do for the next couple of days.' He went into his bag. 'I've got some pictures you might like to see.' He passed two envelopes over to Katy. 'The first lot are of Mrs Munro. The second lot shows Mr Garvie – who's the little guy – and his two mates.'

Katy looked at the pictures, and passed them to Archie and Adam.

Archie whistled. 'She's a stunner, isn't she?'

'She sure is,' Davie replied.

Archie studied the other set. 'These guys look tough. I'd hate to meet that big bruiser on a dark night.'

Davie held up his hands. 'That's all I've got. What do you want me to do now?'

Katy looked over at Archie. 'Can we keep going for a few more days? There's got to be a story here.'

'Do you mean for your gossip column?'

'No! I mean a proper story. Don't you think so?'

'These look real tough guys. I don't want Davie or his people in danger.'

Davie scoffed. 'Oh, we keep well out of sight. Now, the three guys are due to leave on Sunday, and the woman on Monday, so it's only three more days or so. But it's up to you. We can keep watch if you want. But if you prefer to call a halt, it's fine by me.'

Archie glanced over at Katy, then back to Davie. 'Well, okay, let's keep it going. But for Chrissake, stay clear of these guys. Right?'

'We will. Okay, lads and lasses, I'll leave you to it.' He rose, shook hands with everyone, and left the room.

Katy stood up, and packed away her notebook and the pictures. 'We'll get off too, Archie. Thanks for that. It was *very* interesting.'

'Okay, but can I also remind you two to stay away from these people? These guys look like they could dish out real violence. Keep well away. Agreed?'

Katy and Adam both nodded.

'Right, good night. And take care!'

They wandered back to Katy's house.

'That was quite a session,' Adam said, as they stood at her gate. 'Phew, you just don't realise what's going on around you at times.'

'Anyway, well done, you, for tonight.' She put her arm up around his neck, and kissed him impulsively on the lips. 'Good night. Sleep tight.'

He pulled her back towards him, and kissed her back, more deeply. 'Good night, and thanks for that.'

'Oh, you're welcome.' She skipped up the path, looked back, and blew him a kiss from the door. He really was a nice guy.

Chapter 11. Sunday Morning

The day of action at last, thought Strang, as he woke just after five. It had been a bit of a drag in Ayr. He didn't like these 'unfortunate accident' scenarios. They took so much planning, and the team kept going over the details of how they'd do this one on board the motor yacht.

He'd wanted his usual 'suicide' scenario, but Titch had argued against it. 'The guy's one of the richest men in the area, with successful businesses. What reason would he have to commit suicide? In any case, we don't have access to his handwriting without a lot of hassle. Sorry, Strang, it has to be this way.' And in the end, Strang reluctantly agreed.

The problem with the 'unfortunate accident' scenario was that they had to kill the target with one blow in a way that would match the subsequent 'accident' without suspicion. In the one instance where they'd already used this method, on a farmer in Norfolk, it should have been easy. The target had a weekly card game at a nearby farm, with lots of booze, and then staggered his way home along a track that crossed a main railway line at an open level crossing. A train would hit him as he crossed the line.

But it became too complex to achieve. In the end, Spike thumped the target on the forehead, then they manoeuvred the body into place as though he'd tripped over the end of the sleeper block, and fallen onto the track. They had to make sure his boot showed the mark of where that happened, and his forehead had to leave blood on the ground between the tracks at the point where he fell. And then the train sliced him in half as it passed. They'd got away with it, but Strang still thought the 'suicide' option was easier to organise and execute.

They left the house just before six, with Strang and Spike dressed from head to toe in black, with belts that carried the tools and essentials they needed for the day. Titch drove them towards the harbour. Strang, in the passenger seat, watched the passing scene.

Titch said, 'Uh-oh. I think we're being followed.'

The others turned to look. 'Is it the cops?'

'Don't think so. It looks too small for a cop car. Let's just keep driving, and see if I'm right.' He turned away from the harbour route.

A few minutes later, he said, 'He's definitely following us. Let's turn into this factory area and find out what's going on. I'll drive round a corner. You jump out and I'll pull over just ahead. He'll come round the corner and stop when he sees me, and you grab him.'

'Okay.' Strang prepared to jump from the car.

Titch drove around a corner and stopped. Within seconds, Strang and Spike stood in the shadows as Titch drove twenty yards further on.

Moments later, the small car nosed round the corner with its lights off, and stopped. Strang leapt over to it, opened the driver's door, dragged the occupant out, and held him up by the throat against a factory wall. He was just a young skinny guy, hardly out of his teens.

'Who the hell are you, and why are you following us?' Strang snarled. The young guy trembled with fear.

Titch reversed his car, walked over to the group, and punched the young guy in the stomach. The young guy doubled over and groaned.

Strang held him upright again. 'Come on, talk! Who are you?'

'D-Da-Danny,' he stuttered.

'Danny who?'

'D-Danny Watson.'

'And why are you following us, Danny Watson?' Titch asked.

'I'm a private detective working for a local newspaper reporter. She's writing an article for her gossip column, and wants to know more about Mr Preston's new girlfriend.'

'Who's Preston's girlfriend?'

'She's not who she says she is. That's what we're trying to find out.'

Titch looked at Spike with anger in his eyes. He punched the young guy again. 'How do you know that?'

'We checked with a mate in Perth.'

Titch shook his head in frustration. 'So what's that got to do with us?'

'You left a package for her at the hotel the other day. The reporter wanted to know your connection to her, and what you're doing here.'

The group stood in silence for a few moments, and waited for Titch's next move.

Titch stood on tiptoes, with his face close to the young guy. 'And what *are* we doing here, Danny boy?'

The young guy shivered. 'We don't know.'

Titch snarled, 'Listen, you've got it wrong. We're just here on holiday. We don't know this woman.' He paused. 'Have you or your mates talked to the police?'

The young guy looked puzzled. 'The police? Why would we talk to them?'

'Right. That's good.' Titch put his face up to the young guy again. 'You've upset me by following us. But this is your lucky day. I'm going to let you live.' Strang felt the young lad shake beneath his grip. 'But let me tell you, Danny boy, if you talk to the police or *anybody* about us, then I'll come back and cut your bloody balls off. Do you understand?' He turned to Spike. 'Got any tape handy?'

'Yeah.' Spike went into a pocket of his belt, and brought out a roll of thick tape.

'Right, tie up his wrists and ankles and his mouth too. We'll leave him in the boot of his car.' Titch looked around. 'Take the car around the back of these factories. This area will be deserted today, but they'll find him tomorrow, and we'll be gone by then.'

'Okay.' Strang pulled the young guy from the wall, and forced his hands behind his back. Spike taped him up, and Strang lifted him and crammed him into the boot of his car. Spike got in, and drove off.

Strang stood silently beside Titch until Spike joined them again. 'What now?' he asked.

Titch looked up at Strang and Spike. 'Bloody gossip column!' he snarled. 'Of course, Preston's the most eligible bloody bachelor in town. Everybody wants to know about his new girlfriend. Should have thought of that. Shit!' He turned to Spike. 'If her cover's blown, I think we've got to get her out of here.'

'Yeah, good idea.'

'But it seems it's just a nosy reporter trying to get a story, and using an amateur detective. And they don't know why we're here. They haven't talked to the police. I want to complete the job today, but Maggie won't be there to soften up Preston, and get him drunk as we planned. It might make it more difficult for you guys.'

Strang shrugged. 'Don't think it's a problem, given what we know.'

'With Maggie gone, will Preston still go out on his boat?' Spike asked.

Titch thought for a moment. 'Good question. But all the evidence says he's a creature of habit. He'll still go, even just to drown his sorrows.'

Strang laughed. 'Very punny.'

'But what if Preston doesn't appear as usual?'

Titch rubbed his chin. 'I think if he doesn't appear by, say quarter to three, you just abort the mission. Phone Uncle Albert and let him know. We can always come back next weekend if we have to. I don't need to leave Girvan till three, so I'll phone him before I go, and if he hasn't heard from you, I'll assume we're still on, and sail out to meet you. Okay?'

'Okay.'

'Right. Let's get you two on the boat before it gets light. What did you do with his car keys, Spike?'

'Just threw them over a wall.'

'Fine. Let's go.'

They piled into the car and headed for the harbour. Titch said, 'This car's probably marked too. I'll change it before I head to Girvan.'

Strang looked out at the dark town. He hoped they could complete the job today. He didn't want to come back next week.

As before, Strang and Spike crept down the walkway, and onto the *Lady E*. Spike locked the door behind him, and they made their way to the forward cabin. In the quietness, they heard Titch's car start up and head off. It was going to be a long wait.

***

Maggie woke just before seven, and stretched. It had been a good night last night. Better than she'd expected. Preston's pals were a cheerful group, and their wives seemed to accept her. One of the wives, Mandy, kept asking her about life in London, and in different circumstances, Maggie would have quite liked being part of that group. And she'd also got on well with Preston's mother on Friday night.

As she and Preston said good night in the hotel lobby last night, she thought he'd go further for the first time. But after a long hesitation, he just kissed her and left. That was okay. It suited her. But she'd hooked him, no question. She didn't have to lead him any further. And she'd tantalise him later with the silk nightdress. After all, she was good at that sort of thing. She wouldn't be surprised if he proposed to her. She'd need to think how to handle that.

It might be nice to just live a normal life for a change. At times like these, she had a pang of regret about her shadow life. But she'd always been a rebel, taking advantage, doing her own thing. And her brother, Alex, was the same.

She thought back to when she turned eighteen. She'd hated her life then. A dead-end job in a dead-end office, where the owner kept patting her bum as he passed. She hated where she lived. She hated her name. Apart from Alex, she hated her whole bloody family. The only things she liked were magazines about clothes and make-up and film stars. She quite liked her looks, and thought she could be as good a model as some of the girls in the magazines. And she loved Ginger Rogers. She'd go to any cinema where her films were playing, and soak up her beauty and talent.

Then she found out from a fan magazine that Ginger Rogers' real name was Kathy McMath, a name as bad as hers. So, she decided to change her name too.

Alex told her the easiest way was to just adopt the name, address and date of birth of someone else around the same age. He could get her IDs for any name she chose. And few people would ever question her. Most people accepted others at face value, and just assumed they were honest. In any case, checking someone's ID was a complicated process that most people just wouldn't do.

So she got the details of three other girls, Margaret Ralston, Jean Mathieson and Greta Reid, whose names she liked, buggered off to London, and left her old name – Cathie McCabe – far behind in Glasgow.

Life in London was tough, though. She tried every agency she could find, but there were hundreds of other aspiring young models and actresses, and she picked up only occasional modelling, bit-part acting, product promotion or exhibition-hosting jobs. And in the latter she found the keys to her golden future. The two biggest weaknesses of men: their ego and their inherent stupidity in sexual matters.

She'd got a job as a hostess on a large stand at a construction equipment show at Earl's Court. She had to give out leaflets to passing delegates, entice them onto the stand, serve them free cigarettes and booze, and introduce them to one of the salesmen to do his spiel.

She was astonished to find, when she handed out leaflets, at least half the men would then say, 'You're so beautiful, darling. How about meeting after the show? I've got a big expense account. Take you wherever you want. And then I've got a nice hotel room where we can have some fun. How about it?'

She always replied with a smile that she already had a date, but thanks anyway. Then thought to herself, *how stupid could these guys be?* In the main they were overweight, with bad breath and rotten teeth, and just plain ugly. Yet they thought they were God's gift to women. It was as though they thought all single women were raving nymphomaniacs who only wanted to grab their crotch. Very strange. However, it meant a few words of flattery from her could get them to do whatever she wanted.

Three weeks later, she got another job as a hostess at a grand dinner for senior bankers in the City. There she met Armin, a very handsome man in his forties from Switzerland, and a very senior – and very wealthy – banker. This was more like it, and she agreed to join him later at his flat. She treated him well, and he then installed her in a flat in South Kensington, with an allowance, in return for which she provided him with 'special' services every Tuesday and Thursday evening. She also sometimes joined her brother in Scotland to entice a target he'd identified for very lucrative robberies. Life became very comfortable for her.

However, once the war started, her brother thought he'd made an error in his last robbery, and disappeared into the army using a false ID. She felt very much on her own for a while. She also felt guilty at not helping with the war effort, and answered an advert for a secretary at the War Office. She got the job, and became a valued member of Brigadier Paterson's team. It was therefore easy for her to talk about life in London.

A knock at the door jerked her from her thoughts. She got up and peeped out. It was one of the hotel staff. 'There's an urgent call for you at reception, Mrs Munro.'

'Oh, right. Give me a minute and I'll be right there.' She threw on a top and a skirt, and headed downstairs. The receptionist indicated a phone at the end of the desk. She picked it up. 'Hello?'

'Hi, it's me.' It was Titch. 'Are you on your own?' She glanced round. 'Yes.'

'Look, we think your cover's blown. A local newspaper's doing a story on you as Preston's new girlfriend, and thinks your Jean Munro ID is false. They've also linked you to us, because someone saw me deliver a package to your hotel last Wednesday.

'We think you should leave now, and get back to London. Just tell them your uncle has taken ill, and you've got to go this morning. Use the guy we lined up in the nursing home in Chelmsford last week.'

'Right, I'll do that. What about you?'

'Oh, we're fine. They don't know why we're here, so we'll still go ahead. See you in London tomorrow.'

'Okay, bye.' She hung up the phone, and stood for a moment with her back to the receptionist. She changed her expression, and tried to force tears into her eyes. She turned, and stared blankly at the girl.

The receptionist looked over at her. 'Are you okay, Mrs Munro?'

Maggie stood as though stunned. 'It's my uncle. They've rushed him to hospital. I need to get to him.'

'Oh, I'm sorry. Is there anything we can do?'

'When's the next train to Glasgow?'

The girl glanced at the clock. 'Oh, the next one will be eight fifteen now.'

'Okay. Could you get me a taxi for eight o'clock please? And make up my bill.'

'Yes, Mrs Munro.'

Maggie dashed upstairs, had a quick wash, dressed and packed. She came back downstairs just before eight, and saw the taxi at the door. She paid her bill. 'Could you do me a big favour, please?'

'Of course, Mrs Munro.'

'Would you get a message to Mr Preston? He'll be on the golf course now. Tell him they've rushed my uncle to hospital, and I've gone to be with him. And tell him I'll call him later today or tomorrow.'

The girl had taken a note. 'I'll make sure Mr Preston gets this.'

'Thank you so much.' She picked up her case, and went out to the taxi.

***

It was a fine, clear morning. Richard stood at the side of the golf course, making practice swings. Daniel and Johno strolled up. Daniel smiled. 'That was a real stunner you brought last night. She'll keep you busy.'

'You can say that again,' Johno added. 'She's a real honey. Mandy was *very* impressed. Says she'll need to buy a new hat soon.'

They all laughed. Matt Lawson joined them. 'Good morning. All set?'

Johno grinned. 'Yeah, we're just ribbing Richard about Jean. Where did you meet her?'

'She came into the shop on Monday, and we just clicked. It's been a magical week. We're going out on the boat this afternoon.'

Daniel snorted. 'That's a first. Must be serious.'

As they walked on to the third tee, a member of the ground staff came running up to Richard, and handed him a note.

He grimaced. 'Shit!'

The others stopped. 'What's wrong?' Matt asked.

'Jean's just had a message. She's had to go to her uncle in hospital. She'll call me tomorrow. Dammit!'

Matt patted his shoulder. 'Oh, too bad, mate.'

He now regretted last night even more. She'd clearly been ready to go further, and so had he. But he couldn't get the words out. He'd been so desperate to see her in that beautiful silk nightie, to hold her, caress her and to love her. But he'd flunked it, and the moment passed. *Shit!* And he'd planned to raise the subject of marriage on the boat today. *Dammit!* He could kick himself.

He sloped over to the tee. 'Oh, come on. Let's get on with it.'

***

Davie stumbled into the bathroom and splashed cold water on his face. He'd maybe had one too many at his wife's party last night. He staggered downstairs, and put the kettle on. He needed a cup of tea.

He sat back, closed his eyes, and savoured the hot drink. He glanced at the clock. Almost nine o'clock, and no word from either Danny or Fred, his nephews. Danny was tailing the unknown men in Bellevue Road, and Fred was tailing the woman, the false Mrs Munro. *Sunday morning. Everyone's slow to start.*

He let his brain grind into gear. *Didn't feel right, though.* If anything, Danny contacted him too often on a job. *Better go and see him.* He went upstairs, washed, shaved and dressed, and then his phone rang.

'Hi, Davie, it's me.' It was Fred.

'How's it going?'

'The lady's on the move, Davie. I'm in Glasgow now. She got a taxi from the hotel at eight, and got the eight fifteen train. I expected her to come out of St Enoch's and head up towards Buchanan Street Station if she was going to Perth. But she's now in Central Station. She bought a ticket, and the way she's hanging around Platform One, I think she's heading for London Euston. I can't follow her there, Davie. Don't have enough money, and I've got Jamie's do this afternoon.'

'Don't worry, Fred. Just check she gets on the London train, and then head back. Okay?'

'Okay, Davie. Oh, by the way, I think our Mrs Munro's also being tailed by the police.'

'What? You're joking.'

'I'm not, mate. You know that detective we worked with last year on the Donaldson case? Jackie Grant?'

'Yeah.'

'Him and a female cop are following Mrs Munro.'

'You sure?'

'Definitely. They've bought tickets too, and are stood watching her.'

'Well, just check they get on the London train, and let me know.'

'Okay, will do. Oh, that's them on the move now, Davie. They've announced the train, and they're all moving to Platform One. The cops are well behind her, but they're definitely on her tail.'

'Okay, that's great, Fred. Just get back here, and I'll see you later.'

He hung up. His brain struggled to work out what was happening. He picked up the phone, and asked for another number.

'Morning. Egerton Hotel. How can I help you?'

'Is that you, Ella?'

'Yes, who's this?'

'It's Davie Watson. Your favourite ex-cop. How are you this morning?'

'I'm fine. But that's not what you're on to ask me.'

'No, you're right. Remember we talked about Mrs Munro? Is she still with you?'

Ella's voice dropped to a whisper. 'No, she's gone. Got a phone call that her uncle was rushed to hospital. She had to get back to him.'

'Oh, right. Do you know who called?'

'I don't know. I assume it was a relative, '

Davie thought for a moment. *Nothing further here.* 'Okay, Ella. Thanks for that. I owe you one.'

'You mean another one.'

He laughed. 'Yeah, you're right. Another one.'

Well, well, well … An urgent phone call? Very suspicious. And why were the cops tailing the woman? This was getting messy. And he still hadn't heard from Danny. He picked up his car keys, left the house and headed for Bellevue Road.

The house looked very quiet. The men's car had gone, and there was no sign of Danny or his car. He walked over to the house and rang the bell. There was no answer. He banged on the door, and listened for any noise. He'd prepared an excuse if someone had come to the door. But there was no response.

The door of the adjacent house opened and an elderly man came out. 'They've gone, mate. Left early this morning, about six. I happened to be up for a pee at the time. Might be back later, of course.'

'Thanks. Appreciate that. I'll check back later.'

Davie walked back to his car. *What now?* The men were due to leave today anyway. It was the last day of their rental. So, had they gone home already? But they were from London, and Danny wouldn't tail them too far if they left town. Or had they gone to Girvan where they'd parked their motorboat? That was more likely. But why hadn't Danny phoned by now? It was only a forty minute run down there. And were the cops tailing the men too? He headed home.

His wife was in the kitchen. 'Oh, you're back.'

'Any phone calls.'

'No. It's all quiet.'

'Mmm.' He pursed his lips.

'Something wrong?'

'Don't know yet.' He went into the lounge and sat next to the phone. Sometimes there was a point in a case when he needed help. And he was now at that point. He checked the phone book, and got the number.

'Tom Hamilton.'

Davie took a big breath. 'Tom, it's Davie Watson here. Remember me?'

'Of course, Davie. What can I do for you?'

'I think one of my investigations is running across one of yours, and I'd like to talk it through with you. Maybe get your advice?'

There was silence for a minute. 'Okay. Do you want to come over here?'

'Yeah, thanks. See you in ten minutes.'

***

It was Tom's turn on call this weekend. Only once in every eight weeks, so it wasn't too bad. He called the office just before eight for the latest news. All quiet. Then his phone rang. It was Jackie.

'We're at Ayr station, sir. Looks like our Mrs Munro's heading for Glasgow. We'll follow her and call you from there.'

'Thanks, Jackie. Do we know why she's on the move? She was supposed to stay till tomorrow.'

'No idea, sir. A taxi appeared, and she got into it.'

'Okay. Call me from Glasgow.'

Wonder why she's on the move? He called his favourite manager at the Egerton. 'I hear Mrs Munro has checked out early. Any reason why?'

'Don't know, Tom. Ring you back in five minutes.'

Sure enough, she rang back within a few minutes. 'She got a phone call that her uncle had been rushed to hospital, and she had to go to him.'

'Oh, right. Do we know who called?'

'No, we don't.'

'Okay, thanks, Marjory. Appreciate it.'

He sat and thought. If Mrs Munro *was* Cathie McCabe, there wouldn't be a real uncle. It sounded as though someone had been spooked enough to call her, and get her out. But who and what could that be? His team on the job, Jackie and Anne, were experienced, and would stay well out of sight. It was unlikely to be them. Maybe the call was from Cathie's brother, Alex, whom Tom thought would be nearby, but hadn't surfaced yet. What would spook him at this time in the morning? He realised there must be something happening in parallel that he didn't know about. *Shit. That was bad news.*

Jackie rang from Glasgow Central. 'She's bought a first class ticket to London Euston, sir. Looks like she's catching the ten o'clock train. We'll carry on following her, if you're okay with that?'

'Yeah, that would be great, Jackie. I'll make sure you're well compensated.'

'Thanks, sir.'

'Does the train stop on the way to London?'

'Yeah, hang on. It stops at Preston and Crewe. Looks like a fast train.'

'Okay, I'll alert our SB guys at these stations just in case she gets off on the way. And I'll organise a couple of cars to meet you in London. I want to know where she goes and where she lives.'

'We'll do our best, sir.'

'How's she dressed?'

'Grey tailored suit with matching hat, coat, gloves and shoes, with a grey leather handbag and a grey leather suitcase. Pretty classy-looking.'

'Is she on her own? Have you seen any sign of a man with her?'

'We haven't, though we haven't looked especially.'

'Well, if she's who I think she is, her brother won't be far away.'

'Okay, we'll keep an eye out for him, sir. Need to go now. Talk to you later.'

Tom spent the next few minutes talking to the duty inspectors for the SB regions that covered Preston and Crewe. They each agreed to have a team meet the train, and follow the woman if she got off there. Technically, he was supposed to get approval for his team to go into another region on duty, but their previous SB commander had changed the culture, and they now operated more like a national team, and trusted each other. He wouldn't bother the boss with this so early on a Sunday. He'd just run with it.

He called his Met contacts in London, and organised a couple of cars to meet the train at Euston. One to follow the woman, and one to pick up Jackie and Anne.

He sat back and thought it through. He had taken all the action he could, but it still bothered him that he didn't know the full story.

His phone rang. It was Davie Watson, wanting to talk. *Was this the missing link?*

Davie had been a good cop, and since his retirement, seemed to have a successful business as a private detective with local newspapers. Tom had worked with him a couple of times, and found him straight and honest, which wasn't always the case with some of the other PDs in the area.

When he arrived, Tom showed Davie into the front room. Davie opened up immediately. 'I know how it works, Tom. You can't tell me too much, but I'd like to talk to you about a problem I've got that seems linked to a job you're doing. Is that okay?'

'Sure.' Tom waved. 'Carry on.'

'On Tuesday night, I was commissioned by the *Gazette* to find out more about a woman visiting the town and staying at the Egerton. She was Richard Preston's new girlfriend, and the reporter, Katy Young, who does a gossip column for the paper, wanted more details. The woman registered at the hotel as Mrs Jean Munro from Perth.'

Tom leaned forward. *Well, well. How about that?*

'Now, I'm part of a network of PDs around the country, and had a mate in Perth check her out. He found there *is* a woman of that name living at her address in Perth, but she's not the woman at the hotel. However, while I was at the hotel on Wednesday, talking to the receptionist, a man arrived and left a package for Mrs Munro. I followed him. He and two mates had rented a house in Bellevue Road for a week, ending today.'

Tom was *very* interested now. *Maybe this was the elusive brother.* His own tail on the woman hadn't started till Friday morning. 'Who's the letting agent?'

Davie checked his notes, and wrote out the agent's name and number. Then he went on. 'Now, other than that visit, there has been no physical contact between the woman and these men. But somehow, they're connected. I checked out the man's name and address. He's from London, and these are his details.' He passed them to Tom. 'And guess what? His name and address are also false. There *is* a William Garvie at that address, but he's a bus driver who was on duty this week. I've got pictures of them here. Garvie's the little guy.'

He passed over the pictures. Tom studied them. A little guy, a big bruiser of a guy, and a middle guy. All of them tough. 'Hang on a minute, Davie.' Tom pulled out the photo of the Glencairn cup-winning team from his briefcase. 'Do any of these three guys resemble anybody in that football photo?'

Davie examined the pictures. He used a magnifying glass to look more closely at the football team. 'I think the middle guy is maybe the same as this guy here in the football team.'

Tom took the photos and studied them again. 'I think you're right, Davie. And I'd call that a breakthrough.'

Davie raised his eyebrows. 'That's good. Pleased to hear it. Shall I go on?'

'Of course.'

'Now, while the woman has more or less just socialised with Preston and his pals over the last few days, the three guys rented a motorboat – the *Cassie* – in Troon on Thursday, and sailed it down to Girvan. On Friday, they went out in it. But it's still there today. Now, why do that if they're leaving today?'

'Good question.' *Christ, how have I missed this?*

Davie went on. 'And they don't do much either. They look tough, Tom, and the big guy walks like a cat. They've got to be ex-military. I watched them at Ayr harbour yesterday. They had a good look at Preston's motor yacht, the *Lady E*. Now, most people give it a good look – it's pretty spectacular – but this was more than casual.'

Tom tried to remember the yacht. 'What does it look like again?'

Davie hesitated a moment. 'Erm, forty feet long, painted white, with the wheelhouse and rear saloon in shiny brown wood.'

'Carry on.'

'This morning, I have two of my guys – well, my nephews – tailing these people. Fred followed the woman to Glasgow, and he told me your guys were on her tail too.'

'What? He saw our people that clearly?'

'Yeah, well, we worked with Jackie Grant on the Donaldson case last year, so we know him, and Fred also recognised the girl detective with him. So that's when I began to think this might be too big for me, and gave you a call.'

'Okay, I understand.'

'But the thing that really worries me, Tom, is my other nephew, Danny. He was tailing the men and he's just disappeared. I've found out the men left Bellevue Road around six this morning, but I don't know where they are. And Danny should have phoned in by now. I'm worried his disappearance might be linked to this woman taking off.'

Tom thought for a moment. 'Well, it could be, Davie.' *Damn right it was.*

'Shit! I warned him to stay well clear.' Davie punched his knee.

Tom knew now there *was* a link between the woman and these men, since they included her brother. This was what he'd been missing. But what were they up to? He knew that Cathie and Alex McCabe robbed rich men, and probably bumped them off if they had to. So Preston must be their latest target. But now Cathie and the men had gone. Did that mean the plot had blown, and the robbery was off? Or had it already happened?

He checked the phone book and made a call.

'Ayr Golf Club. Good morning.'

'This is Inspector Hamilton from the county police. Is Mr Preston on the golf course, this morning?'

'He is, sir. Teed off with his friends around eight o'clock. Can I give him a message?'

'No, thanks. I'll catch him later. Bye.'

So, Preston was still okay. Something else must have spooked the group. Maybe it had to do with the missing Danny. He had to take control if he was to catch this lot.

He turned to Davie. 'Okay, first let's see how we can help. Was Danny in a car, on a bike, or on foot?'

'He was in his car – a small Morris Ten.' He wrote on his pad and tore it off. 'This is his reg number.'

'And the men? Do you have their car details?'

Davie dug into his folder. 'Here they are. It's a large grey Austin.' He passed over the paper.

Tom picked up the phone, and got through to the duty sergeant at Ayr Police Station. 'Joe, it's Tom Hamilton here. Put out an alert on two cars and their occupants, please?' He gave the relevant details. 'Focus on Ayr and the surrounding area. There's a possibility they may be in Girvan, but I'll call them direct. Let me know if anyone finds anything.'

'Yes, sir.'

He gave the same message to Girvan Police Station, and asked them to check if the *Cassie* still moored in Girvan harbour.

'We just need to wait now, Davie.'

'Thanks, Tom. I appreciate it. Is there anything else you can tell me? I mean, why check on Preston?'

Tom hesitated. 'You know how it is. Davie. Let's just say some of these guys are persons of interest.'

Davie grimaced. 'That means you don't have enough to nail them, right?'

'Yeah. I suggest you go back home and try to relax.'

Davie scrawled his number, passed it over, then stood up. 'Thanks anyway, Tom.'

Tom showed him out, then came back and phoned the letting agent.

'You know the three guys that rented your house in Bellevue Road?'

'You mean Mr Garvie and his mates?'

'Yes. Are you likely to see them again later today?'

'Don't think so. They were due to leave no later than ten this morning, and just put the keys through the door. I haven't been round there, but I assume they've gone.'

'Right, make sure no one goes into that house, including yourself, until we have a look at it. We think these men might be involved in some sort of crime.'

'Is it serious?'

'Well, I can't say yet, but we want to check for prints and so on. Stay available and we'll call you later?'

'Yeah, sure. No problem.'

Tom rang off. He couldn't do much more here. Probably best to go down to the station, and be on hand if news came in on the cars.

The phone rang as he was ready to leave. The Girvan police sergeant confirmed the *Cassie* still at Girvan harbour. No one around. All quiet. No sign of the cars there either.

Where the hell were they, and what were they doing?

***

Strang glanced at his watch. Eleven o'clock. Still three hours to go before they expected Preston to arrive. He glanced over at Spike on the other bunk. He looked as though he was dozing, but Strang knew, from past experience, that he could spring into action in an instant if he had to. They'd trained for that.

He lay and listened to the sounds around him – the lapping of the water when a boat passed, the sound of an occasional car, people shouting on the other side of the harbour, the sounds of small aircraft passing overhead. He'd seen the sign for Prestwick Flying Club on the way down. Clearly, Sunday was their busy day.

It would be nice to fly. He'd seen films of it at the cinema. You got a great view of the countryside, but you couldn't see much detail from up there. But he'd still like to try it. Maybe next year.

***

Just after half past twelve, the duty sergeant, Joe, came into Tom's office. 'A patrol car has just found the grey Austin in a cul-de-sac off Woodfield Crescent, in the northern part of town, sir. I've got a car ready to take you there, and we've allocated DS Wendy Stirling to help you.'

Tom jumped up. 'That's great, Joe. Thanks.' He grabbed his briefcase, and dashed out. Joe was playing politics. This was him making sure one of his people was in on the case. Tom had met Wendy before, and she had a good reputation. She was already in the car.

'Hi, Wendy. Good to see you again.'

'And you, sir. What's the background?'

On the way, he told her the essential information. They arrived, and parked next to the patrol car.

'What have we got?' Tom asked the patrol man.

'Got the key here, sir. It was under the car. But we haven't opened it yet. Wanted to wait for you first.'

Tom pursed his lips. 'Okay, thanks.' He walked round the car. It all looked normal. 'Have you checked underneath? Just thinking about a booby trap.'

'We did, sir. Looks all clear to us.'

'Okay, give me the key, and stand back just in case.'

Tom put the key in the driver's lock, and turned it. The lock clicked open. He gingerly opened the driver's door. Nothing happened. He went to the back of the car, and opened the boot lid. 'Okay, I think we're all right. Let's have a good look at this.'

He searched the car. There was nothing suspicious. The glove box contained the car manual and papers from the rental company. The name on the rental agreement was William Garvie with the address Davie had given earlier. There was nothing under the seats, and the boot was clear. The car was clean – too clean. He turned to Wendy. 'Could you get the prints boys to check this car, please? I don't expect to find much, but let's just check anyway. Oh, and while you're at it, ask them to check out the house in Bellevue Road, please? Here's the letting agent's details. I'd like to be there when they go in, so find out when that would be.'

'Yes, sir. Will do.' She went back to their car.

Tom stood and thought. Why would Garvie leave the car here? It was a quiet spot near a play park. There would be no passing traffic, though, and Garvie could have banked on the Austin not being found quickly.

He turned to the patrol man. 'Have we checked with any of these householders whether they saw anything?'

'We did, sir, while we were waiting for you. The woman in that house there – a Mrs White – saw a man leave the car here about nine o'clock. He came back a while later in another car, and transferred bags over. He hasn't come back since.'

'Good. I'll have a word with her.'

Wendy came back. 'The prints boys will be here in half an hour, sir. And after they're finished here, they'll go on to Bellevue Road.'

'Right. Let's check Mrs White. She saw something.'

They walked over to the house, introduced themselves and showed their warrant cards. Mrs White, a heavy-built woman in her mid-fifties, bustled around getting them seats.

Tom pulled a photograph from his briefcase. 'We'd like you to check if the man you saw this morning with that car is one of the three men in this photo.'

She looked at the picture. 'Yes, this smaller man. It was definitely him.'

Tom took the photo back. 'Thanks very much, Mrs White, that's very helpful. Now, you told our patrol that the man came back with another car. How much later?'

She thought for a moment. 'I would say less than an hour – maybe forty-five minutes?'

'And did you see anyone else with him at all?'

'No. He was on his own the whole time.'

'Can you tell me anything about the second car? Did you see the registration number?'

She shook her head. 'I'm sorry. It was just a black car, and I didn't see the number.'

Tom sighed. That's as much as he was going to get here. He stood up. 'Thanks again, Mrs White. If there's anything else you remember, then please call me at any time.' He gave her a card.

They left the house and walked back to their car. Tom leaned against it, and pondered. 'So where would Garvie get another car from? Has to be over there.' He pointed to a compound, fenced off on the other side of Woodfield Crescent, with bunting and faded flags fluttering in the breeze. 'Let's go see what we can find.'

They drove back round to the main road and entered the car lot. The office block had a sign above it, 'Woodfield Motors'. Another sign on the office door, giving their business hours, stated 'Sunday – Closed'.

Wendy said, 'I suppose Garvie could have stolen the second car.'

'Yeah, it's possible. But the way the PD, Davie Watson, described them, they seemed to do a lot of planning. Stealing a car doesn't quite fit that.'

They heard hammering from a building behind the office block, and walked round the side. They went through a half-open wicker door, and entered a large workshop, with several cars in various states of repair. Tom shouted, 'Hello?'

A middle-aged man in faded blue overalls rose from the floor on the far side. He walked towards them, wiping his hands on a rag. 'Can I help you?'

Tom and Wendy introduced themselves, and showed their warrant cards. 'Are you the boss around here?'

'No. He's not here right now.'

'Do you know where he is?'

'Yeah, he's away getting his dinner.'

'Could you ask him to come back? We'd like to talk to him.'

'About what?'

'We'll talk to *him* about it.'

'Okay, this way.' He sauntered to a door in the far wall, and along a corridor into the office block. Tom and Wendy followed.

Tom asked the boss's name.

'It's Andy Crawford.'

The man picked up a phone, and asked for the number. 'Hi, boss. We've got the police here. Can you come back?'

He listened for a moment, then handed the phone to Tom. 'He wants to talk to you.'

Tom took the phone. 'Mr Crawford? Inspector Hamilton here. We'd like to talk to you about some enquiries we're making. Could you get back here, please, sir?'

'What's it about?'

'Let's talk face-to-face, sir.'

'Okay. I'll be about ten minutes.'

'Thank you, sir.' Tom replaced the receiver and turned to the man. 'He'll be here in ten minutes. Will we just wait here?'

The man shrugged. 'As good as anywhere. I'll leave you to it then.' He sauntered off back to the workshop.

Tom sat on a chair, and thought how he'd handle Crawford. He glanced over at Wendy, who was going from desk to desk examining papers. Neither spoke.

Within ten minutes a black Humber saloon drew up, and a man got out. He was dressed in a sports jacket and flannels, and an open-necked shirt, with the collar over the jacket. He seemed a pleasant enough chap.

Tom heard him unlocking the main office door, and stood up. The man came into the office with a half grin. 'Hi, I'm Andy Crawford. What can I do for you?'

Tom and Wendy introduced themselves. Tom said, 'We're investigating an incident, and wondered if you met this man this morning.' He pulled out the photo of the three men, and pointed to Garvie.

Crawford took the photo and stared at it. There was a long silence. Too long, thought Tom. Why was he taking so long to answer? *That was very suspicious.*

'Yes. I met him this morning.'

'And did he rent or buy a car from you?'

Again, there was a long silence. 'Yes. He bought an Austin Twelve.'

Wendy spoke from the other side of the office. 'Is this the Bill of Sale for it?'

He nodded.

'Why is it signed and dated with tomorrow's date?'

He grimaced. 'Well, we're not allowed to trade on a Sunday. We got into trouble with the council six months ago. But the guy was desperate. He had to get to Langholm this afternoon to seal a big deal, and his gearbox had failed. It was the only way he could get there on time. Please don't tell the council.'

Tom thought, Langholm? Where the hell was that again? Somewhere in the Borders? What the hell did Langholm have to do with all this? And who was he seeing there? 'Could I see the paperwork, please?'

Wendy passed it over. The buyer's name was Trevor Wickham, of 23 Bartholomew Road, London, NW1.

'Did he show you ID?' Tom asked.

'He did. He showed a driver's licence, ID card and passport. It all checked out. Is there something wrong?'

Tom leafed through the paperwork. The purchase price was ninety pounds. 'And how did he pay?'

'With cash.'

'Do you still have the cash here?'

'Yes. It's in our safe till tomorrow.'

Tom turned to Wendy. 'Ask the prints boys to check this cash, please.'

'Will do, sir.'

He turned back to Crawford. 'Make sure you keep that cash separate until our guys have checked it.'

'No problem.'

'Were these two other guys with Mr Wickham?'

'No. He was on his own.'

'Did you take him out to the car?'

'Yes, I did.'

'Did you see these guys hanging around outside?'

'I didn't. I think there were people standing at the bus stop. But I didn't pay much attention.'

'Okay, not to worry. You've been very helpful. I'm not concerned with any problems you may have with the council, but if Mr Wickham contacts you again, would you give us a call, please?' He handed over his card, and Wendy gave hers too.

Tom and Wendy left the office, and went back to their car. Tom radioed Joe back at the station. 'Joe, put out an alert on this car and its occupants, please.' He gave Joe the details. 'Cover the Ayr and Girvan areas, and pass the information to your opposite number at Langholm. It's in the Borders somewhere.'

He sat back and glanced at his watch. Nearly half past one. What the hell was going on with these guys? And was Langholm a serious lead, or just another fairy tale like the name and address? He was pretty sure if he checked, the ID for Mr Wickham would turn up false too. Yet the little guy carried full ID for the man, just as he had for William Garvie. So he was up to something. But what? *And where was Danny?*

***

Katy stood at the window, watching for Adam. As soon as he appeared, she dashed out and grabbed his arm. 'We need to go round to Archie's place. He wants to see us.'

'About what?'

'I don't know. But he said it's urgent. Maybe we have a story breaking at last.'

Archie showed them into his front room. 'I just wanted to let you know that I've had a very distraught Davie on the phone. His nephew Danny was following the three men, and he and the men have all disappeared. He's scared to hell that something serious has happened to Danny. He should have heard from him hours ago.' Katy's hand flew to her mouth in shock. 'And Mrs Munro has also scarpered. She's on her way to London as we speak, with the police on her tail.'

Katy whispered, 'Oh, my God. What's going on?' She thought Archie looked angry. *Was he blaming her?*

'I wish I knew. But your gossip column story's now looking a lot more serious.'

Well, that wasn't her fault. But it sounded like one big story. 'Well, you can't blame me for that, Archie.'

He glared at her, then took a deep breath. 'Oh, I'm not blaming you, Katy. But a young man might be in big trouble, and it's kind of our fault for starting it off. These guys are dangerous. Maybe Danny just got too close.'

Katy felt a knot in her stomach. Davie had asked if they wanted him to continue to follow the men, and they'd agreed. So it *was* her fault. 'So, how do we help find him?'

'Don't think there's much *we* can do. The police have an alert out for him.'

'What's that mean?' Adam asked.

Archie glanced over at him. 'It means they have every car and patrol in the area looking for him.'

Katy thought for a moment. 'Why are the police tailing Mrs Munro, Archie? They don't just tail people because they have a false ID, do they?'

'Well, probably not. They must have something else of interest on her to follow her to London.'

'Wow. There's got to be a story there, Archie!'

Archie snapped. 'Is that all you care about, Katy?'

She was startled. *It was her job, after all.* Maybe she'd better back off on the story angle. 'Sorry. I didn't mean to upset you. Let me ask again. How can we help?' She delved into her satchel. 'I've still got the photos here. The clue to what's happening must be in Girvan.'

Archie looked puzzled. 'How do you work that out?'

'Well, Davie told us Garvie had moved the motorboat to Girvan on Thursday, and his mates had driven the car down there. They must plan to use the

Chapter 12. Sunday Afternoon

Sandra Maxwell thrilled at the view of the estuary as the car breasted the hill south of Kilmarnock. She knew Tom Hamilton was on duty this weekend, and thought she'd better let him know she was now in his area. She patched through to him on the radio telephone. 'Hi, Tom. Just to let you know I'm now near Ayr. I'm seeing our informant at two. How are things with you?'

'Fine, ma'am. Well, maybe not so fine. Got a problem here, and I'm stuck with it. Would like to talk it through with you, if you have a minute. Where are you?'

'We're nearly at Prestwick Airport.'

'That's great. As you come through Prestwick into Ayr, there's a used car lot a few hundred yards on your right called Woodfield Motors. It's got loads of bunting and flags around it. We're right there.'

'Okay. Will do.' She gave her driver the directions. As they turned in, she saw Tom standing beside a police patrol car. She got out, and went over to him. 'What's the problem?'

Tom brought her up to speed on the events of the morning, and showed her the pictures of the three men. 'I think that guy there matches this guy here.' He pulled out the Glencairn football team photo. 'And *that* guy is Alex McCabe.'

Sandra examined the pictures. 'You might be right. So where are we now?'

'There are still too many unknowns, ma'am. We don't know why the woman scarpered, or where the men are. And Danny's disappearance sounds serious. Something's spooking this lot, and we don't know what it is yet. Preston's still okay so far, if he's the target. I think I have to stick with it until we find out what the hell's going on. Do you agree, ma'am?'

'Yeah, stay on it, Tom. If Garvie's changed his car, it means someone identified the old one. And that must be the missing Danny. I hope he's okay. He's probably the key to it all.'

Sandra turned as a young woman joined them. Tom said, 'Superintendent Maxwell, this is DS Stirling.'

They shook hands. 'Pleased to meet you, sergeant.'

'And you, ma'am. I'm sorry, may I interrupt?'

Sandra indicated for her to go on. 'The prints boys have checked the car, sir, and it's clean. They're now here to check the cash. It should take ten minutes or so. Then they'll go to Bellevue Road.'

'Thanks, Wendy. I'll be ready.'

Wendy excused herself, and walked back towards the office building. Sandra watched her go. 'I don't remember her. Is she one of ours?'

'No, ma'am. The duty officer at Ayr allocated her with the car. It's just them keeping an eye on us.'

'Oh, I thought we were past that.'

'Well, not down here, ma'am.'

'Okay, I'll leave that to you. Keep me informed, Tom. But remember, I'm flying on the new helicopter thing this afternoon from three o'clock. I don't know whether you'll be able to contact me, but here's Colonel Chuck Campbell's number. Try that if you have to.' She scribbled the info on a note.

'Fine, ma'am. Hope you enjoy your flight.'

'So do I. But I need to go now. Talk to you later.'

Sandra got back into her car. It looked like Tom's story on Thursday had been right. Good lad. But she had to leave that to him for the moment. She'd other things to worry about.

She arrived at Janet's flat, and looked around. 'Oh, Adam not here?'

'No. He got a call from his girlfriend just after lunch. I suppose she takes priority over us.'

Sandra laughed. 'Oh well. That's us put in our place. He's got a girlfriend already? Settled in well then?'

'Yeah, he's doing fine. He seems to enjoy life down here. He coaches a football team, has a girl, enjoys his job. Life's good for him now.'

'I'm pleased to hear it. But I wanted to get back to you over Adam's lip-reading of Mr Preston.'

'Oh, yes. Is it all resolved now?'

'Well, sort of. We've resolved the matter to our satisfaction.'

'Oh, right. Did you find out who the captain was?'

'We did, but I don't want to go into detail.'

'Oh, I see. And what about us? Adam and me?'

'You didn't come into it. We presented it as a comment by a waiter on the meeting in Manchester. After all, we have a duty to protect you.'

'Well, thanks for that. And, of course, as long as you're happy. That's the main thing.'

Sandra smiled. 'So, how are you and Mr Preston?'

'Oh, I'm doing fine. I now work with him full time. The job has more responsibility than I expected, but I enjoy being back in business again.'

'That's good.'

'And Mr Preston's also doing well. He's got himself a new girlfriend, and gone gaga over her. He's even taking her out on his boat this afternoon. That's a first.'

'Oh, really? In what way?'

'Well, Richard usually goes out on the boat himself on a Sunday afternoon. I think he sails down to Ailsa Craig and back. That's his "me" time. But now even that has changed.'

Sandra remembered Tom talking about Preston's routine on a Sunday. But she couldn't tell Janet that Preston's trip with his girlfriend wasn't going to happen today. That would set too many hares running. 'My goodness, it must be serious then.'

'Seems to be. Good luck to him. He deserves it.'

'Well, I'm glad your relationship with him is still okay.' She stood up. 'I'd better get going. I've another appointment. Give my best regards to Adam. Sorry I missed him.'

'Will do.' They shook hands, and Janet showed Sandra out.

***

Strang lay and listened to the padding footsteps above his head. He glanced over at Spike, lying wide awake, his eyes moving with the footsteps. Strang heard two men talking, one on board, the other on the harbour side. Then the sound of mooring ropes landing on the deck. A few moments later, the twin diesels sprang into life, and the boat moved away from the harbour.

Strang rose and went to the cabin door. It had two circular brass grills, which he'd set slightly open, and allowed him to peer through past the galley, and see the saloon. He imagined the man in the upper wheelhouse, steering the boat out into the estuary. He returned to his bunk, with a thumbs-up sign to Spike. At last it was nearly time for action. Another hour or so to go.

***

Tom asked the letting agent to open the door, and stepped inside. The keys were lying on the floor as expected. Wendy followed behind him. They went slowly from room to room. The place was clean and clear. There were no obvious signs anyone had stayed there. Tom realised he'd be lucky to get any usable info from the prints boys, but waved them inside anyway.

Then his driver came to the door. 'Call for you, sir.'

Tom went to the car, and picked up the phone. It was Joe from the police station. 'A patrol car crew has just found Danny Watson's car hidden behind a factory in the Heathfield Industrial Area, sir. They also found the key on some waste ground. Danny was tied up in the boot, but seems to be okay at first sight.'

'Thank Christ for that. I'm on my way. Call his uncle, Davie Watson, at this number, and ask him to meet me there.' He gave Joe the number.

Tom and Wendy, together with one of the prints boys, headed off to the north end of town again.

They arrived just after the ambulance, and found Danny sitting at the open door of the patrol car. 'I'm Inspector Tom Hamilton. How're you doing?'

Danny glanced up then looked away. The ambulance men came over and began to examine him.

Tom left them to it, and went over to the patrol men. 'How was he?'

'He was tied with this tape, sir. Ankles and wrists. And gagged.' He held up pieces of tape. 'He's a bit traumatised, and won't talk. He says they'll kill him if he talks to the police.'

Tom looked back at the lad. *Poor bugger*. But he *had* to find out what Danny knew. It was urgent.

Just then, Davie and a woman arrived, and ran over to Danny. They hugged him, and then stood aside for the ambulance men to continue their checks.

Davie came over to Tom. He had tears in his eyes. 'Thanks, Tom. Really appreciate it.'

Tom put his arm around Davie's shoulders. 'I know you're emotional about getting him back, Davie, but I need you to do something for me right now.'

Davie looked up with alarm. 'What is it?'

'Danny won't talk to the police. He says they – whoever *they* are – will kill him if he does. Now, I understand his fear, but I need to know what happened this morning. Can you find out, and let me know?'

Davie nodded. 'Sure.' He went back over to Danny.

Tom stood with Wendy and the patrol men, and tried to stay calm. He had to know what Danny told the men, and whether that triggered the woman heading for London. And he still didn't know where the men were. He glanced at his watch. Nearly half past two. *Come on, come on.* He willed Davie to get back to him.

Ten minutes later, Davie came over to Tom. The ambulance men had got Danny moving slowly, then loaded him and the woman into the ambulance, and headed off to the hospital.

'The lad's shit scared, Tom. He's shaking like a leaf. It's been a hell of an experience for him. But he's given me the gist of what happened.' Wendy pulled out a pad to take notes. 'He followed them from Bellevue Road this morning, around six o'clock. He thought they were heading for the harbour, but they went across the harbour bridge, and worked their way north, ending up here. He was well behind them all the way, and came to the conclusion they were going to break into one of these factory units.

'As he came round a corner, he saw their car up ahead and stopped. Then two guys jumped him, and dragged him out of the car. They held him up against a wall and punched him hard in the stomach, the bastards.

'They asked why he was following them. He said because they linked to Preston's new girlfriend by leaving a package at her hotel. She was the target of a gossip column article in the local paper, and carried a false ID.

'The little guy seemed to be the boss. He did all the talking, and said Danny had got it wrong. They didn't know anything about the woman. He wanted to know whether Danny or his mates had talked to the police, and Danny asked what the police had to do with it.

'Because of that, they said they'd let him live, but warned him not to talk to anyone. They taped him up, locked him in the boot and took off. He's been panicking ever since.'

'Tell him he's done well. We'll put a cop with him to protect him for a few days, but I'm going to need a statement from him.' He turned to Wendy. 'Will you organise that please, sergeant?'

Davie half-smiled. 'Thanks, Tom. Can I go now?'

'Yeah, of course. See you soon.' Tom turned to the patrol men. 'Thanks for your help. Could one of you drive Danny's car down to the station, please?'

Within a few moments, Tom stood with Wendy, leaning against their car. 'What do you make of that, then?' he mused. 'The men say they don't know the woman. Can that be true? Has Davie got this wrong? And anyway, what are *they* doing here? Danny says he thought they were heading for the harbour at one point. Why go to the harbour at that time?'

'Well, most people go to a harbour to catch a boat.'

'That's very clever, Wendy. We think Preston's the target, probably to rob him, and he's got his boat moored in the harbour.'

'So, maybe there's something valuable on board, and that's what they're after.'

Tom thumped the car. 'No, it's the bloody boat! They're out to steal Preston's yacht. It must be worth thousands. I'll bet you these guys are hijacking it. That's what they're doing, dammit. They probably went on board first thing this morning, and hid.'

'Well, Garvie didn't. He's bought another car, and got a motorboat at Girvan. Why do they need that?'

'Good question, Wendy.' He thought for a moment. 'Because they must still have lots of stuff with them that they couldn't hide on board. But two of the guys *could* hide on board, grab Preston, and hijack the boat. The little guy takes all their stuff out in the motorboat to meet them. That's it!'

'So, what about the motorboat?'

'They just abandon it. Someone will find it.'

'And what do they do with Preston?'

'Depends how ruthless they are. They either tie him up, take him with them, and abandon him somewhere, or they throw him over the side.'

'Is there a market for stolen boats, then?'

'There's a big market for stolen cars, Wendy, so I assume there must be one for stolen boats. They've probably got it sold already. Hijack it, and sail it to a little bay somewhere in Ireland. No one would know until Preston failed to return later tonight. And these guys would have gone by then. Very clever, huh?'

'So, what should we do?'

'I wonder if Preston has a radio phone on board. We could call him and warn him, if it's not too late.'

He leaned into the car, picked up the phone, and asked Joe to connect him with Mr Preston's home.

'Hello?'

'Hello. This is Inspector Hamilton from the police here. Who am I speaking to?'

'Ben here. No one else around, I'm afraid.'

'Do you know if Mr Preston's out on his boat today?

'He is, sir. Saw him off myself about an hour ago.'

'Does he have a radio telephone on board?'

'He does, sir. But he won't have it switched on.'

'Oh? Why's that?'

'He never wants interrupted when he's out on a Sunday, sir.'

'Can you check if it's switched on?'

'Well, I'll try, sir, once you ring off.'

'Okay. I'll ring you back in two minutes. What's your number?'

'One two three, sir.'

'Right, if you get through to him, will you tell him to return to Ayr harbour immediately? It's very urgent.'

'Will do, sir.'

Tom rang off, waited two minutes, and then rang the number again.

'It's Inspector Hamilton. Did you get Mr Preston?'

'No. As I said, sir, the phone's switched off.'

'Okay, thanks for checking, Ben.'

Tom hung up. *Dammit.*

'What now?' Wendy asked.

'Good question.' If they'd hijacked Preston's yacht, he couldn't do much about it now. He glanced at his watch. After three o'clock. But maybe he could stop the little guy Garvie. He picked up the phone, and asked Girvan police to check if the *Cassie* still lay in Girvan harbour. 'If it is, then stop anyone using it until I get there.' He turned to Wendy. 'Are we finished here?'

'Yes, I think we're clear, sir.'

'Right, let's get back to base.' The driver had just turned the corner when the phone rang.

'Patrol at the harbour says the *Cassie* left ten minutes ago, sir. I'm told there was one man on board, carrying one small bag.'

Shit! Missed him too.

Wendy said, 'If he's only got one bag, maybe he's coming back there. And he must have left a car there.'

'You're right. Let's get to Girvan.' Whatever was going to happen would happen at sea. And he couldn't do anything about that. Or could he?

He turned to Wendy and smiled. 'I think I know who could help us here.' He picked up the phone.

***

Sandra stood at the door with the sign 'USAAF United States Army Air Forces' and glanced at the helicopter thirty yards away. It wasn't very big.

Chuck Campbell emerged. 'Hey, Sandra. Great to see you. Looking forward to your flight?'

She smiled. More like a grimace. 'Well, a bit nervous, to be honest.'

He laughed. 'Ah, nothing to worry about. Come on, let's get you ready.'

He showed her into the building and through to a large room with benches and lockers round the walls. Items of uniform equipment hung from lockers. 'You've got to change into a flying suit. We've taken a guess at sizes, so let's check them out.' He walked over to a locker and lifted down a flying suit. 'Here, try this.'

She took the suit. It was a plush grey material with padding, and the USAAF insignia on the left of the chest. It also carried a label sewn on the right side that read 'MAXWELL'.

She laughed, and held it against her chest. 'Looks about right.'

'Good. Try these flying boots.' He passed them to her with thick socks.

She sat and tried them on. 'Yep, they feel fine.'

'Right, I'll leave you to it. Take off your outer clothes. The flying suit's warm. Leave your clothes in this locker, and take the key with you.' He left the room.

The suit felt strange to wear, but very comfortable. The boots were comfortable too. Chuck was standing waiting for her in the corridor, already changed into his flying gear.

'Hey, you now look the part. Well done. Now, let's get weighed, and register the flight. Here's your Mae West. You need to wear this in the aircraft when flying over water.' He gave her the life vest, and they walked into an adjacent office, where an officer weighed them, and completed the paperwork. Chuck signed it.

'Right, we're all set to go.' He gave her a grey solid flying helmet with visor and microphone, and led the way out to the helicopter. He walked all round it, looking at the machine, then helped her fasten the life vest. It was bulky, but light. She climbed onto the right hand seat, fascinated by all the controls.

Chuck got in the other side and settled himself in the seat. 'Okay, let's get these on.' He fitted the helmet over his head. She did the same. 'It's quite noisy when we're flying, so we communicate via the radio system. Let's plug you in here.' He leaned over, plugged the lead from her helmet into the control panel, and did the same with his. He turned the key. 'Can you hear me okay?'

She smiled. 'Yes, loud and clear.'

'Good. I'm going to just walk you through the controls so you know what's what. But first, from a safety point of view, just follow my instructions. We're in a protected cabin here, and this aircraft has utility floats that allow it to float on water. No need to panic.'

She took a deep breath.

He described the various controls and then said, 'We're now ready to go. You okay?'

She took another deep breath. 'Yes, I'm fine.'

'Okay.' He pressed a button, and the engine sprang into life. The rotor above her head began to turn. He turned to her and smiled. 'We're going on a mission.'

'To do what?'

'To take aerial photos of Culzean Castle and Turnberry to send framed copies over to the general. I think he'd like that, and it might help our case for investment.' He pointed down to the panel in front of her. 'We've got two cameras, one for stills, and one for movies. Once we're up, I'll switch them on, and show you how they work. You take the pictures.'

She laughed. 'Okay.'

'Right, I'm going to lift her twenty feet to make sure you're happy.' He pulled on the lever at his side. The engine got louder and they lifted into the air. He held the position for a minute or so. 'You okay?'

She nodded, and tried to steady her breath.

He glanced down at flight notes he'd attached to his thigh, asked the control tower for permission to take off, and gave directions and numbers. She heard the instruction come in. 'Clear for take-off, US five two.'

'Roger.' He lifted the lever, moved the joystick in front of him, and operated the foot pedals. The machine lifted slowly into the air and turned towards the south. Sandra thought flying looked complicated, having to operate levers, read dials, and talk to control. But to her surprise, she found it fun. She sat back to enjoy the flight, and watched Ayr pass below them, with all the tiny people enjoying the beach and the sunshine.

Within a few minutes, they were hovering over Culzean Castle. Chuck leaned over and switched on the cameras. The images from the cameras appeared on screens in the lower panel in front of her. 'The controls for the still camera are in this hand-controller on your left, and for the movie camera on your right. We'll take a couple of photos of the castle. Let's get into the right position to show the general's apartment.' He manoeuvred the helicopter. 'Right, zoom in and see if it's clearer.'

She pressed the 'zoom +' button and the image on the screen enlarged. It went too close in, so she pressed the focus control. She then clearly saw a man standing on a path. 'Wow, that's amazing!' She zoomed out until they got a good view of the castle apartment, and refocused. He nodded, and she clicked the button to take the picture. He moved the helicopter, and nodded again. She set the picture in the frame, and clicked.

'That's good. Let's do the same at Turnberry.'

They went through the same procedure, and got great photos of the hotel, with the golf course and the lighthouse. She was enjoying this.

Just then, the radio crackled. It was the USAAF controller. 'We have an urgent call for Superintendent Maxwell from an Inspector Hamilton. Can she take the call? Over.'

Chuck turned and mouthed, 'Okay?'

She nodded.

'Roger, control. Put it through. Over.'

Tom came on the line. 'Sorry to bother you, ma'am, but we've moved on a bit in the last hour. We found the young PD assistant. The three men beat him up, but he's okay. From what he said we think two of the three men boarded Preston's yacht, the *Lady E*, before it sailed. The other one's on a motorboat named *Cassie* moving out from Girvan. We think they're going to hijack Preston's yacht to sell it, and maybe dump Preston overboard. These guys – or at least one of them – has form for this sort of thing. It looks like whatever they're doing will happen at sea. I know you're flying over the estuary. Is there any way you can find Preston's boat, and see what's going on? Over.'

She turned to Chuck. He nodded. 'Yes, Tom. What does the boat look like? Over.'

'It's a motor yacht, around forty feet long, painted white, with the rear cabin and saloon in polished brown wood. He's probably heading for Ailsa Craig. Over.'

'Okay, Tom. We'll see what we can find. Over.'

Chuck talked to the control tower, swung round to the west, and headed towards Ailsa Craig.

***

Strang lay on the bunk. The engines had stopped for half an hour now. He glanced over at Spike on the other bunk, and smiled. They knew what Preston was doing, but they wouldn't interrupt him. They wanted him languid and relaxed for the next stage.

Then they heard him on deck as he stowed the sea anchor, and then the engines started up with a soft rumble. The engine note got louder, and the boat moved faster in the water.

Strang got up from the bunk, and stretched his aching limbs. He went into one of the pouches on his belt, and pulled out a handgun. Spike did the same. They moved out from the cabin, and tiptoed past the galley into the saloon. Strang peered up into the upper wheelhouse. Preston had his head back against the seat with his eyes closed. *Perfect*.

Strang crept up behind Preston, and put the gun to his head. 'Don't move, and don't say anything.'

Preston lifted his head, and looked round. 'What the . . .?' He saw the gun and stopped, fear in his eyes.

Strang glanced up. They were heading to the left of Ailsa Craig, still some distance away. 'Right, lock the steering, and very slowly move down to the saloon.' Strang knew he looked menacing, and added to it by putting on his most scary voice.

Preston put the lock bracket on the steering wheel, and rose from the chair. Strang stood back, and let Preston descend to the saloon. He paled when he saw Spike, holding his gun.

Spike smiled. 'Take a seat, and let's have a drink.'

Preston unlocked the drinks cabinet, pulled out a bottle of Black Label, and three glasses.

'No, no. Just one glass,' Spike said. 'We don't drink.' He gave a wide smile again. Strang thought

Spike was coming across as a likeable chap, trying to put Preston at ease.

Preston put two of the glasses back in the cupboard, and sat back, waiting. He looked at Strang and Spike in turn, and glanced at their guns. 'Can we talk about this?'

Spike shook his head. 'No. We don't talk either.'

'If it's money you want, just tell me. I'll make sure you get it.'

'No, we don't want your money. Fill the glass and drink it.' This time, Strang noted his smile was a bit more forced. Spike was getting impatient.

Preston swallowed the whisky. 'Well, if you don't want money, what *do* you want?'

'In good time. Fill the glass again, and drink it.'

Preston drank from the glass. 'Is this a hijack?'

'Yeah, something like that.'

The boat was heaving now as it got further out in the estuary. Strang sat on the same side of the saloon as Preston, and watched him become more and more sozzled. He and Spike wore thin rubber gloves, but from habit they avoided touching anything. Strang rested his elbow on the table in front of him.

Preston slurred, 'Not an easy boat to hide, this one. It's a one-off. Why don't you let me give you the money you'd get for it? I'll double it.'

'I've already told you we don't want your money. Now, if you had to go on deck in this weather, would you wear a safety harness?'

Preston's head lolled forward as he nodded. 'Yeah. And a life jacket.'

'Where are they?'

'In the locker to the left in the wheelhouse.' He was now well drunk.

Strang stood up, went to the locker, and pulled out a life jacket and the safety harness. He brought them back to Preston. 'Put them on.'

Preston struggled into the life jacket, then into the safety harness.

'Fill the glass, and drink it again,' Spike ordered.

Preston did so. Strang looked at the bottle of whisky. It had been almost full when they started. Now it was only a quarter full. That was a lot of whisky, and should do the trick. He signalled to Spike.

'We're going on deck now. Where would you attach the safety harness?'

Preston lifted his head, squinted at Spike, and then his head lolled back down again. 'To . . . to one of the stan . . . stan . . . stanchions.'

Spike stood up. 'Right, up you get.'

Preston tried to stand, but collapsed on the floor. Strang lifted him. 'Come on, pal. This way.' He guided him towards the side door to the deck. Preston tried to resist, but Strang had a strong grip on him.

Preston was now so drunk he could hardly stand. Strang manoeuvred him out onto the deck. Preston's feet were now sliding away from him, and Strang had difficulty holding him upright against the swaying and yawing of the boat.

Spike bent down, grabbed one of Preston's feet, and slid it hard against the deck, leaving a black scrape mark on the polished surface.

Strang then gripped Preston's body, and lined him up to smash his head against the rail stanchion where they had attached the safety harness. Spike grabbed Preston's legs, and Strang forced Preston over to test where his head would hit. He tried it again from a slightly different position. He only had one chance to get it right, and he wanted to make sure Preston's temple hit the stanchion hard. He also had to be upwind of Preston when he hit so he didn't get any blood spatter. He tested it again. Then Spike let go and moved upwind. Strang held Preston's limp body still, then smashed his head against the stanchion. There was a burst of blood from the side of the head, and Preston collapsed onto the deck.

Strang heard an engine roar above him and looked up. There was an aircraft flying hundreds of feet above them. But in that instant, the boat heaved in the heavy swell, and both Strang and Spike had to grab hold of a rail. Preston's body slid towards the stern. Neither Strang nor Spike could catch it, and the body slid into the water, and dragged behind the boat.

Strang shouted, 'Can we get him back on board?'

Spike shook his head. 'No, leave it. It's just part of the accident now.'

Strang hadn't checked whether Preston was dead because of the distraction, but with the body dragged along behind the boat, he realised Preston would never survive that pounding. Job done.

He looked around to see where they were. The mass of Ailsa Craig was coming up on the right, and he could see the outline of the lighthouse, which faced the mainland. There were a couple of sailing boats coming from the other side of the island, heading back up the estuary. He then saw Titch approaching in his motorboat from the left. Strang went into the wheelhouse, took the lock bracket off the steering wheel, and eased the engines back so that Titch could get alongside.

Titch threw a rope over the rail, and Spike tied it to a bollard. The two boats bumped together as they moved through the swell.

Strang continued to drive the boat south past the lighthouse, and then turned towards the island. The charts they'd checked earlier in the week showed a shingle beach just south of the lighthouse. He lined up the boat to the beach, and increased the engine speed.

Spike had already jumped over into the motorboat, so Strang put the lock bracket back on, took a last look to make sure they were heading in the right direction, and then untied the rope and jumped over to Titch's motorboat. He assumed that when the yacht hit land, the overload would cut off the engines.

The three of them patted each other's shoulders. Titch passed the bag with water and food in it, then headed back towards Girvan.

***

'Is that it over there?' Chuck asked, pointing to the right.

Sandra peered in that direction. *God, it was amazing how small these boats appeared from up here.* Then she saw the white motor yacht.

Chuck swung the helicopter round, and came up behind and to the side of the yacht. Sandra manoeuvred the cameras so they focused on the yacht, and zoomed in. 'Yes, that's it. The *Lady E*. But the wheelhouse looks empty. Why would that be?'

'Probably running on auto.'

Sandra checked where the yacht was heading – straight through the gap between Ailsa Craig and the mainland. She looked back at the cameras, and noticed movement in the wheelhouse. 'There's someone in the wheelhouse now.' She tried to focus the camera. 'No, he's disappeared again into the cabin.'

A few minutes later, she saw movement again. This time it was a heavy-built man, dressed in black, holding and dragging a man in sweater and slacks, who she identified as Mr Preston, onto the deck, followed by another man in black holding a gun. She clicked the still camera, and started the movie camera. She sat, fascinated, as the smaller man tried to place Preston's foot on the deck. Then the large man held Preston, and smashed his head into one of the rail stanchions. She winced as she clicked the still camera again.

Just then, Chuck seemed to lose height slightly and adjusted the flying position to bring it back into line with where they'd been. 'Oops, just an air pocket.'

The two men in black looked up at the helicopter, and Sandra clicked again. She was sure these were two of the men in the photo Tom showed her earlier. What the hell were they doing? They seemed to have killed Preston, and his body had slid along the deck, and fallen into the water. The two men then looked over towards the mainland. 'What are they doing now?'

Chuck pointed. 'It's a small motorboat, coming alongside. Can you see what it's called?'

Sandra studied the view from the still camera. 'It looks like *Cassie*. That's the boat these three guys hired in Troon, and that little guy steering it is the third member of the gang.' She clicked the still camera.

One of the men jumped onto the motorboat, while the other bigger man turned the motor yacht towards Ailsa Craig. Sandra snorted. 'What are they doing?'

'I think they're beaching the motor yacht on Ailsa Craig. Why would they do that? And with the guy's body dragging along behind?'

Sandra continued to operate the still camera and caught the third man jumping off the motor yacht, and embracing the two others in the motorboat. The smaller boat pulled away, and turned towards the mainland. 'Where are they heading?'

Chuck checked the charts. 'I reckon they're heading towards Girvan.'

Sandra watched as the boats separated, with the motor yacht now heading straight for Ailsa Craig. 'I need to talk to Tom. Can we call him?'

'Yeah, no problem,' Chuck said, and started calling his control tower. In a few moments, the duty officer at the station came on the line. *The wonders of modern communications,* thought Sandra.

'This is Superintendent Maxwell here. Can you patch me through to Inspector Tom Hamilton, please? It's very urgent. Over.' The motor yacht continued on its steady progress towards Ailsa Craig.

'Ma'am, Tom Hamilton here. Over.'

'Tom, it looks like the three guys in the photo you showed me have just murdered Mr Preston on his yacht, and it's now headed for Ailsa Craig. They're heading back to Girvan in a small motorboat. Arrest them. They'll get there in half an hour or so. Over.'

'Right, ma'am. I'm almost in Girvan now, so I'll organise that. Over.'

'Thanks. Oh, and at least one of the men is armed, so have armed officers available. Over.'

'Will do, ma'am. Over.'

Chuck guided the helicopter behind the motor yacht as it drove onto the shingle beach. The body of Preston floated in the sea behind the boat. Chuck flew towards a flat area just south of the boat, and landed. They took off their helmets, and ran across the shingle towards the motor yacht. Two men ran from the lighthouse.

They all arrived at the boat at the same instant. The helicopter engine had wound down, and all was quiet. Chuck shouted, 'There's a man's body in the water behind the boat. Can you help me?'

Sandra watched as the three men pulled on the safety harness wire, and dragged the body into shallow water. The lighthouse men lifted the body onto the beach. Chuck kneeled down and pressed his fingers to Preston's neck. He looked up at Sandra. 'He's still alive. Where's the nearest hospital?'

One man said, 'Best one's Ayr County Hospital.'

'Right, I'll take him there. Do you have a stretcher?'

'Yeah, I'll get it,' said the other man, and dashed off.

Sandra examined Preston as they released the safety harness and life jacket. He had severe bruising at the temple, and blood still oozed from the wound. It looked very serious. The man arrived with the stretcher, and they gently lifted Preston onto it, and tied the retaining straps. The two men carried the stretcher to the aircraft.

Chuck opened the door, and folded the passenger seat forward to give extra space. 'Let's get him in here.' The men slid the stretcher into the cabin. Chuck jumped in from the other side, strapped the stretcher down onto the floor with mesh panels, and tightened them to make it secure.

He turned to Sandra. 'Okay, we're ready. But I've a weight limit, so I need to leave you here.' He turned to the men. 'Thanks a lot, guys, for your help. Can you call ahead and ask the hospital to get ready for him? How far is it, anyway?'

'About twenty miles or so.'

He turned to Sandra again. 'With a bit of luck I'll be back for you in about forty-five minutes. Okay?'

She nodded. 'Get going.'

He jumped into the pilot's seat. Within a few seconds, the rotor blade turned, the helicopter lifted off from the beach, and headed towards Ayr. A minute later, it was just a distant speck in the sky.

Sandra watched it disappear. 'I'm Superintendent Maxwell of Glasgow Police, by the way.'

'I'm Fraser.'

'I'm Will. What's going on?'

Sandra hesitated. 'I'm not too sure myself right now. It's a long and very complicated story that I don't want to go into, if you don't mind.'

'No, no. That's okay.'

'Do you have a ladder I can use to climb onto the boat? I'd like to have a quick look around. Make sure there's no one else there. And do you have a pair of rubber gloves?'

Fraser nodded. 'Yeah, sure, and I'll call the hospital as well.' He ran off towards the lighthouse.

'I'd like to use the telephone myself.'

'Sure. No problem.'

Fraser came running up with a small wooden ladder, and gave Sandra a pair of rubber gloves. As they walked over to the boat, she asked, 'Do you think it's stable sitting there?'

'Yeah, I think so.' He gave it a thump on the side.

Sandra climbed the ladder onto the starboard side deck. She wanted to stay well away from the port side deck, where all the action had taken place. She sat down on the cabin roof and took off her flying boots, then explored the boat in her thick socks.

She noticed the ignition keys still in the dashboard, and removed them. The main cabin was luxurious, with plush sofas and shiny wooden fittings. A bottle of Black Label lay on its side on the table in a pool of liquid held by the raised edge. She bent down and smelled the liquid. Whisky. A glass stood on the table against the raised edge. That would be useful for fingerprints.

She had a quick look round the rest of the boat, and satisfied herself that, at least in the main public areas, there was no one else remaining. She came back on deck, put on her flying boots, and climbed down from the boat.

Will and Fraser stood waiting for her. 'Are there just you two here on the island?'

Fraser nodded. 'At the moment. Our third member is on weekend leave. He'll be back tomorrow morning. And, of course, the quarry men will arrive tomorrow.'

'The quarry men?'

'Yeah, the guys that run the quarry. They're here Monday to Friday.'

'I need to make sure no one else goes near that boat until our forensics guys have checked it out. Can you do that for me?'

'Well, *we* won't go near it, but I can't answer for the quarry men. They'll probably want to climb all over it.'

'Well, in that case, I'll get a team over here tonight. Is there somewhere they can stay?'

'Yeah, there are a couple of visitor cottages at the quarry. They could stay there. It's pretty basic, but it should be okay for a night or two.'

'Right, thanks. Let's go and phone now.' She walked towards the lighthouse.

Fraser asked for Ayr Police and handed the phone to Sandra. She got patched through to Tom again.

'Tom, Preston's still alive, but only just. Let the family know he's had an accident on board his yacht, and has a head injury. He's been taken by helicopter to Ayr County Hospital. Don't go into details. I'll do that later. Also put a police guard on him 24/7, please. The yacht has crashed onto Ailsa Craig, and we'll get the coastguard to organise its recovery. But I need a forensics team over here on the island tonight to check the boat. And I need to talk to them before they start. Can you organise that for me? They can stay over here. Tell them to check with Fraser at the lighthouse.'

'Will do, ma'am.'

'How's it going in Girvan with the three men about to arrive?'

'I'm at Girvan harbour now, ma'am. We've assembled a total of eighteen officers, from both on-duty and off-duty personnel, all in plain clothes. And there are three of us armed. If your timing's right, they should arrive here within the next ten minutes or so. We've also found their car. DS Stirling's eagle eye found it parked in a side street just off the harbour. They had altered the reg plate with some clever painting from PBL318 to

RBU516. We're just organising a coal lorry to double park and block it in. We'll be very careful, ma'am, and keep members of the public well away. We'll make the harbour appear normal and surprise them, and then cuff them quickly.'

'Sounds good, Tom. But take care. These guys are very dangerous.'

'Yes, ma'am. What are we charging them with? Is it attempted murder?'

'That's right. We've got the whole thing on film from the helicopter.'

'Crikey. That's going to be a surprise for them, eh?'

'Hope so. Better let you get on. See you later.'

Sandra rang off. She felt frustrated at not being there with Tom and the team. She just had to be patient. Fraser made tea, and she sat looking out at the estuary. She glanced at her watch. Almost four o'clock. Maybe twenty minutes before Chuck got back, then ten minutes to Girvan. Tom was a good lad, but she thought of the complications in arresting armed men in public, and just hoped it went okay. *Fingers crossed.*

***

Katy sat on a bench at Girvan harbour. It was still bright, but now cool, and people were beginning to drift home. Adam seemed bored, and Archie looked . . . well, his usual mixture of passive tolerance and patience.

Just then, she heard someone with a loudspeaker shouting from behind her. She turned and saw four people come from the south-west corner of the harbour. 'This is the police. Please clear the harbour. This is the police. Please clear the harbour.'

Katy's heart leapt. They were not in uniform, but something was happening, and she was on the spot to get the story. *Brilliant!* The few people around began to move up the side streets away from the harbour. But she wanted to see what would happen.

She stood up. 'Come on. Let's go over here.' She walked towards the houses that bordered the harbour. She knocked on a door, and an elderly lady answered. She put on a big smile. 'Hi there, I'm Katy, from the *Ayr Gazette*.' She showed her press card. 'I'll give you five pounds if you let us come in and sit at your window.'

The woman looked at her in amazement. Katy put on an even bigger smile. 'And we'll put your photo in next week's paper. How about that?'

The woman seemed bewildered, but nodded. 'Okay, then. Come in.' She opened the door wide. The three of them entered the house, and went over to the window.

Katy had a panoramic view of the harbour, so pulled binoculars from her bag, and laid them on the table. Then got her notebook, and went to the woman. 'Could I have your name, please?'

'Mrs Thornton. Mrs Annie Thornton.'

'And may I ask how old you are, Mrs Thornton?'

'Seventy-two.'

'And what's your address here?'

'It's 17 Harbourside, Girvan.'

'That's great, Mrs Thornton. Archie here will organise the five pounds and the photo. Okay, Archie?'

Archie shrugged. 'Okay.'

They settled down at the table. Adam picked up the binoculars, and checked the harbour. Katy leaned over and looked out. There were just a few couples strolling around, and a few men standing over at the closed pub. They must all be cops, she thought. *Wow, this is big*. She placed her notebook and pencil on the table.

***

Strang sat back in the motorboat as it thumped its way through the waves towards Girvan. He'd had some water and sandwiches, and felt better, though it was bloody cold out here on the water. He took off his belt, put it in Titch's bag, and gave his belly a good scratch. That was the hard part done, but like all these jobs, he could never fully relax until he got back to his flat in London. And that was still a long way off.

It seemed slow progress towards Girvan, and Strang wondered whether the tide was against them. But soon they saw the harbour ahead, and Titch steered the boat towards the entrance. He followed the harbour wall on the right, and turned round the corner to the mooring position they had on Friday.

Strang climbed up the ladder on to the harbour, and tied the mooring rope. He turned and caught the bag Spike threw up to him. Then Spike and Titch joined him. Titch smiled at Strang, and patted his shoulder. 'There you go. Another one complete for Uncle Albert.'

Strang and Spike both laughed, and followed Titch across the harbour to the side street.

Spike said, 'I'm glad to be on dry land again. Don't make a great sailor.'

Strang chuckled, trying to visualise Spike in a sailor uniform. 'I think you'd suit bell bottoms.'

Spike smirked at the thought.

They entered the side street, and walked up to the car. Titch snorted. 'Shit. Bloody coal lorry's blocking us in. You two get into the car. I'll go find the driver.'

Strang threw the bag into the boot, and climbed into the back of the car. Spike got in the front. Strang looked round, but Titch had disappeared behind the lorry.

Strang eased back in the seat. 'I used to be a coal man myself. Years ago, when I was fifteen. Only lasted four days, and that was four days too long. What a bloody job. Lifting hundredweight bags of coal into people's houses, and dumping them in the bunker. The coal dust went everywhere. You finished the day like one of them . . . what do you call them . . . erm, minstrels. You know, where only your eyes are white. Everything else is black. Jesus, it was tough. There were no good bits. The boss knew all the prick-teasers on the route, and he took them for himself.'

Spike glanced back. 'Prick-teasers?'

'Yeah, you know. Women in flimsy blouses and no bra. Thank Christ I don't have to do that for a living.'

Spike chuckled. 'Prick-teasers! That's a good one.'

They sat for a few moments. Strang leaned back, closed his eyes and idly thought about these far-off days. Then Spike said, 'What the—'

He opened his eyes just as the car doors were yanked open, with shouts from a group of people outside the car. 'Armed police! Keep your hands in the air. Armed police!' Three men had guns pointed straight at them, one of them showing his warrant card. 'Keep your hands where we can see them!'

Strang sat upright and held his hands up. *Shit!* How did this happen so quickly? There had been no one within two miles of them out at sea. They'd even made sure they did everything on the port side, so no one on the lighthouse could see what was going on. Titch had always warned them to say nothing if they were ever arrested. Don't answer any questions. Let the buggers prove their case. He regretted putting the bag in the boot now. His gun was still in his belt there. *Dammit!*

The guy with the gun pointed at Spike said, 'Right, you in the front. Keep your hands where I can see them, and slowly – very slowly – get out of the car and lie on the ground. Keep your hands high!'

Strang watched Spike place his feet outside, and slide off the seat onto the pavement. They cuffed his wrists within seconds. The man with the gun knelt on

Spike's back and searched his pockets. Then said, 'You're under arrest for the attempted murder of Richard Preston. You have the right to remain silent, but anything you do say will be taken down and may be used in evidence. Do you understand?'

Spike murmured something.

'Do you understand?' the man shouted.

'Yes.'

Only attempted murder? thought Strang. They hadn't killed Preston then? It meant they'd have to come back up here again to complete the job. *Shit!* That's why he hated these 'unfortunate accident' scenarios. Other guys manoeuvred Titch from behind the lorry, with his hands cuffed behind him, and placed him on the pavement not far from Spike. *Shit, that was a blow.*

The man with the gun came to the rear door, and crouched down. 'Right, the same for you. Keep your hands where I can see them, and slowly come out of the car and lie on the ground. Now!'

Strang put one leg out, but couldn't turn his body and get his other leg on the ground without levering himself with his hands.

'Come on, move!' the man with the gun shouted.

Strang had got himself stuck in the position, and couldn't move as ordered.

'Come on, lean out the car, and get on the ground. Now!' the man shouted.

Strang attempted to lean out the car. The young guy holding the door open reached in and tried to pull him out. Strang hated people touching him, and reacted by grabbing the young guy in a choke-hold, twisting him round, then falling out on top of him. Then he felt his body crushed by half a dozen men, and his face hit the pavement. They cuffed his wrists behind his back. The men dragged him away from the car onto the pavement, and cuffed his ankles. He tasted blood on his lips.

'Get the ambulance round!' shouted the man with the gun, and one of the group ran off. Strang glanced round. The young guy struggled to his feet, looking pale and scared. Strang heard the man with the gun read him his rights, and shouted 'Yes' in reply. What the hell was going to happen now?

***

Katy, Adam and Archie watched the three men walk towards them from the harbour. Katy recognised them from Davie's picture, and wrote rapidly in shorthand. Adam observed them through the binoculars. The men patted each other's shoulders, and Adam got his own notebook out, and scrawled something.

Katy asked. 'What did you see?'

He continued to watch. 'I'll tell you later.'

The men walked up the side street beside the house, and out of sight. She rose, went outside, and peeped round the corner. Two of the men had got into a car a few yards up the street, and the other smaller man had gone round the side of a coal lorry. A group of men rushed into view, and quickly surrounded the car, some holding guns. *Wow. Guns in Girvan.* That sounded like the basis of a headline. There was lots of activity around the car, with one man cuffed on the ground. Then there was a huge scuffle to get the other man out the car. She began to form the story in her head. A man came up behind her, showed his police warrant card, and told her to move away. She went back into the house, and told Adam and Archie what had happened.

'This looks like serious stuff, Katy. Be careful what you write.'

'How do you mean?'

'Just make sure you run it past me and Kenny before you go too far.'

Katy pursed her lips. They were always telling her what she couldn't write. It was a great story. Armed police in Girvan? She *had* to write it.

Chapter 13. Sunday Evening

When the helicopter came back, Sandra gave the keys for Preston's yacht to Fraser, thanked both men for their help, and walked over to join Chuck in the aircraft.

'How did it go?'

'Okay. A doctor examined him before they lifted him out, and mentioned an induced coma. I guess they know what they're doing.'

'That's good. I hope he'll be okay.' She paused. 'You know, I've been thinking. It's very strange these guys just seemed to want to kill Preston. As far as we know, they didn't rob him – he still had his wallet on him – and they didn't hijack the boat. I had a look on board. There was a bottle of whisky that had been well drunk with only one glass there. I think Preston must have been blind drunk when they manoeuvred him out on deck. It smells to me like a contract killing, Chuck. Why would anyone want to kill Preston? Who has he upset to that extent, I wonder?'

Chuck glanced at her with a smile. 'Do you want me to answer that?'

'Any ideas would help right now.'

'He's a big businessman, right? Then he's upset an even bigger businessman, either by doing or not doing something. And that's what I've learned from lots of Hollywood movies.'

She laughed. 'Thanks for that.' But maybe there was a grain of truth in what he said. She made a mental note to check out that Triumph group again.

'You're welcome. Hey, could you call ahead, and get your people to clear a landing area for us? We'll be there in a few minutes. What's your man's name again?'

'Inspector Tom Hamilton.'

'Oh, yeah. That's it.' Chuck got on the radio, went through the various links, and a couple of minutes later Tom came on the line.

'How's it going? Over,' she asked.

'We've got the three men cuffed safely. One of them has minor injuries. We've got an ambulance man checking him right now. Other than that, we're fine. We've checked the car. These guys had two handguns. So you were right. Their other bags are here too. Looks like they were heading off from here. Over.'

'Well done, Tom. That's great. We'll be with you in just a few minutes. Can you clear a space for us to land at the harbour, please? Over.'

'No problem, ma'am. Will do. Over.'

She clicked off and watched the coastline coming closer. Within minutes, they hovered over Girvan harbour. To her surprise, there weren't many people around. The police had cleared an area just south of the harbour. Chuck lowered the helicopter onto the ground.

Chuck and Sandra disconnected their comms gear, climbed out, and took off their life vests. Tom came over towards them, and shook hands. 'Great to see you again, ma'am. Enjoy the flight?'

'Yes, fine. This is Colonel Chuck Campbell. Inspector Tom Hamilton.'

Chuck said, 'Right, I'll wait here for you, Sandra.' Now that the rotors had stopped turning, a small group had begun edging closer towards the aircraft. 'Any chance of a couple of your guys to help keep the crowd clear?' He touched the aircraft. 'She's still very precious, you know.'

'Yeah, no problem.' Tom gestured to a few of his people, who formed a cordon around the helicopter.

Sandra looked around, taking in the scene. 'Okay, lead the way, Tom.'

As they walked towards the side street off the harbour, Tom grinned and said, 'Is that you over your fear of flying now, ma'am?'

She stopped and turned to him. 'You know, Tom, until this moment, I hadn't even thought about that. Thank you so much!' She playfully hit his arm.

As they approached the tape stretched across the entrance to the narrow street, she heard someone from the crowd call, 'Sandra!'

She turned, saw Adam, and went over to him. 'Hello, Adam. What are you doing here?'

'I'm here with my friends, Katy and Archie, from the local newspaper. We've been tracking these three men you've just captured.'

Now that *was* news. Sandra shook hands with Katy and Archie. 'I'd like to talk to you in a few minutes. Could you remain here, please?'

They all nodded. Adam said, 'Oh, and when the three men came ashore, they patted each other's shoulders, and the little guy said this to the others.' He pulled out his notebook, tore the last page off, and gave it to Sandra.

She took the paper and read it. "There you go, another one complete for Uncle Albert". 'Thank you, Adam, that's very helpful. Don't talk about this to anyone, please. See you in a few minutes.' She stowed the note in her pocket.

A policeman raised the tape, and she and Tom walked up the street towards the three men, who now sat against a wall, five yards apart, hands cuffed behind their backs. It looked like a good operation by Tom and the team. The three men were the ones she'd seen earlier in Tom's photo – the little guy furthest up the street, the middle-sized guy in the middle, and the big guy with the bruised face nearest them.

'Okay, so who do we have here?'

Tom pulled out his notebook. 'The little guy's carrying two IDs – William Garvie and Trevor Wickham. The middle guy's carrying an ID for Andrew Barnes, and the big guy for Robert Francis. They're all from London, and you know what? I don't believe any of them.'

Sandra pursed her lips. 'So we don't know who they are. Well, don't let that stop us. Book them with whatever IDs they've got. Take photos and prints, and we'll talk to the Met in the morning. Where are you taking them?'

'To Ayr, ma'am. We've got the right cells there, and we can remand them in court in the morning. We're just waiting for the cars.'

'Fine. But I was thinking coming over here, Tom, that this has the smell of a contract killing. Maybe rather than set too many hares running tomorrow, we should just charge them with assault on the young investigator, with other charges pending? What do you think?'

Tom thought for a moment. 'Yeah, sounds like a plan. It would give us a chance to find out who they are, and what's happening with Preston. We could also have a look at the film from the helicopter, and make sure we've got them bang to rights.'

'Okay, let's go with that. Good job, Tom.'

Sandra looked at the three men, faces expressionless. They were tough nuts – clearly ex-military – but were they really just a bunch of contract killers with false IDs? *This was going to be a tough one to solve.*

***

Strang lay against the wall while the ambulance man worked on his face. The man cleaned the bruises, and then rubbed cream on them. His fingers were very soft for a man – he must have done this a lot. The man put a dressing on the side of his cheek, and began to pack his bag to leave. He stood and said to one of the cops, 'That's him okay now. Clear to move.'

Then there was an engine noise in the air. An aircraft hovered above the harbour beyond the end of the street. It slowly descended and touched down. He recognised it as the same aircraft that had been flying way above the boat. It had American insignia, the star and the letters USAAF. That was their equivalent of the RAF. *How the hell were the Americans involved in this?*

A few minutes later a tall, dark-haired woman came up the street talking to the cop who had held a gun at them. She was dressed in grey coveralls with flying boots, and her uniform carried the USAAF logo. She stood a few yards away, but he could see the name tag 'MAXWELL' on her chest. Preston must have been involved with American forces. Surely Maggie would have sussed that? *Bugger it!* He hadn't been happy with this job, but now with the Americans involved, it took the whole thing to a new level. *They'd bloody missed that. Say nothing.*

***

Katy watched the tall woman in the USAAF flying suit walk past the tape and up the side street, and turned to Adam. 'Who's she?'

Adam smiled at her in a way she'd come to recognise when he knew something she didn't. It infuriated her. 'She's Superintendent Maxwell of the Glasgow Police, the head of Special Branch for the West of Scotland.'

Katy scribbled in her notebook. 'Wow. And how do you know her?'

Adam hesitated. 'Well, she's a kind of distant relative, I suppose. Let me think ... She's the sister of my aunt's brother-in-law's wife. I think that's right.'

'And why's she wearing an American uniform, and flying in that amazing machine?'

'I've no idea. Why don't you ask her?'

'I will.' She continued scribbling. 'Are you going to tell me what the note said that you passed to her?'

'You heard her say not to tell anyone.'

'But you said you'd tell me later.'

'That was before she told me not to. I can't disobey a police order.'

Katy bit her lip. She got annoyed when he didn't share things like that. But now she realised that Adam had probably passed on a lip-reading note to the superintendent. There was a story in the middle of all this, and she only knew bits of it. She had to be careful not to probe too far, though, in case it blew back on her. And she didn't want that. She'd just wait and see what Superintendent Maxwell had to say.

Ten minutes later, the superintendent returned with a colleague in plain clothes. 'This is Inspector Tom Hamilton. Is there somewhere we can talk?'

Katy led the way over to Mrs Thornton's house, and rang the doorbell. She put on her welcoming smile to Mrs Thornton. 'Can we use your front room again for ten minutes, please, Mrs Thornton?'

The old lady stepped aside. 'Of course.'

The five of them went into the house and settled in chairs at the window. The superintendent said, 'Would you tell us why you were tracking these three men?'

Katy jumped at the chance to tell her story, and hoped she might get something back that she could use as an exclusive. She told about her gossip column, and her need for more information on Mr Preston's new girlfriend. She explained that the paper had hired a private detective – Davie Watson – to get that information, and he'd linked the woman to the three men. So they'd also tailed the men. She said that Davie had found out both the woman and the little guy had false IDs, and the whole thing had become one big intrigue. They'd also discovered the men had hired a motorboat and moved it to Girvan, and while they didn't know what the men were using the boat for, they'd come down to Girvan because they thought something would happen there.

'One man went out in the motorboat this afternoon and three came back. Do you know what happened out there?' she asked the superintendent.

Maxwell just looked at her with no expression. Katy didn't want to interrupt. She'd found the best way to get an answer was to wait for it. But then Maxwell turned to Hamilton. 'Do you know Davie Watson, Tom?'

'Yes, ma'am. I met him this morning. He's the PD I mentioned earlier.'

'Oh, right. The one with the missing nephew.'

'That's right, ma'am.'

Katy jumped in. 'What happened to Danny? Did you find him?'

Hamilton nodded. 'Yes, we found him. A bit shaken up, but safe and well.'

'Oh, that's good. What happened to him?'

'I can't say. It's part of an ongoing enquiry.'

Katy turned to Maxwell. 'And does that apply to whatever happened out on the water?'

'I'm afraid it does.'

'Is there any information you *can* release?'

Maxwell hesitated. 'We had a report this morning that a young man had disappeared.'

'This was Danny Watson?'

'That's correct. When our team found the young man, it emerged he'd been assaulted by three men. Our team very quickly established the three men involved, and we set out to find them, and question them about the matter. We now have them in custody, and we expect them to appear in court tomorrow morning.'

Katy scribbled in shorthand as Maxwell spoke.

'I'd like you to limit your reporting of these events to what I've just said. If you agree, then I'll give you an exclusive interview on further matters that might be uncovered later. Do you agree?'

Katy looked at Archie and smiled. He nodded back. She asked, 'Would this include what happened out at sea, and info on Mr Preston's new girlfriend?'

'It may do. We still have to complete our enquiries. So, what do you say?'

Katy felt there was respect on both sides. 'I agree.'

'Thank you. I appreciate that.'

'May I ask you something else?'

'Of course.'

'Why are you wearing a US Air Force uniform, and flying in a US aircraft?'

Maxwell laughed. 'Oh, that's pure coincidence. You understand that, as a country, we work in conjunction with the US military on a wide range of mutual interests. As part of that, I was invited to experience one of their new Sikorsky helicopters, to assess its suitability for police work.'

'And how was it?'

'Just amazing. And very impressive.'

'Thank you, Superintendent. I look forward to talking to you again.'

'Me too. Goodbye for now.' Maxwell rose, shook hands with everyone and left.

Katy watched Maxwell cross the harbour towards the helicopter. 'Wow, what a woman,' she murmured.

***

Maggie closed the door behind her, dropped her case and bag in the hall, and heaved a sigh of relief. She went through to the large lounge, with picture windows, and switched on the standard lamp. She glanced out the window. A tall man in a coat and hat talked to Ned, the maintenance man, whom she herself had spoken to on her way in.

She flopped down into an easy chair, and sank into its comfortable shape. It had been a long journey from Ayr, made even longer by having to wait an hour for a taxi at Euston. And she could still smell the tang of smoke on her clothes from the steam engine. She'd go and have a bath in a minute.

She'd also have liked a chat with Tamsin next door, who was always so cheerful. But Saturday and Sunday were her busiest days. She would see her tomorrow, though. They always got together on a Monday evening for drinks and nibbles, and a long chat. Maggie enjoyed hearing about the latest peculiarities of Tamsin's clients, and they always had a good laugh.

Armin owned their flats, and the girls paid only a peppercorn rent. Maggie entertained him every Tuesday and Thursday, and an occasional Sunday, for intense love-making. She assumed Tamsin provided services to his colleagues or clients. He always said he wasn't bothered about the rent because he made lots more money in a year on the capital appreciation. He was also a very considerate lover, and Maggie enjoyed being with him. It was an exceptional relationship, because they each did their utmost to satisfy the other. She looked forward to seeing him again on Tuesday.

The doorbell rang. She eased herself out of the chair. Maybe Tamsin, or more likely her maid, Betsy, had seen her arrive. She opened the door. Two men and a woman.

Cops without a doubt. The tall man nearest the door had talked to Ned a few minutes ago. 'Miss Greta Reid?'

She nodded. 'Yes?'

'I'm DS Jon Price from the Metropolitan Police, and this is DS Jackie Grant and DC Anne Dixon, from Ayrshire County Police.' They each held up their warrant cards. 'We're making enquiries about a recent incident in Ayr, Scotland. May we come in?'

She wanted to say, 'No, bugger off,' but realised that might not be sensible. She opened the door wider. 'Sure, come in.'

She showed them through to the lounge. They all sat down, and the three police pulled notebooks from their pockets. 'First of all, can I just check your full name is Greta Reid?' Price asked.

'That's correct.'

He turned to Grant, and he in turn asked, 'During your visit to Ayr this week, you were registered at the Egerton Hotel as Mrs Jean Munro. Why was that?'

'Well, that's my real name.'

The two men glanced at each other. 'Your real name?' Grant asked, 'Isn't Greta Reid your real name? That's on the board downstairs.'

'No. Greta Reid's my stage name.'

'What's a stage name?'

'Well, when I came to London many years ago, I did a variety of modelling work, stage work, and exhibition hosting. In common with most models and aspiring actresses, I used a stage name – Greta Reid. I made lots of friends, and we all just knew each other by our stage names. That's just the way it was. And one very special friend arranged the lease for this flat in my name, and used Greta Reid, not realising it was my stage name. I've just stuck with it ever since.' She shrugged. 'It doesn't make any difference to me.'

'And who's this very special friend?'

'That's a step too far. Check the property register.'

Grant looked miffed at her response, but asked, 'Do you have evidence your real name is Mrs Jean Munro?'

'Of course. I have my marriage lines and birth certificate somewhere.'

'Is it possible to see them?'

'They're probably in the bureau over there.' Maggie stood up.

DC Dixon jumped out of her seat. 'If you tell me where they are, I'll find them.'

'Why would you say that?' Maggie sneered at her. 'Are you scared I've got some ulterior motive in going to the bureau? Come with me if you like, but it'll be a lot quicker to let me look for them.'

The girl blushed, but accompanied Maggie over to the bureau. Maggie checked through several drawers and sections of the bureau, and found the papers. 'Here we are.' She handed the certificates to Grant. 'That's my birth certificate as Jean Mathieson, and that's when I became Mrs Jean Munro. Satisfied?'

Grant examined the documents, and handed them to Price. 'So, are you still married, divorced, or what?'

'I'm widowed. My husband went missing in the Cairngorms in '39 and was declared dead in '41. We assume he fell off a mountain somewhere, but his body was never found.'

'This certificate gives your address as 40 Atholl Gardens, Perth.'

'Well, that was my address then.'

'So, when did you come down here?'

'Oh, I first came here in '36. But about two years later I met James, and moved to Perth. When he went missing, I was devastated. I couldn't stay there and came back here just before the war started.'

'Why did you use the Perth address when you registered at the hotel in Ayr?'

'I didn't. I used "Care of Reid" at this address, as I always do.'

'You didn't. You used the Perth address.'

Maggie shook her head. 'I didn't.' She thought for a moment. 'No, I know what happened. The girl asked me for an ID card and I gave her it. She then registered me, copying my name and address from that.' She searched her handbag. 'This is my ID card, and it still carries my Atholl Gardens address. It's just an oversight. I haven't travelled from London since before the war, and just forgot about updating it. I'm sorry.'

'I see. Just an oversight, then.' Grant looked very disappointed.

The doorbell rang. 'I'll get it,' said Dixon, and jumped from her chair.

They heard the man at the door say, 'That's DI Hamilton returning DS Grant's call. I thought I better let him know.'

Grant stood up. 'I better take this.' He walked from the room.

Dixon came back and sat down.

Hospitality for the police was not Maggie's scene, but she said, 'Would you like a drink? Whisky, gin?'

They both shook their heads. *Well, bugger them.* 'Mind if I have one?'

'No, go ahead.'

Maggie got up, made herself a gin and tonic, and came back to her seat. *God, that tasted so good. Just what I needed.*

They sat in silence. Maggie noticed Dixon wore a small solitaire engagement ring. She'd seen that ring before. On the train from Glasgow. When she went to the toilet. That girl had been on the train. So the girl and Grant had tailed her from Ayr. Now why would they do that? How had she come under suspicion, and for what?

A few minutes later, Grant returned and called to Price, 'Can I have a word?'

Grant, Price and the girl, Dixon, all gathered in the hall, and whispered together for a few minutes. Maggie watched Grant tell the others something significant. They came back into the lounge and sat down.

Maggie felt a pit in her stomach. 'Everything okay?'

Grant looked over at her. 'I'm afraid not. Mrs Jean Munro, I'm arresting you on suspicion of being an accomplice in the attempted murder of Richard Preston this afternoon. You have the right to remain silent, but anything you do say will be taken down and may be used in evidence. Do you understand?'

Maggie sat staring at him. *Oh, shit*. She struggled to keep her face straight but concerned. Then she laughed. 'No, I *don't* understand. That's ridiculous! Richard Preston and I kind of . . . well . . . fell in love this week. There's no way I'd hurt him. That's just so stupid! How can you even think that?'

'That's as may be, Mrs Munro, but my instructions are to take you back to Ayr.'

She laughed again. 'It's nonsense. You know I can have you for wrongful arrest?'

'I'm aware of that, Mrs Munro. But I would ask you to get ready to go.'

'Well, I need to leave a note next door. That'll only take a minute.'

'Okay, as quick as you can please.'

She went to the bureau and wrote a note to Tamsin. 'Because of a misunderstanding in Scotland, I've been arrested in the name Mrs Jean Munro and taken back there tonight. Please contact AF soonest and ask him to organise a good lawyer for me.' She asked Grant the name of the main police contact, and location. Then continued the note. 'The police officer in charge is a DI Tom Hamilton at Ayr Police Station. Love G.'

She stood up. 'I'll leave this next door. Come with me if you like.'

Price stood up, and went with her across the hall. Betsy opened the door.

'Betsy, could you please make sure Tamsin gets this note as soon as possible?'

'Yes, ma'am.'

'Thanks. I'll be in touch.'

Maggie turned and walked back into her flat. She went into her bedroom to change, and emerged a few minutes later, ready to go. Within the hour, she was in a closed compartment on the way back to Ayr with two police officers.

She leaned back in the seat, and closed her eyes. How the hell had they worked out that she was an accomplice in an attempted murder? And their statement meant Richard Preston was still alive. So that hadn't gone to plan either.

They'd been so careful. There had been no physical contact with Titch and the lads after she met Preston. There had been a couple of phone calls, but they'd been from public phone boxes, so that wasn't it. So how had anyone made a link? Titch had said someone had seen him deliver a package to her hotel on the Wednesday. Some nosy bugger must have been at the hotel, and then followed him. And that's how they'd got a connection between them. *Shit!* And she hadn't needed the money in the end. That was a mistake.

But she'd had *another* package delivered on the Wednesday, and several on the Thursday after her wander round the shops. Maybe she could use *them* to introduce confusion into the picture?

She'd already covered the phone call to the hotel that morning by calling the young male nurse in Chelmsford from Euston Station. He'd taken such a shine to her when she visited her old 'uncle' two weeks ago, and he'd agreed to confirm to anyone who asked that he'd called Maggie that morning in a panic about her uncle. But he'd mistaken the old man's symptoms. He'd have done it for free, but adding a £20 reward, and a dinner date with her, had sealed the deal.

What she had to do now was to develop a scenario to convince the police the nosy observer had made a mistake. That someone else had delivered her package. That was her best chance of walking away from this. She worked out the gist of it as the train thundered north. That only left the knotty problem of her ID – Mrs Jean Munro – or Miss Jean Mathieson as was, which might be more difficult to resolve.

***

Sandra changed and returned to the flight operations room carrying her flying suit and boots. Chuck had already changed. 'That's the paperwork all complete. You're free to go. Enjoy the experience?'

She smiled. 'Thank you so much. It was fantastic. An amazing machine. And so versatile. We should use it for police work across the country.'

'Yeah, you're right. Glad you enjoyed it. And the rescue of Preston was a first for us.' He paused for a moment. 'Do you have time for dinner tonight, as we talked about?'

'I'm sorry, Chuck. Not tonight. I need to get to the hospital, and see Preston and his family. And follow up with Tom. Maybe another time, huh? You have a great phrase for it – take a . . . ?

He laughed. 'Rain check. Sure, I'll give you that. But first, we'll see you tomorrow.'

'Look forward to it.' They had agreed on the way up from Girvan it would be easier to see the film in the USAAF screening room, and Sandra could then decide which bits of it she wanted. Their tech boys would then produce it in the appropriate format.

Chuck showed her out to her car. She asked her driver to take her to Ayr County Hospital, picked up the phone and connected to Janet.

'Hello, Janet. Sandra Maxwell here. I don't know whether you've heard, but Richard Preston was injured on his yacht today, and is now in Ayr County Hospital.'

'Oh, my God! What happened?'

'There was an incident on board that I'll tell you about later. I'm on my way to the hospital now. Can you meet me there?'

'Yes, of course. Where?'

'Let's meet at the entrance for emergencies.'

'Okay, I'll be there as soon as I can.'

'Good. Oh, and please don't tell Adam or his girlfriend about this for the moment.'

Fifteen minutes later, Sandra arrived at the hospital, and asked for Richard Preston at the emergency arrivals desk. The woman went to check, and Janet rushed in. 'What happened?'

'We're just waiting to find out where he is. Some men attacked him. By chance, I was in a helicopter in the area, and we flew him here as soon as we could. But he has severe head injuries, and was unconscious.'

Janet's hand flew to her mouth. 'Oh, my God. Will he be all right?'

'I don't think anyone will know at this stage. But the family will need lots of support. That's why I asked you to come over.'

'Well, there's only really his mother.'

'She'll need your support over the next few months.'

'Months? Oh my God. Who'd do such a thing?'

'We have the people responsible. But I need you to keep the information about an attack and these people private for now. Can you do that?'

'Yes, but why would they attack Richard?'

'We don't know that yet.'

The receptionist returned with a young man. 'Mr Preston's now out of theatre, and in the Intensive Care Unit. The porter here will take you to it.'

'Thank you.' Sandra and Janet followed him as he led the way through the hospital.

Outside the ICU, Janet exclaimed, 'Oh, it's Mrs Preston and Ben.' She ran over to an older woman and a man sitting waiting.

Mrs Preston embraced Janet, and sobbed on her shoulder. 'Oh, Janet. It's terrible.'

Janet held Mrs Preston, and tears streamed down her cheeks too. Sandra stood a few feet away, and let them comfort each other. Ben also stood to the side.

After a few moments, the two women separated, and Mrs Preston wiped her eyes with a handkerchief. 'We're just waiting for the doctor.'

Janet held the older woman's arm. 'Is there anything we can do?'

'Just stay with me.'

'Of course I will.' Janet guided Mrs Preston back to her seat. She turned and waved Sandra over. 'Mrs Preston, this is Superintendent Sandra Maxwell of the Glasgow Police. She's leading the police investigation, and was in the helicopter that rescued Richard.'

Mrs Preston looked up. 'Thank you so much.'

'Oh, you're welcome, ma'am.'

Sandra went over and introduced herself to the policeman on duty outside the ICU. They chatted for a few minutes about his duties.

Ben came over to her. 'Excuse me, ma'am. May I ask about the boat?'

'Of course. It beached on Ailsa Craig. At the moment the boat is a crime scene, and we have to leave it like that until our forensic team have examined it. That may take a couple of days. After that, I guess the coastguard will organise a recovery.'

'If it's okay with you, ma'am, we'd like to organise our own recovery via our insurance company. We'll arrange for Denny's of Dumbarton to recover it. They did work on it last year, and they're very good.'

Sandra shrugged. 'As you wish. That's not a problem once we're finished.'

A few minutes later, a tall man, wearing a theatre gown and cap, emerged from the ICU, and came over to the group. 'I'm Doctor Johnston. I've been looking after Mr Preston, and would like a word with you. Please come in here.' He opened an office door.

'You're all Mr Preston's friends and relatives?'

Janet spoke up. 'Yes, this is Mr Preston's mother; we're close friends; and this is Superintendent Maxwell from Glasgow Police. She's in charge of the case, and was in the helicopter that rescued Mr Preston.'

'That rescue – getting Mr Preston here within half an hour of the incident – was the best thing that could have happened in the circumstances. It has given him the best chance of recovery.'

The group all turned round to look at Sandra, and Mrs Preston leaned over and touched her arm. 'Thank you,' she mouthed.

The doctor went on, 'Mr Preston has suffered what we call a traumatic brain injury from an impact to the left temple. We've treated the surface wound as best we can, and sedated him. We're helping his breathing with pure oxygen, and we'll keep him in that state at least overnight, and for most of tomorrow.

'Now, unfortunately, we can't see into his head to assess the internal damage, but I want to explain the possibilities for recovery, as we know them at this time. Is that okay?'

They all nodded.

'I have to tell you that such injuries can result in a wide range of outcomes, from full recovery to severe disablement or worse. And we won't know which for some time. However, there are hopeful signs. His pupils respond well to light, which is a good sign. But I think you should prepare for some level of ongoing problems. These could be physical, cognitive, emotional or behavioural, or a combination of them.

'I'm not an expert on this condition, so you may want to check with such an expert. We're quite happy for you to do so. Alternatively, I can act on your behalf, and contact Dr James Murray in Glasgow, who is, in my view, one of the best in the country. He's very experienced in these TBI cases, but he's expensive.'

Janet stepped in again, after glancing at Mrs Preston. 'I think we'd like you to do that, if you don't mind.'

'It's not a problem. I'll call him tomorrow. Now, once Mr Preston recovers consciousness, which may take a few days, you should prepare yourselves for an extended period of rehabilitation, depending on the damage done. I should also say that even in the best of cases, there are often long-term consequences on emotions and lifestyle, which may last for many months, or even years.

'We'll do our best while he's in our care, but Dr Murray might want to move Mr Preston to his specialist unit in Glasgow to help with rehabilitation, once he can be moved.'

Janet nodded. 'We agree with whatever you and Dr Murray think best, of course.'

The doctor looked round the group. 'Well, I'm sorry it's not better news. I don't think you need to stay here. If Mr Preston's condition changes, we'll call you. Please give me your contact details when we finish. Is there anything else you want to know?'

Everyone shook their heads. Sandra thought Mrs Preston looked much better than she had earlier. And Janet seemed to take the lead on behalf of the family.

'Right, one last thing, if I may.' The doctor looked at Sandra. 'You've placed a policeman on duty here, I assume for Mr Preston's protection. Now, that's not usual for us in this department, and I'd like to know why, so I can reassure our staff.'

'I understand your concerns, doctor, and those of your staff. Maybe we can talk about that later?'

The doctor pursed his lips. 'Okay.' He stood up, and everyone else gathered their things and prepared to leave. As they left the office, Sandra saw Tom Hamilton standing talking to the policeman on guard. She was glad he'd come along.

The doctor turned to Mrs Preston. 'We're limiting access to immediate family only. Would you like a quick look to see him for yourself?'

'Yes, thanks. I'd like that.'

The two of them disappeared into the ICU while the others waited outside. Sandra walked over to Tom. 'Hi, thanks for coming. Let's talk once the family has gone.'

'Yes, ma'am.'

'The doctor's nervous about the police guard. We need to work out how we minimise their inconvenience, but still protect Preston.'

They discussed the matter between themselves for a few minutes, and came up with what they thought was a workable solution – to apply ID checks on anyone entering the ICU, but use common sense.

Janet interrupted their discussion. 'Can I ask you something, Sandra?'

'Of course.'

'I need to tell the staff at the shop about this tomorrow morning. How much do you want me to say?'

Sandra thought for a moment. 'Limit it to Mr Preston being injured and in hospital. You could say the police are investigating, and you'll let them know more later. Okay?'

'Okay.'

A few minutes later, the doctor emerged with a tearful Mrs Preston and a senior nurse comforting her. The family slowly gathered their things and left.

Sandra and Tom discussed the police presence with the doctor and nurse. 'I'd ask you to keep this confidential. Mr Preston was the victim of what we believe was a targeted serious assault today. But we don't yet understand why. While we have three men in custody, we believe there's still a credible threat to Mr Preston, and that's why I want police protection in place here. I'm happy to discuss with you the best way to do this with minimum inconvenience to you and your staff. But I believe our presence is necessary to deter any further such approaches to Mr Preston. I hope you understand.' She went on to outline her and Tom's solution to their interference problem.

The doctor and nurse exchanged glances, and nodded agreement to Sandra's solution. After the discussion, they left to go back into the ICU.

Sandra pointed to the row of seats, and she and Tom sat down.

'I wanted a word, ma'am, and when I heard you were here, I thought I'd come over and catch you. I think I've made a mistake.'

Sandra raised her eyebrows. 'Oh? What makes you think that?'

'I spoke earlier to DS Grant, who trailed Mrs Munro to London.'

'Oh, right. I'd forgotten about her.'

'He told me her ID checked out. She was exactly who she said she was, and had the certificates to prove it. He asked what he should do, and I told him to arrest her on suspicion of being an accomplice in the attempted murder of Preston, and bring her back here.

'I've been thinking about it, and I might be wrong. Grant called me from Euston. The woman's saying it's all ridiculous, that she and Preston fell in love, and shouting wrongful arrest. Maybe I just took my hunch she's really Cathie McCabe too far.

'I did a test with the football team photo with a couple of my guys, and neither of them picked out Alex McCabe as one of the men. And when I thought it through, the assumption that Mrs Jean Munro was a false ID came from the DI in Perth, and the link between the woman and the three men came from Davie Watson, and maybe they got that wrong too. I could have relied on their reports too much because they confirmed my original suspicions. Sorry about that, ma'am.'

She took a deep breath. 'We all follow hunches, Tom. And sometimes we follow them a step too far. We've all done it. So don't beat yourself up. No one's gone to the gallows yet. Where's the woman now?'

He glanced at his watch. 'They're still on their way here. It'll be a couple of hours yet before they arrive. I've just had a meeting with the local prosecutors, and they're happy to go with the assault charge for the men in the morning. But they're questioning where the woman fits in. They don't want to take her to court yet. They want to see evidence that she lured Richard Preston into danger. And we don't have any. They just don't see a case against her. That set me thinking.'

Sandra needed him to calm down. 'Well, let's not do anything hasty. Just run with what we have, and see what happens tomorrow. We can hold her for a couple of days. If we've made a mistake, we admit it and correct it. Don't worry. Okay?'

He nodded. 'Okay, ma'am. Thanks.'

They stood up, gave the policemen a wave, and left the building.

'I've got the forensics team waiting to go out to Ailsa Craig tonight, ma'am. You said you wanted a word with them first.'

'Oh, right. Let's do that now.' She went into Tom's car, and spoke on the phone to the forensics team. She described what had happened on the yacht, and asked them to take as many detailed photographs as they could on the port deck. She also wanted them to check for fingerprints in the cabins. She recalled the single glass and the bottle on the table, and asked them to lift prints off them.

In the back of her car on her way home to Glasgow, she thought about what Tom had said. She was concerned a couple of his detectives had failed to connect the photographs. Maybe she should keep Tom away from the ID issues in the case. Sometimes it was like that. You followed a hunch you were certain was right, and it turned out to be wrong. You always felt bad when your instincts let you down. But they needed to keep their focus, and check out the woman in more depth to be sure. The important thing was to lock down the case against the three men, whoever they were. And she also had to check out the reference to Uncle Albert that Adam had lip-read. She was following a hunch herself that the attack on Preston was a contract killing, and she needed to be careful how far she took that.

By the time she got home, she'd worked out a rough plan on how to approach the case, and then relaxed with a glass of wine. It had been quite a day. She couldn't remember any instance where a senior police officer had actually witnessed a serious crime in action. They usually dealt with crimes after the event. She admitted to herself it was unsettling to see the casual, calm approach of the killers. But the helicopter flight had been amazing.

Her phone rang. It was Tom. 'Just to let you know, ma'am, all three men have clammed up. They're answering "no comment" to all questions. The woman's doing the same. Looks like we're going to have to work round them to build the case.'

'Thanks, Tom. Well, we've had to do that before. See you in the morning.'

She hung up and grimaced. He didn't have to call her about that. It was a sure sign he'd lost confidence in himself. That was a pity. He was one of her key people. She would also have to deal with *that* in the morning.

Chapter 14. Monday

Sandra Maxwell arrived in her office early to firm up her plans. Normally, she started with a victim, and worked through the three basic aspects of a crime – motive, means and opportunity – to identify the perpetrator. But, in this case, she had the means, opportunity and perps on film. Only the motive remained unclear.

In most violent crimes, the victim and perp knew each other. In this case, she had no obvious link between the three men and Richard Preston, except maybe the mysterious Mrs Munro. The three men had also planned the attack very carefully. They had staged an accident on board the yacht that, if she hadn't seen it herself, would have led any investigator to conclude that a drunken Mr Preston had slipped, banged his head, and drowned in a remote location. He'd only survived because Chuck had got him to hospital within a few minutes.

The men hadn't left anything to chance. They had worked together, and killed before. Maybe in the Army. They'd planned and executed a murder attempt, on behalf of 'Uncle Albert', if Adam had got that right.

Which led on to why, and who paid for it? Preston, part of the foiled plot to kill the PM, already swam in murky waters with some powerful and wealthy people.

She thought back to Chuck's half-flippant remark about an even bigger businessman. She had enough experience of such men to know self-interest had top priority with them. Their attitude in the main was 'bugger everybody else', wrapped in a cloak of respectability. And they could get very nasty with each other under the guise of 'No hard feelings, mate. It's not personal, it's just business'. She had to find a link between the paymasters and the three men, and it wouldn't be easy. They'd use shady lawyers as middle men and pay in cash. But she'd still try.

She decided to have three teams on the case. The first – the main team – would focus on the three men. Who were they and what was their motive? That team, led by Bill Jamieson, would have to liaise with the Met in London.

The second team, led by Sam Turnbull, would focus on the woman. Who was she, and did she have any link to the three men? Was she involved in the case at all?

The third team, a senior team led by her, would look at any link with paymasters. She'd use Tom as her assistant back at base to coordinate the teams, and liaise with the Preston family in Ayr as necessary. This would help him rebuild his confidence.

With such a heavy input from London, she needed the boss to agree, and arranged a call with him for nine o'clock. She would then meet with her three inspectors at ten to plan their actions. Bill and Sam could then get started while she and Tom went to Prestwick to see the film. She'd also take Jim Hannah, a senior procurator fiscal with the Crown Office, who often guided her on how to present cases in court. The film would form the core of this case.

Just before nine o'clock, her phone rang. 'Your call to Commander Burnett, ma'am.'

He came on the line with his cheerful Yorkshire accent. 'Hello, Sandra. A call from you first thing on a Monday means something important has happened up there. Tell me about it.'

She had already prepared her notes. Burnett liked to see the whole picture within the first couple of minutes, then the relevant details. She took him through the various strands of the story in a very concise way.

'Blimey. Quite a story, Sandra. Not often we see murder in action, huh?'

'That's true, sir. My first question is whether I can still lead this case, since I'll need to be a key witness? I mean, the senior police officer is usually a witness anyway to cover police strategy and procedures, but in this case, I actually watched the incident happen. Will that give me a conflict?'

Burnett was silent for a moment. 'I don't think so. The evidence will come from an objective source, the film. Any evidence you give will relate to how you filmed it from the helicopter. I don't see a conflict, but you should check with one of your friendly prosecutors. You have different rules on corroboration in Scotland.'

'Okay, sir. I'll do that. I also wanted to check whether we could still lead the case from SB. I think this incident might link back in some way to when the Triumph group targeted the PM. Can we still keep responsibility for *this* incident on that basis?'

'Yes, I think so, Sandra. We need to deal with the USAAF involvement anyway. But we should keep our chief constables in the loop as usual. We may need resources from them anyway. On that issue, I think you should include Brian Walker from London in your meeting this morning. He knows better than most what it takes to find out things down here, and it'll speed up the process for you. I'll make sure he's available for you.'

'That would be good, sir. Lastly, I believe this was an attempted contract killing. I say that because the men didn't try to rob Preston or steal his boat. Their sole purpose was to kill him. But, I don't think we should go public with that at this stage. It would raise too many questions about why they targeted the victim that we can't answer.

'Now, I have no sympathy for Preston. He only has himself to blame for getting into this mess in the first place. But in this instance, he was probably the innocent party, and we should try to keep it that way until we gather more evidence on the paymasters. I think we should charge the men with attempted murder during a failed robbery – the theft of Preston's boat. I realise it will all come out soon and trash his reputation, but I just feel there are too many unknowns right now. What do you think, sir?'

There was a long pause. 'Yeah, that might work well for us if it gives the paymasters a false sense of security. Okay, but check it out with the prosecutors first.'

'Right, sir. Talking about paymasters, what about Sir Anthony? He's got to be involved in this somewhere. Should we haul him in again for questioning?'

'Oh, he's a slippery bugger that one, Sandra. His hands will be well clean. He'd just contact one of his dodgy lawyers, and let them handle it. If it *is* a contract, he may have paid for it, but he won't know any details. But I'm up for doing the same as we did before. Haul him in and give him a fright.'

'Okay, sir. Once we know where we stand, we can talk about it again.'

'Looks like you've got it all well under control as usual, Sandra. Keep me in the picture. Give me a call at five o'clock each day for the next few days, and let me know if you need any lubrication from this end.'

He rang off. She relished Burnett's positive approach. Then her phone rang again.

'Inspector Hamilton for you, ma'am.'

Tom came on the line. 'Just to let you know, ma'am, a bunch of lawyers has just shown up asking for me at Ayr Police Station. They represent their client, Mrs Jean Munro, and demand time with her. And, get this. They're led by Mr Vince Pastrano, KC.'

Sandra's jaw dropped. 'What? Pastrano himself? You're kidding! What the hell's going on?' Pastrano was the best and most expensive criminal defence lawyer in Scotland, famous for representing local crime lords – and getting them off the hook.

'Good question, ma'am. Pastrano also made the point that any aspects of Mrs Munro's defence that concern activities in London were to be directed to her representative there, a Mr Josh Calman, KC.'

'Jesus!' Calman was probably the most expensive defence lawyer in the UK. 'Are we missing something here, Tom? Is this woman some sort of master criminal? Who the hell's paying for these top guys?'

'Another very good question, ma'am, '

'What's Pastrano doing now?'

'I couldn't get you because you were on the phone, but he had all the right paperwork, so I had to let him meet with her. As far as I know, they're still there.'

'And do they represent the three men too?'

'No, ma'am. No mention of them. Only the woman.'

'Bloody hell, Tom. We *must* be missing something. That woman must be hell of important to someone big. Let me know once Pastrano leaves. I've met him a few times, so I'll contact him, and see what it's all about.'

She hung up the phone. Vince Pastrano she knew at first hand – a very clever and *very* smart lawyer. Josh Calman she knew by reputation – even more so. This woman had suddenly become a lot more significant.

***

Katy went out early to buy a *Daily Record*. She'd hardly slept after she and Archie had talked to Kenny, and he agreed she could write a piece for the paper. Archie had fixed it for her. She found it on page three.

'Guns in Girvan
by Katy Young, Ayrshire Reporter

Armed police detained three men at Girvan harbour yesterday after an assault on a 20-year-old man earlier in the day. Inquiries continue.'

Dammit! She'd written two paragraphs, but Archie had warned her the sub-editors might compress it. Every word was precious in a daily paper.

Still, she had a by-line in a national daily. She called Adam to tell him the good news. 'Hey, well done.'

She skipped back to her house, and flopped down on the sofa to savour the moment.

***

Janet called a full staff meeting on the ground floor at nine o'clock.

'I have some bad news for you all this morning. Yesterday, Mr Preston had an accident on his yacht, and suffered a severe head injury. We don't know all the details yet, but the yacht crashed onto the shingle beach on Ailsa Craig.

'He's now in Ayr County Hospital under sedation, and may be there for some time. I'm sure all our thoughts and best wishes go to him for a fast recovery.

'Meanwhile, we should all carry on as normal. I'll give you updates on his condition as I receive them. We'll split his duties among the other members of the board for the moment. Thank you for your time.'

The staff muttered as they went off to their departments. Janet thought it wouldn't take long for the rumour mill to start, so she would stay close to them for the rest of the day. She then went off to the *Gazette* office and the Egerton Hotel to give the same message.

***

Maggie sat on the bunk in her cell. She hadn't slept well. They'd served breakfast that tasted better than it looked. Now she wondered what would happen.

She'd thought through where she might be vulnerable, and blessed Alex's advice – always make sure your tracks are covered. This was when that advice really mattered. She hoped Tamsin had contacted Armin.

The door unlocked, and the policeman said, 'Right, out you come. Your lawyer's here, and wants to talk to you. So, whenever you're ready.'

She stood up. 'Give me a minute. Must look my best.' She brushed her hair, applied her make-up, then put on her suit jacket. 'Right, let's go.'

There were two men and a woman in the meeting room. One man rose and came over to her as the door closed behind her. He shook her hand. 'Mrs Munro, I'm Vince Pastrano, and I'm your lawyer. These are my assistants, Alastair and Becky. Our job is to get you off these charges, and out of here. Now, please sit down and tell us how you think these charges have been levelled against you.'

He pulled a chair out for her. She was already impressed with him. Well dressed in a light grey suit with red tie and matching handkerchief in his top pocket. Good-looking too – maybe Italian stock – with hair just a touch long. In his late forties. She relaxed and told her story. Pastrano asked a few questions as she talked. The others took copious notes.

When she finished, Pastrano sat and thought for a moment. He lifted one hand with his index finger up, and pursed his lips. 'Okay, now let me tell you what will happen. You're innocent, and we're going to find witnesses who will support your story.'

'Witnesses?'

He smiled. 'There are always witnesses, my dear, and our job is to make sure their recollections match what you say. Now, let's go through the whole thing again, step by step and in detail. Let's start with your background in London. Oh, and by the way, your lawyer in London is a friend of mine – Josh Calman – a very good man who'll look after your interests down there. Let's get started.'

***

Sandra and her three inspectors, Bill, Sam and Tom, sat round a table. She held a telephone connected to Brian Walker in London. She liked Brian. They'd worked together on the Aquila job a few years ago, when they had nailed a bunch of German spies.

She summarised the case for Brian's benefit, and then went through her plans. 'Let's talk about team one – focused on the three men – led by Bill here. I've radio-telegraphed their pictures and prints to you, Brian. Have you got them?'

'Yep, got them, Sandra.'

'Good. Let's call them the little one, the middle one, and the big one. We need to know who they are, and their motive for this attack. They're all carrying London based IDs and I've sent you the names, addresses and dates of birth, Brian.

'Now, we've been told by the PD that the William Garvie ID is false. The name, address and date of birth match a real person, but he's a bus driver with London Transport. Their other IDs are probably also false, but we need to confirm that, okay?'

'Okay, Sandra.'

'Let's keep in mind, though, that in this country, it's not a crime to impersonate someone other than a police officer or lawyer. It's only a crime if you then use the false ID to commit a civil or criminal offence. So let's make sure we focus on the offence. But if we *can* find their true identities, it might lead us to their paymasters.

'If all their IDs match real people, then they won't be chosen at random. There must be a common link between the real guys that might lead us to where our crooks got these names, and maybe even further. Can you put a team on this, Brian?'

'Yes, will do.'

'The next thing about these three men is their background. I watched them in action and they were calm and calculated in killing. That probably means they're ex-military, maybe ex-commandos. Can you check out military records, Brian? With a bit of luck, their prints could give us their real names.'

'Yes, we'll check that out.'

'Then, lastly, their motive. I believe this was an attempted contract killing, because they didn't try to rob Mr Preston or steal his boat. But we're not going public with that. It would raise too many awkward questions that we can't answer. Publicly, it will be an attempted robbery that went wrong, but internally we'll treat it as a contract killing.

'I have it on quite good authority that, when the three men landed at Girvan, the little guy said to the others, "There you go, another one complete for Uncle Albert." Can you put a request out around all the London divisions, Brian, to see if anyone has heard anything about an Uncle Albert in the context of contract killing?'

'Right, will do, Sandra.'

'In the meantime, we'll follow any clues at this end. But the men just say "no comment" to all questions, so they're not going to give up any info easily.'

She paused for a drink of water, and to let the information soak in.

'Now, let's move on to team two, led by Sam, and focused on the woman. She has very eminent and expensive lawyers – Josh Calman in London, and Vince Pastrano up here. So, someone's putting *lots* of money into freeing her.

'I'd expect Pastrano to tell me within days that we have no case against her. That's his style, and very often, he can prove it, or at least introduce a level of reasonable doubt that gets them off. We need to be very sure of our facts if we think she's part of any conspiracy.

'I have to say, the links between the woman and the three men are flimsy at best. As I see it, we only have two. The first is the PD I talked about before, who says the little guy delivered a package to the woman's hotel last Wednesday. Now, he's an ex-cop, but they can make mistakes too. We'll follow that one through at this end.

'The second is the phone call the woman received at the hotel that her uncle was ill. The timing of that call matches an assault by the men on the PD's assistant, who told them about the woman's false ID, and their suspected link to her.

'The men denied any link, but, if we assume a conspiracy, then the phone call could have been from one of the three men to warn that her cover was blown. We need to check that story out.'

'Do we know who and where the uncle is? I assume if he exists, then he's down here in the London area.'

'No, we don't, Brian. According to DS Grant, who tailed the woman to London, she made a phone call from Euston Station before joining the taxi queue. That could have been to a hospital or nursing home.

'If we're honest, guys, we probably jumped the gun when we arrested her. She claims she and Preston fell in love, and we'll check that from here. But she's now shouting wrongful arrest, and has clammed up.

'However, we do have some evidence – circumstantial at best – that the woman may be the sister of the middle one of these three men. The two of them might have a history of assaulting and robbing rich men. Again, we'll check that from here.

'Lastly, Brian, could you check her IDs in London – Jean Mathieson, Mrs Jean Munro and Greta Reid. See if we have anything on her.

'DS Grant thinks her IDs are valid, but the PD says her ID for Jean Munro in Perth is false. We have to know either way, and we'll check that out from this end.

'But, if we can't prove she lured Preston into a deadly situation, or any link between her and the three men, we'll have to let her go, false ID or not.

'So, that's our plan, gentlemen. Any comments?'

The four men just murmured in agreement.

'Okay, thanks for your help. We'll talk again at four. I've got to report to the boss each day at five.'

Ten minutes later, Tom popped his head round her door. 'That's the three men charged with the assault on Danny Watson, ma'am. They've pled not guilty, and are remanded in custody pending further enquiries.'

'Who represented them?'

'Only the duty solicitor, ma'am.'

She chewed her lip. 'That's very strange. Thanks Tom.' The woman had Pastrano and Calman. Lots of legal power. The men had the opposite. None of it was quite what she expected.

***

They sat in the second front row in the briefing room, Sandra between Tom and Jim Hannah. Typical American comfort, she thought. Soft, almost cinema-like seats with arms, and with a desktop that folded up from the side if you needed to take notes.

Chuck sat at the side in the front row. 'All set? Okay, Bob, let's roll it!'

The lights dimmed. The film was way better than Sandra expected. Because of the zoom effect, it seemed they looked down from just a few feet above the incident. She now relived it without the distractions of operating the camera, shocked again at the casual violence the men used towards Preston.

The film caught the men's faces as they looked up towards the helicopter, and there was no doubt it was the three men they had in custody. It continued after the men jumped onto the motorboat, and followed the yacht as it crashed onto the shingle beach at Ailsa Craig. She shivered at Preston's body trailing behind it.

At the end, Chuck turned to them and smiled. 'Happy with that?'

The three of them sat silent for a moment. Sandra shook her head. 'I can't believe the clarity. We must have been hundreds of feet above them.'

'Yeah, that's correct. But we use these cameras for detailed surveys, and for covert surveillance, so they're very special.'

Sandra turned to Jim Hannah. 'What do you think, Jim? Is that enough to convict them?'

He nodded. 'I've never seen anything like it. Clearly an attempted murder in action. Rock-solid proof of guilt in my view, caught by modern technology.'

'What about you, Tom?'

'It's just amazing, ma'am. There's no doubt without that, it would be very easy to assume Preston just had an accident on deck. Brilliant.'

Chuck stood up. 'We've made a copy for you.' He handed Sandra a metal film canister. 'The film is 35mm in size. That's our standard for these films. But we can transfer it over to any size you need to show in court. Just give us the size, and we'll do the rest.'

Sandra took the film canister. 'Thanks, Chuck. We'll get back to you on that.'

He also gave her a large envelope. 'These are the still photos you took at the time. You might also find them useful.'

She pulled out the photos, and passed them to Tom and Jim. They showed the key moments when Sandra had clicked the still camera and captured the action. 'That's great, Chuck. We can't thank you enough.'

'No problem. Do you need us to give evidence?'

She looked at Jim. 'If we need to explain why Sandra was on a US helicopter, it may be useful.'

'Okay, just let us know.' Chuck showed them out.

In the car heading back towards Glasgow, Tom said, 'Wouldn't our jobs be a lot easier if we had evidence like that every time?'

Sandra nodded, and wondered if the day would ever come when they'd use a helicopter for police work.

***

At four o'clock, Sandra and her team sat round the table again. Engineers had now rigged up a way of hearing Brian through a separate loudspeaker. Sandra still had to use the handset to talk to Brian, but she thought it a small step forward to make life easier.

She started. 'Right, let's deal with team one, the three men. I can tell you all that Tom and I saw the film today with a senior prosecutor, and he says it's rock-solid evidence of guilt. It's going to blow them away in court, no matter who they are. Right, Bill, on you go.'

Bill cleared his throat. 'We've checked the house they used last week, their cars, their motorboat, and Mr Preston's motor yacht, and have no useful info from any of them. It's like they've never been here. They're also giving "no comment" answers to all questions. So, we've no further info on them from this end.'

'Okay, Bill. That's a pity. Brian, can you update us from your end?'

'Yes, Sandra. We can confirm the IDs the three men carry relate to real people who live and work in London. I've sent you the details. None of them knew someone had borrowed their identities, or could identify the men. They have no common links, except they all rent their property from a company called Camden Hill Lettings.

'We found it's part of a group owned by a family called Daly, who seem well respected in the area. They support local charities, including police charities.

'Around forty people work in the lettings company. We found they don't lock their records away at night. So, anyone in the office can see any record at any time. No one we spoke to recognised the three men. But one of the three could easily have a girlfriend who works in the typing pool, for instance, who could pass them ID details of anyone they want. And she'd be hard to find.'

'Is there an Uncle Albert in the Daly family?'

'The boss of the lettings company said he only had three relatives called Albert. One, in his late fifties, runs a newspaper shop near Camden Town tube station, and has done so for over thirty years. There's a young man in his early twenties, studying to be a teacher. The other is a baby. We interviewed the two adults, and found them just ordinary guys. Not crime lords. They couldn't identify any of the three men either. But I'll come on to another aspect of Uncle Albert in a minute.

'Okay, sorry to interrupt.'

'The three men's prints don't match any of our records. We contacted the Army records branch. But they can only search their records by text. In other words, if you give them a name, address or date of birth, they'll provide a record that may include fingerprints. But they can't work back from prints to give the name, address and date of birth. They don't hold their print records in the same way as ours. So that's a dead end, unless we want to examine the fingerprint records of all three and a half million soldiers they had during the war. They also don't carry commandos' records separately.'

'That's a bugger, isn't it?' Bill said.

'It sure is. So the search for the three men's real identities has drawn a blank so far. We could publish their photos in the local paper and see if anyone calls in. But I know you might not want to do that because of other aspects of the case, Sandra.'

'Yeah, I want to keep a low profile for the moment. Let me have a think about it, Brian.' She herself had never had much success with that newspaper approach.

'Fine, Sandra. To finish off this section, we trawled our divisions for any reference to an 'Uncle Albert'. We had a response from a desk sergeant at Bow Street. Four weeks ago, his cops pulled in a drunk, charged with breach of the peace. He had started a fight in a local pub because his girlfriend had dumped him. He took exception to a group enjoying themselves at the next table, who had toasted 'Uncle Albert' in champagne. He agreed, when he sobered up, he'd been stupid. The cops that attended had taken a note of the person assaulted at the next table, but it'll take time to find the cop and get details. I'll get back to you later on this Sandra. Sorry I can't be more positive.'

'Well, thanks for that, Brian. Do you have any joy from team two on Mrs Munro, or Greta Reid, or whoever she is?'

'A couple of points here. We did a trawl through our SB records, and found we knew Miss Greta Reid.'

'What? You're kidding! In what respect?'

'Three years ago, we did a major search for someone leaking secrets to the Germans. It included members of a Whitehall committee, and their personal secretaries. One of the secretaries was Miss Greta Reid.

'I've read the files. She aroused suspicion because she lived in a luxury flat in South Kensington, way above her pay grade. Now, that's not unusual down here, Sandra. Lots of daughters of wealthy families took low-paid jobs in Whitehall to help with the war effort. But we checked her out anyway.

'We found she came from a plain background in Glasgow, and had a sugar daddy who visited her on Tuesday and Thursday evenings. We didn't know who he was, so we followed him, and lost him twice in various tube stations.

'The boss gave us permission to do a false stop and search the man. He was a Swiss national, Armin Fischer, and a senior executive at a Swiss bank. He had a flat in the city that he used during the week, and a large family house in Sevenoaks, Kent, where he joined his family at weekends. That's also not unusual for London, Sandra, and we cleared the girl on the leaked documents.

'Now, this man, Fischer, comes from a village called Aesch, near Basle, in Switzerland. We've just checked who owns the block of flat where Greta Reid lives. It's a company in the British Virgin Islands called Aesch Investments. This man Fischer is a multi-millionaire, and we believe he's funding all these expensive lawyers to get his sugar babe out of jail.'

'Wow! That makes sense. And the money's being funnelled via the British Virgin Islands company?'

'That's what we think. But of course, we can't prove it, or even find out who's behind the company. We think this Greta Reid is a kept woman, and has been for years. So, why did she go to Ayr last week? Was it just for a break as she said, or was she part of the plot against Preston? And that's something we think you guys have to work out from your end.'

'Fair enough, Brian. Thanks for doing such prompt work. Now, Sam, what about the woman at this end?'

'The woman's saying nothing to us now, ma'am. Like the men, she's gives "no comment" to all questions. As to why she came to Ayr, we've talked to various people at the Preston store, and at the hotel. We found Mrs Barbour the most open and helpful.'

'Oh, yes? What did she say?'

'She said Preston introduced himself to Mrs Munro as she shopped in the store. They seemed to just click, and it developed into a love match. Mrs Munro had also blended in with Preston's friends. She had come to Ayr, as a neutral place, to decide between Perth and London. It also gave her the chance to see a distant aunt in a local nursing home, and that checks out too. Mrs Barbour said Preston had fallen in love with Mrs Munro, and wanted her to stay in Ayr as his wife. So that ties up with what Mrs Munro told DS Grant.

'With regard to her ID, the birth certificate for Jean Mathieson seems genuine. We found an aunt of Jean's in Glasgow. She said the Mathieson family emigrated to Canada in the thirties, but there was a big bust-up because Jean didn't want to go. In the end, Jean stayed with her for a few weeks, then went off to London with her boyfriend, a pleasant lad called Alex. The aunt then lost touch with her. However, she looked at a picture of Mrs Munro, and said she was *not* Jean Mathieson. She didn't know the woman in the photo.

'We showed her the photo of the football team, but she couldn't identify anyone as Alex, the boyfriend. We've phoned the police in Toronto to find out more about Jean's family, but no response so far. We're sure, though, that Mrs Munro is *not* Jean Mathieson as was.'

'Wow, a good piece of work, Sam. Well done.'

'Thanks, ma'am. Turning now to Mrs Munro. The Perth registry office can't find their copy of her marriage lines. They say that's not unusual as they sometimes had problems with marriages in outlying villages. This one took place in a small village called Findo Gask. We went there to check their records. On the day in question, they had one marriage, but it *wasn't* between Jean Mathieson and James Munro. We believe they would have recorded the Munro marriage in the same way if it *had* taken place. So, we think Mrs Munro has fake marriage lines, and that's why Perth registry has no record.

'Her ID card with the Atholl Gardens address is also fake. She uses Jean Mathieson's date of birth on it, and it *would* have been her address had she married James Munro. We met the real Mrs Jean Munro, who currently lives there. We showed her the photo of our Mrs Munro, and asked her if she was the mysterious Janice, girlfriend of James Munro, when he went missing. But neither she nor her husband had ever met the girl, so that was a dead end too.

'Just to finish off this section, ma'am, we also checked her ID for Greta Reid. We found a woman in Glasgow called Greta Reid with the same date of birth. She thought the woman in the photo was a school friend of hers called Cathie McCabe. So, we believe that McCabe "borrowed" the IDs of Jean Mathieson and Greta Reid when she moved to London. The pity is that we can't find the real Jean Mathieson.'

Sandra looked at Tom. 'Feel better now?'

'I certainly do, ma'am, thanks.'

Sandra looked at the others. 'So, to nail this woman now, we have to prove a link to the three men. Where are we with that, Sam?'

'This link had been suggested by the PD, Davie Watson. He followed a man who had left a package for Mrs Munro at her hotel last Wednesday. We spoke to the girl who Davie was talking to at the time. She says that when he heard the man mention Mrs Munro, Davie glanced up, and she looked round. But by then the man was already walking out towards the door. He wore a gabardine coat and a hat, and they didn't see his face.

'She couldn't recognise the man as one of the three men in the photograph. She also said there were other people around the door at that time. The other girl, who took the package, could not identify any of them either. In my view, there's at least some doubt that Davie followed the right man.

'Therefore, on the evidence so far, the woman's IDs are false, but there's nothing that would stand up in court that would link her to the three men. And, in any case, she didn't lure Preston into danger, because she was travelling to London at that time. She might be part of the gang, but we just can't prove it.'

'Okay, Sam, thanks for that. And if Vince Pastrano also thinks we can't prove it, he'll want her released.' She glanced at Tom and raised an eyebrow.

'Thanks, guys. I appreciate all your inputs. I'll go over them with the boss in a few minutes. In the meantime, keep an open mind and follow the evidence.'

She hung up the phone, and watched her team leave the room. She had to keep a detached view of the evidence, and follow it if credible. But sometimes it didn't always deliver what you wanted.

***

Sandra updated Burnett at five o'clock. He was pleased about the film, and agreed it would be great if they'd that sort of evidence in every case. 'I'm told the RAF has a couple of these Hoverflys at their new training school. I'll check if we can use them on special operations. I'll also have a word with Brian on his Uncle Albert lead. Keep in touch.'

Sandra wrote up her notes. She was happy about the film. The ID issues paled into insignificance against it.

But she'd still like to know who the men were. It might lead to other crimes they'd committed.

Tom knocked at the door. 'Excuse me, ma'am, I've just had a call from that reporter in Ayr, Katy Young. She's looking for a quote for tomorrow's paper. Is there anything you want to tell her?'

'Yeah, let's try to keep control of the news a bit longer. She's probably been in court this morning so knows the men's names, and the assault charge on Danny Watson. Now that we've got the film, I think we can go a bit further with her. Jim Hannah is charging them with assault on Preston tomorrow.'

She pulled her pad in front of her and wrote a note. 'Following their arrest at Girvan harbour on Sunday, three men, all from North London, are expected to be further charged with assault on a 42-year-old man near Girvan. Police inquiries are continuing.'

She handed the note to Tom. 'Give her this. If she doesn't know it's Preston, then don't tell her, but if she asks if it *is* him, then don't deny it.'

'Okay, ma'am. Are we not going with attempted murder at this stage?'

'Jim Hannah's holding off for another day to see if there's big-money lawyers involved. At the moment, they're still using the duty solicitor, and we can't figure out why. Once we go with an attempted murder charge, then it's a remittance to the High Court, and all hell breaks out in the papers. But I think it might break tomorrow or the next day.'

'Fine, ma'am. I'll get back to her with this.'

Just after he left, her phone rang. 'It's a Mr Pastrano for you, ma'am.'

Well, that didn't take him long. The phone clicked. 'Mr Pastrano. Good evening. What can I do for you?'

'Ah, Superintendent Maxwell. Good to talk to you again. How are you this fine evening?'

She could imagine him with a smile on his face. He was a smarmy bastard at times, but it went over big in the courtroom. 'I'm fine.'

'I wondered if we might meet this evening – say for half an hour?'

'To do what?'

'To talk about your case against my client, Mrs Jean Munro. We have serious concerns about the case. In fact, I'd go so far as to say I think your people have made a mistake here. And I'd just like to explain that to you, so you don't waste any more time and effort on it.'

She knew he had lots of staff. And they worked fast and efficiently. 'What do you want from me?'

'I don't want anything from you, Superintendent. I'd like you just to listen to what I have to say, and then make up your own mind on the action you might take.'

She thought for a moment. So he wasn't looking to pump her for information. In any case, he knew from the past she wouldn't tell him anything. It sounded okay. 'All right, Mr Pastrano, I'll do that.'

'Excellent! How about in say half an hour, at the second-floor cocktail bar in the Central Hotel?'

'That's fine. See you then.'

'Look forward to it, Superintendent.'

As she packed her things and got ready to leave, she thought he must be very sure of his ground if he wanted to talk this early. After all, he'd only started on the case that morning. He sure didn't waste time.

***

He waved to her from a table at the far end of the bar. She'd met him here before – and at the same table. This must be his favoured watering hole. He held out his hand in welcome. 'Ah, Superintendent, good to see you. May I get you a drink?'

'Sparkling water, with lemon, but no ice, thanks.'

He caught a passing waiter and ordered her drink, then settled alongside her. He went into his briefcase, and pulled out a large white envelope. 'This is for you, Superintendent. It gives all the details of the contacts and conclusions that I'd like to cover. May I start?'

She took the envelope and laid it on the table. 'Please do.' Her drink arrived and she picked it up. 'Cheers,' and settled into the seat.

He raised his glass. 'Cheers,' and took a sip. 'Now, I may well cover ground you already know, but if I may, I'd like to explain the case as I see it. Is that okay?'

She nodded, and took a sip of her own drink.

'My client was shocked when your people arrested her last night. She'd met Mr Preston purely by chance. He introduced himself when she was in his store. And over the last week or so they became close. She thought he might even propose marriage. But it seems someone linked her with the men involved in his attempted murder, and she has no idea how that happened.

'This morning, my team has gone through every minute of her stay in Ayr. In the end, we focused on packages delivered to Mrs Munro last week at her hotel. These included table mats and other gifts she had bought in local shops. The shops said they'd used their own junior staff, or a local odd-job man, Sammy McKay, to deliver the packages during Wednesday and Thursday. Our team interviewed them all, including Sammy.

'We also talked to the hotel receptionists who were on duty these days. One of them accepted a package for Mrs Munro early on Wednesday afternoon, delivered by Sammy. At the time, the other girl was standing talking to a private detective – an ex-cop called Davie Watson – about Mrs Munro. When they heard her name, they both looked round, but the man was already walking out the door. She says they didn't see his face, but she thought it was Sammy, whom she vaguely knew. Davie left the hotel by a side door.

'We also interviewed the PD, Davie. He'd asked the girl about Mrs Munro on behalf of a journalist at the local paper, who writes a gossip column. He followed the man who had just left, though he agreed he hadn't seen his face.

'However, he had photos of a man and his two mates, who had rented a house in the town. We got copies of the photos, and went back to the hotel. The girls on the desk couldn't recognise any of the men. But the barman at the hotel agreed the small man in the photo had been in the bar for at least an hour over lunch time with another man. He left just after two o'clock, the same time as Sammy.

'Therefore, we believe Davie Watson confused the two men, who have similar builds. He followed the wrong man. Now, if this man and his two mates are the ones involved in the attempted murder, then we think that's where the mix-up came from.

'Davie Watson told us these men had acted suspiciously and had assaulted his nephew. But he agreed he *could* have followed the wrong man, and had linked Mrs Munro to these men by mistake.

'In addition, to charge Mrs Munro with conspiracy, you need to show her presence in Ayr had changed Preston's routines, and that she lured him into danger. Now, we've talked with Mrs Barbour, Operations Director at the Preston store.

'She said that, after meeting Mrs Munro, he did change his routines on the Monday, Tuesday and Wednesday. But on the Thursday, Friday, Saturday and Sunday, he followed the exact same routines he followed every week.

'And on the Sunday, when the incident happened, Mr Preston had played golf in the morning, and gone sailing in the afternoon, as he always did. On that day, Mrs Munro wasn't even in Ayr. So, how could she be part of a conspiracy against Mr Preston?

'We think you have no case against Mrs Munro, and you should release her without charge right now.'

Sandra thought about what he'd said. It largely matched Sam's statement earlier. Pastrano wouldn't state these as facts unless he had witness statements to back them up. She knew Pastrano would find every crack in the prosecution case – *her* case – and widen it to become a reasonable doubt. And that's all he had to do to win. She also knew some witnesses recalled events in proportion to the number of five-pound notes in front of them. Would Pastrano go that far? It would depend on the stakes involved. But in this case, the stakes seemed very high.

'Why did she leave the hotel early?'

'She got a call from the nursing home in Chelmsford where her uncle lives. He'd taken a turn for the worse, and the nurse suggested she see him as soon as possible. However, when she arrived at Euston, she phoned the nursing home, and found it a false alarm. So she just went home. Our associates in London have interviewed the young nurse concerned, and he has confirmed making the call.'

'How did he know where to contact Mrs Munro?'

'She'd visited the nursing home just two weeks ago concerned at her uncle's condition. She left her contact numbers then.'

Sandra assumed that Josh Calman's team had taken the Chelmsford statements. They would operate in the same way as Pastrano. On the face of it, the link between Mrs Munro and the three men looked an open-and-shut mistake. But she wouldn't admit that to him. 'Let me check your info from our end, and if it matches we'll see where we go. Be assured I won't hold or charge any innocent person.'

He nodded. 'Thank you, I accept that. But you had the three men up in court this morning on assault charges, not attempted murder. And you didn't put Mrs Munro up in court at all. Does that mean you still have doubts about what happened?'

She smiled at him. 'Come on, Vincent, you know I won't answer that. But while she's answering "no comment" to all our questions, it's difficult to pull it all to a conclusion.'

His lips thinned. 'Well, we believe we can prove without a doubt, there's no link between Mrs Munro and the three men. So, on that basis, and on the fact that she was away from Ayr on the day of the incident, we believe she has no case to answer. I'll give you tomorrow to confirm this, and get back to me. But we're prepared to go to court and present that evidence. If you have any other issues about Mrs Munro, then please ask me. We'll help you get answers to clarify her position. Is that fair?'

'At this point, that's fair.'

'That's all I ask. Thanks for listening.'

'You're welcome.' She observed him as he started to chat about other matters. Did she trust him? Probably not. But he was a very sharp lawyer. She'd have to be very sure of her evidence if she wanted to hold Mrs Munro for much longer. If she couldn't link Mrs Munro to the three men and the incident beyond a reasonable doubt, she'd have to let her go, even with her false IDs.

She called the office from her car, and found Tom and Sam still there. She asked them to stay on for a few minutes, and then went through Pastrano's evidence with them. They agreed a course of action for the next day to confirm his details.

Tom also confirmed, with the forensics team now finished on the Preston motor yacht, he'd now cleared Ben to arrange for the yacht's recovery.

Chapter 15. Aftermath

Sandra and her team met at four o'clock on Tuesday. Sam said, 'Our teams have interviewed all the witnesses on Pastrano's list, ma'am. They've all confirmed their stories. The only real question mark was with the young male nurse in Chelmsford.'

Brian cut in. 'Yeah, Sandra. He confirmed making the call about her uncle's condition. But it all just seemed too pat to us. We couldn't disprove it, though.'

Sandra brought the meeting to a halt. 'Okay. Thanks Sam and Brian and your teams. It looks like you've confirmed Pastrano's conclusions. We can't link the woman to the three men, and have no evidence she lured Preston into danger. So we should release her without charge. In these circumstances, her false IDs don't come into it. Let's arrange the paperwork tonight, Tom, and release her in the morning.'

***

Katy came in early on Wednesday and finished her gossip column for the week. She'd left a space at the top to insert an item on Mr Preston's new lady friend, but Archie had called her late last night. He told her the police had detained Mrs Munro on Sunday night as an accomplice in the attempted murder of Mr Preston. However, they would now release her this morning without charge. They couldn't link her to the three men, and had no evidence she lured Preston into danger. Katy realised the story was now not suitable for her gossip column, and filled the space with something else.

But she'd been stunned to hear of the attempted murder charge. Adam had told her Mr Preston had had an accident on his boat on Sunday, and was now in hospital. But he hadn't said anything about attempted murder. *My God, what was going on?*

Kenny was shocked when Katy told him, and called Janet Barbour. But she didn't know about the attempted murder charge either. Katy looked at the photos of the woman and three men on her desk. 'Can we run any story on this, Kenny?'

'No. It's still only hearsay. Is there any chance you can call your new best friend, and get a statement on what we've heard? We go to press tonight.'

Katy's heart thumped. If this was true, it was a huge story. She picked up her phone and tried to get Maxwell, but she wasn't available. Kenny stood beside Katy's desk, and put his hand to his chin. 'Shit. We're running out of time.'

One of the staff photographers, Sandy Moffat, came past her desk. 'Hi Katy, Kenny. What's new with you guys?' He looked at the photos. 'What's this you're working on?'

Katy glanced up at him. 'At the moment it's a dying story, because there's no link between this woman and these three men.'

'Let's have a look. I know that woman. Saw her last weekend, and she was with these three guys.'

Katy's jaw dropped. 'You're kidding, Sandy. Where did you see her?'

'My brother Vic and I were in the taxi queue at Ayr station. Vic had just bought a new camera in Glasgow. A car drew up and she got out of it. The driver was that little guy there, and he got her case out of the boot. These two other guys were also in the car. Might even have a photo of them. You don't see many stunners like her in Ayr.

'She joined the queue beside us, and Vic chatted to her. She was here for a week and asked about the area. When the next taxi came, we let her take it, and she asked for the Egerton Hotel. Why? Is it important?'

She stared at him. 'Important? It's one of the very few times I could kiss you. Can you get the photo?'

'Sure. I'll be about half an hour or so.' He rushed out the door.

She picked up the phone, but Kenny stepped forward. 'Who are you phoning, Katy?'

'I'm phoning Maxwell to let her know we've got a link between the woman and the three men. That's important for her to know.'

'Right. Could you just hold it for a few minutes. I need to make a phone call first.'

She shrugged. 'Okay. If you say so.'

He turned and headed for his office.

Katy watched him go. *What the hell was he up to?* This photo would be the first step in proving collusion. Just exactly what Maxwell was looking for. She watched Kenny on the phone. *Who the hell was he phoning?*

***

'Daniel, it's Kenny McLeod here. Have you got a minute? I need some urgent advice.'

'Sure, Kenny. How can I help?'

'One of my reporters, Katy Young, has been doing a story for her gossip column on Richard's new girlfriend, Jean Munro, whom I saw you talking to on Saturday.'

'Yeah, quite a woman.'

'Janet told me Richard was head over heels in love with Jean. Could even lead to marriage. They were like lovesick teenagers.'

'Yeah.'

'Well, we've picked up from police sources that Mrs Munro was arrested in London on Sunday night as an accomplice in the attempted murder of Richard on Sunday afternoon.'

'What? Jesus Christ. Are you sure?'

'That's what we hear.'

'Bloody hell.'

'Now, I've just spoken to Janet again, and she didn't know anything about the attempted murder charge. But she told me off the record, that three men attacked Richard on his boat, and he's very seriously ill. He has severe damage to his head, and might not survive.'

'Jesus Christ. Janet called me on Sunday night, and I spoke to Mrs Preston yesterday, but neither of them mentioned attempted murder.'

'Yeah, I think the story's just broke this morning. Anyway, the police seem to have made a balls up. They've no evidence that Jean has any links to the three men, or that she lured him into danger. In fact, she wasn't even here on Sunday. It seems to be a case of mistaken identity somewhere along the line. So, they'll release her without charge this morning.'

'So, what's your problem?'

'My problem is that Katy, with one of my staff photographers, Sandy, has just unearthed a link between Mrs Munro and the three men. Sandy might even have a photograph of them together a week ago. That in itself, doesn't prove she had anything to do with the crime, but it's a big step towards proving some sort of collusion.

'Now, apart from the fact Richard owns the newspaper, he's also a very good friend. If he's that close to death, this revelation might just tip him over the edge. And I certainly don't want that. So, my dilemma is, what should I do about it? Hence the call.'

'Okay, Kenny. You did the right thing. How amenable would Katy and Sandy be to a bribe to stay silent? How much do they earn right now?'

'I'd need to check, but they probably get about five pounds a week.'

'So, how would they react if you offered them a hundred pounds each to say nothing to anyone about their find, and sign a confidentiality agreement? I'd pay for it, Kenny, but you'd have to sign a CA as well.'

'Jesus, Daniel. Is that legal?'

'Yeah, it's legal. The only problem that might arise is if the police asked them direct if they know of any link between Mrs Munro and the three men. Then you move into a grey area. But, if they don't say anything to anyone, that will never arise.'

'Well, I think Sandy would jump at it. Money motivates him. I'm not so sure about Katy. She's more career oriented. She's quite ethical in her own way.'

'Could you do something career wise for her, then?'

'Yeah, possibly. We hooked her up with the *Daily Record* this week, and she was like a dog with two tails when they ran one of her stories. We've already talked to the Features Editor there. He's looking for new talent right now.'

'Sounds good. Let's go for it, Kenny. I'll send you over the money and the CAs.'

'How do I sell it to them, Daniel?'

'Well, if there *is* a photo, you've got to get Sandy to sell it to you with the negative, and sign a CA. Just say it's a big story you're working on, and you need to keep it quiet. He'll be happy with the cash. But he's not to talk to anyone about it. Particularly not Katy.

'With her, you just say Sandy doesn't have a photo, which he won't have because you've bought it. That kills the story. Then concentrate on her. Tell her about the opp at the *Record*, and give her the money for clothes to dress for the city. Then you don't need a CA for her. Would that work?'

'Yeah. That's good.'

'Fine. Come over later with the photo and the signed CAs, and let me know how it goes.'

'Right. Will do. And thanks.'

'No problem.'

***

Katy watched Kenny prowl the outer office. He never did that. *What was wrong?*. Then he grabbed a package from a girl who arrived at the front door, and headed for his office. He pulled the blind down. *He never did that either.* He reappeared, and stood near the front door. *What was he waiting for now?* Then Sandy came in, and Kenny shuttled him into his office. He didn't even look over to her. *What was going on?* Five minutes later, Sandy emerged and went straight out of the office, whistling as he went. Then Kenny appeared and signalled her. 'Katy, could I have a word, please?'

She nodded, and went over to his office. *Now, she'd find out what happened.* 'Did Sandy have a photo?'

'No, no. Forget it. He doesn't have a photo. That woman's a dead story now. Just kill it.'

'But surely he could give evidence?'

'No, he's not sure now. And in any case, the woman couldn't have lured Richard into danger. She wasn't even here on Sunday. I've told you, just kill it. I want to talk about you.'

She raised her eyebrows. 'Okay.'

'Archie and I have been talking about your career. We recognise you need more of a challenge. That's why we got you into the *Record* this week. We've talked with Ed Paton, the Features Editor there, and he's looking for someone like you to join his team. We think you'd be a good fit. Would you be interested in that?'

'Wow. Of course.'

'We'll work out a way to keep you on our books to do your Clayrissa column, but also work for them in Glasgow. What do you think?

'I'd love that.'

'We'll get you in front of Ed to finalise things, but it should be a done deal. However, if you're going to work in the city, you'll have to smarten up. Change out of your sloppy clothes into a business suit and high heels.' He went into a desk drawer. 'Here's a hundred pounds. Use it to kit yourself out.'

'Wow. Thanks very much, Kenny.'

'No problem.'

She left his office and called Adam. 'Are you free for an early lunch?'

'Yeah, can be.'

'Okay, see you in ten minutes at the restaurant.'

All thoughts of the story and the photo had now gone. She was so excited at this opportunity. She hoped Adam would go along with it too. She felt they were more like a couple now, and wanted to share her exciting news with him.

***

Tom watched Mrs Munro escorted from the cells. She was a smart operator, no doubt about it. Very cool and convincing. She'd spun a web of lies and half-truths well enough to allow Pastrano and his team to find and open the gaps that clouded the truth, and allowed her to go free. Sometimes, as a policeman, you knew the truth, but couldn't find the evidence to back it up. *Dammit!*

Pastrano had turned up with a female colleague, and within moments, Mrs Munro stood in front of the desk, with Tom on one side and Pastrano on the other. The desk sergeant went through the formal release procedure.

Pastrano turned and walked over to his colleague. Tom couldn't resist it. He leaned over and whispered in Mrs Munro's ear. 'You're good, Cathie. But I'll get you next time.'

She jumped back, startled. He'd scored a hit. Pastrano came over to her. 'Are you all right?'

She nodded, wide-eyed. 'Get me out of here.'

Tom watched the group move away from the desk, Cathie gliding as usual. She cast a fearful look back at him as she left. That alone was worth all the effort.

***

When Katy got back to the office, Kenny was waiting for her. 'Right, that's the attempted murder charge on the three men now official. They've just been in court. Can you try and call Maxwell again, and get more details. It would give us a great front page if you could.'

'Okay, let's see what we can do.' She called the number. Kenny stood beside her desk, listening.

'Oh, hi, Katy. Sorry I didn't get back to you this morning. What can I do for you?'

'We're all a bit shocked here about the attempted murder charge on the three men. I'm just trying to get the latest information as our paper goes to press tonight. Is there anything else you can tell me?'

'Oh, I see. Well, let me bring you up to date. On Monday, the three men appeared in court charged with assault on a twenty-year-old man. Yesterday, we charged them with an assault on a forty-two-year-old man. Today, they've been charged with the attempted murder of Richard Preston during a failed robbery on Sunday.'

'Robbing him of what?'

'They were hijacking the boat.'

'And where's the boat now?'

'It crash-landed on Ailsa Craig. It's now been sent for repair.'

'So, that's what happened at sea on Sunday, then?'

'That's correct.'

'And where's Mr Preston now?'

'He's in Ayr County Hospital. As I understand it, his recovery may take some time.'

'Oh my God. Is it that bad?'

'I'm afraid so.'

'And was Mrs Munro involved?'

There was a pause. 'Why do you ask that?'

'We heard she had been arrested as an accomplice.'

There was another pause. 'During our investigations, we had a report from a member of the public that there might be a link. But it turned out to be a case of mistaken identity. There's no story for you there, Katy.'

She hesitated. 'Okay. May I ask you something else, Superintendent?'

'Of course.'

'You say the incident on Sunday was a failed robbery. But when I saw the men arrive at Girvan harbour, they didn't appear to have failed in what they'd done. In fact, they were laughing and patting each other's shoulders. How do you explain that?'

'I'm sorry, I can't. That's the way our evidence points right now. And I'd appreciate it if you followed that line in your article.'

That's an odd thing for her to say. But Katy had the feeling she shouldn't push it any further. She didn't want to stray into the previous Preston story, particularly with Kenny listening alongside.

'Okay. Thank you very much, ma'am. I really appreciate this.'

'You're welcome. Katy. Goodbye.'

Katy hung up the phone, and looked up at Kenny. She took him through the conversation. 'I just don't believe that bit about a failed robbery, Kenny.'

'What are you saying then?'

'These guys were happy when they landed. They'd done what they set out to do.'

'Which was?'

Katy thought for a moment. 'I think they went out there to kill him. One man went out in the motorboat and three came back. It means the other two must have already been on Preston's boat when he sailed.'

'Jesus. Why would they want to kill him?'

'Well, that we don't know. But they must have thought they'd succeeded when they landed. We still don't really know what happened out there. And she's not saying.'

Kenny grimaced. 'It'll all come out in court, Katy. Just write the story with what we've got. Our readers want facts, not speculation.'

'Okay, boss. Will do.' She loaded a blank sheet into her typewriter. There was a great story here, but it was just out of her reach. A few weeks ago, Preston had aimed to kill a captain – the unknown captain. Now, he'd finished up as the captain almost killed. And she shouldn't have known about either instance.

Maxwell knew the full story, of course. But Katy realised that, as a journalist, she would never get to know it all. And maybe that was right – for her own good. Guys like Kenny and Archie had an instinct for how far they could go. She was learning it the hard way. There was a point in any situation where your safety took priority. Preston had overstepped that point somehow, and paid the price. But she couldn't say that. Kenny was right. Write what you know, not what you think you know.

She began to type the story under the banner headline 'Preston Sensation'.

***

Sandra raised the issue of 'Uncle Albert' with Burnett later that week.

'I've met Brian about this, Sandra. The man assaulted in the pub was a solicitor, Monty Levine. We asked him about his 'Uncle Albert' toast. He denied all knowledge of it. He said his assailant must have misheard him.

'We thought he was a bit shifty about it, though, and got a warrant to check his home and offices. He works for lots of different companies. The ones we found of most interest were two corporations chaired by our old friend Sir Anthony Hewlett-Burke. Levine seems to do a lot of work for them.

'So we pulled in Sir Anthony again. He also denied all knowledge, of course, and stomped off in a rage. We can't find anything in Levine's notes of an 'Uncle Albert'. I'm afraid it's another dead end.

'There probably *is* an 'Uncle Albert' somewhere, but these people cover their tracks so well. It's impossible for us to pin anything on them. But I hope we've scared Sir Anthony and Levine off just as we did before.'

'That's okay, sir. I just get so angry when these clever crooks get away with it because they have money and contacts.'

'I agree. But the best we can do is warn them off, keep an eye on them, and hope they make a mistake.' '

'Fine, sir. That's just what we'll do.'

***

Six months later, Katy attended court for the Preston trial. Ed Paton, her editor, had asked her to do a daily three hundred word column called 'Katy's View', focused on the people involved in the case. She sat next to Craig Nelson, one of the news reporters, on the Press benches. He described who was who in court.

She watched the three men enter the dock. They looked just as menacing as when she first saw them in Girvan. She knew one of them had a false ID, so they probably all did. There was a definite story there, and she hoped it would come out in court. They were asked to plead on the charge of attempted murder.

To everyone's astonishment, they pleaded 'Guilty'.

Craig whispered, 'Jesus. Why are they doing that?'

Katy shrugged. She had no idea. The judge went on to request submissions from both sides. 'Sentencing will take place one week today.' He banged his gavel.

'What happened?' Katy asked.

'I don't know. They've pleaded 'Not Guilty' at all previous hearings. We expected the same here today, and for the trial to last a couple of weeks or so. But something has changed. I'd love to know what did it.'

They gathered their things, and moved out of the courtroom. In the foyer, Katy saw Sandra Maxwell with a man in uniform. She grabbed Craig's arm. 'Let's go find out.'

Katy put on a big smile. 'Morning, ma'am. It's Katy Young from Ayr. Remember? Good to see you again.'

Sandra turned. 'Oh, Katy. Of course. My goodness, you do look smart.'

'Thanks. I'm working with the *Record* in Glasgow now. This is my colleague, Craig Nelson.'

Sandra shook his hand. 'Pleased to meet you. I'm Chief Superintendent Maxwell. And this is Colonel Campbell of the US Army Air Force.'

They all shook hands.

'Chief, ma'am? Congratulations.'

'Thanks, Katy.'

'May I ask you something, ma'am?'

'Of course, Katy. I wouldn't expect anything else from you.'

'These three men pleaded 'Guilty' this morning. Yet they pleaded 'Not Guilty' at all previous hearings. What changed their minds?'

Sandra glanced at Campbell. Katy pulled out a notebook and pencil.

'Erm. During our investigations, we found evidence that showed, without doubt, these three men had committed the crime. We disclosed it to the defence team a few weeks ago. I assume that changed their minds. And they may get a lighter sentence by doing so.'

'May I ask what this evidence was, ma'am?'

Sandra glanced at Campbell, who nodded. 'It was a film taken from a USAAF helicopter that happened to be flying above the crime scene.'

'Wow. Was that the new hovering aircraft you got out of in Girvan?'

'That's correct.'

'Is it possible to see this film?'

'I'm sorry. It's not available for public view.'

'You said at the time you were assessing the aircraft for possible police work.'

'That's true. And it certainly proved its value then.'

Campbell cut in. 'If you're thinking about doing an article on how our new helicopter can be used in search and rescue or crime busting, let me know, and I'll give you a ride in it sometime. Then you can see at first hand what it can do.'

'Wow. Would you really do that?'

'Sure. We use it every day for training and operations. We can slot you in any time. Here's my card. Call me when you're free, and we'll fix it.'

'Thanks very much, sir. That's brilliant.'

'No problem.'

Sandra stepped in. 'We need to go now, Katy. But we'll keep in touch.'

'Thanks, ma'am.'

Katy watched them go. Maxwell still knew a lot more than she said. But maybe that was the way it had to be. As they exited the building, Campbell put his arm across Maxwell's back, and held her waist. She leaned into him. *That looked cosy. Were these two an item?*

She turned to Craig, and laughed out loud. 'A helicopter ride. Isn't that fantastic? And you've got an exclusive on what changed these guys minds. Can you do me a favour though. Give it a positive spin on the USAAF helping us solve a crime, huh?'

'Will do.' They headed back to the office.

She met Adam as usual that evening. 'Guess what I'm going to do.'

He smiled and shrugged. 'No idea.'

'Have a ride in one of these American helicopters.'

'Jesus. How did that happen?'

She told him about meeting Maxwell earlier in the day. By now, she knew she was in love with Adam. They'd already talked about their future together. But Katy was reluctant to commit, and wanted to enjoy her growing reputation as a journalist.

The five-a-side football team Adam trained had become league leaders by the end of March after a succession of wins. In fact, they hadn't lost a game since Adam started coaching them. They retained that position until the league finished in May, and won the League Trophy to everyone's delight. Katy had written it up in the *Gazette* as 'Spanish Two-Step Wins Trophy'.

***

On a bright June morning, Janet sat in the garden room at Laurel Avenue talking with Mrs Preston. Richard was due back home for the first time since his 'accident'.

'It'll be good to have him back.'

Janet nodded. 'Yes, I want to see him away from the convalescent home. It was very comfortable, of course, and Dr Murray has done a wonderful job. But I think he'll recover better at home now. Do you think he'll ever get back into the business?'

'Well, let's wait and see. I want to talk about that, though. Over the last few months, you've done an amazing job, Janet. The staff are cheerful and motivated. Customers now think it's an exciting place to shop. Most important of all, we're making good money again. I haven't seen Neil Hendry so happy for years. And it's all down to you. I'm reluctant to bring Richard back too early, in case it casts a shadow over what you've achieved. He's very bitter, you know. I want to manage his return very carefully. I think, in a way, it was my fault he fell into this situation.'

Janet raised her eyebrows. 'What? Why, Mrs Preston? It can't be your fault.'

'Well, I think it probably was. I gave him too much freedom, and didn't realise he was misusing it. He should have been happy to run the business, make good money, and have a good life. Yet it seems he wanted something else. I don't know what it was – more status, more recognition from his peers – but his yearning didn't do him any favours.

'I'm glad these men pleaded 'Guilty'. A trial would have been too much of an ordeal for him – and for us. We still don't know what was behind it all, and perhaps we never will. I watched these three men in the dock. Not a flicker of emotion from them. How could these people be so cruel?

'The rot started with that Triumph group. They were a bunch of sharks, and Richard was just too naïve. I think everyone should find their level where they're content, and enjoy it. Not strive for something beyond them that puts them in danger. Ambition is fine, but not at the expense of safety or happiness. I should have seen it earlier. That's why I say I'm probably at fault.'

Janet didn't know the full story either. She was aware, though, that her actions way back in reporting Richard to the police might well have somehow led to his present position. But for her own peace of mind, she had to think positively, block out the past, and look to the future. She remembered Adam's comment, 'Everyone has a secret.' This had to be hers.

'I think you're being too hard on yourself, Mrs Preston. But I agree, let's make sure we introduce Richard in a way that works for him, and not expect too much too soon.'

'Thanks, my dear. I don't know what I'd have done without you. That's why I'd like to formalise your position, and invite you to become Managing Director from the first of July. You're already doing the job, and you've been a godsend to us. I'll also adjust the shareholding, and gift you ten per cent.'

Janet was stunned. 'Oh, my goodness. Thank you so much, Mrs Preston. I'm delighted to accept.'

'It's well deserved, my dear.'

The doorbell rang, and Meg showed Daniel into the room. He kissed each of them on the cheek. 'Richard asked me to come over. I take it he's not back yet.'

'He's due any minute.'

Daniel nodded. 'I think he's done remarkably well. They've now got him to plan his day, pace himself, prioritise things, and problem-solve properly, all to avoid brain fatigue. I mean, when he went there he didn't know which day of the week it was. They've done a fantastic job.'

They heard the car arrive, and went to the door to welcome Richard. His face was gaunt, with a deep dimple in his left temple, but his eyes were bright. He struggled with a walking stick, hugged Janet, and his mother, and shook Daniel's hand. 'Daniel and I are going up to my study, mother.'

Janet watched the two of them slowly climb the stairs. As she and Mrs Preston turned to go back into the garden room, she heard Richard say, 'I need your help.'

She thought, *Oh, my God. What was he up to now. Hadn't he learned any lessons?*

A Note from James Hume

Thank you so much for reading Killing the Captain. If you enjoyed it, please take a moment to leave a review on Amazon or Goodreads. Even if it's only a line or two, it would be *very* much appreciated.

I welcome contact from my readers. If you'd like to hear about new releases, or contact me for any other reason, send a brief email to james@jameshumeauthor.com

I promise not to share your email with anyone else, and I won't clutter your inbox. I'll only contact you when a new release is imminent, or to reply to you.

You can unsubscribe at any time.

With warm regards,

James Hume

Further Reading

Hunting Aquila (An intriguing WW2 spy drama, with a twist)

During World War 2, Churchill stumbles across a leak of vital information from the UK to the enemy and calls in Commander Jonathan Porritt to catch the mole. Porritt has no leads until Jane, a young British translator, unwittingly gets caught up with a German spy trying to flee the country. Can Porritt use his Special Branch teams in Glasgow, Yorkshire, London and Belfast to rescue Jane and smash the undercover spy organisation before Churchill's invasion plans get leaked?

'A proper page-turner full of well-plotted twists and turns. I loved the story, which rattles along at a cracking pace. The attention to detail with impressive research meant the whole book stayed with me long after I'd finished reading.' (Kerry Barrett, Author / Editor)

'Well written spy novel. Grabs you from the beginning to the end. A great cast of characters, both good and bad.' (Kindle customer)

'A brilliant story. I couldn't put this book down and read it in less than a day to the exclusion of everything else.' (Kindle customer)

Available: Now on Amazon

Chasing Aquila (Sequel to Hunting Aquila)

Just after World War 2, Superintendent Sandra Maxwell, Head of Special Branch in the West of Scotland, checks if a suspicious death in Glasgow is linked to Aquila, a German spy organisation that flourished in the UK during the war. She finds that Aquila has now morphed into a sinister new organisation. Can she catch the killer by chasing him across Holland and Germany, capture the head of the organisation, and smash their new activities before they spread to every major UK city?

This deftly plotted, action-packed thriller is full of twists and turns. Carefully weaving fact and fiction, it provides powerful and intriguing lessons that still apply in today's changing world.

'Excellent follow up to Hunting Aquila. Mr. Hume lets the characters grow as the books move forward, with the female main characters showing women in positions of leadership and authority while being human.' (Amazon Reviewer)

'Easy to read, never a dull moment, true to life and no unnecessary sexuality thrown in. Looking forward to author's next book.' (Amazon Reviewer)

'These ww2 stories are really great, even if fiction. Although adding real history takes it to a new level of enjoyment.' (Amazon Reviewer)

Available: Now on Amazon

Avenging the Captain (Sequel to this book)

In preparation.

Potentially available late 2021.

Printed in Poland
by Amazon Fulfillment
Poland Sp. z o.o., Wrocław

boat for something. Why don't we go to Girvan, and see if they're there?'

'Jesus, Katy. The police have an alert out on them. How are we going to find them if they can't?'

'Because we think differently, that's how. Come on, Archie. Take us to Girvan.'

'What, *now*?'

'Yes, now. The woman's on the move. The men have disappeared. Something's happening today. Come on, Archie! Let's go and see.'

Archie pondered. 'Okay. It's probably better than just sitting here worrying. I'll get my keys.'

Within a few minutes, they were on their way south to Girvan. Katy thought she was now doing something useful. And still getting a story.